A BRIEF MESSAGE FROM YOUR SPONSORS

If this is your first foray into the shadowy world of rediscovered black fiction we call the Old School, welcome. If you've got the taste for adventure, we think you're going to like it here. If you're joining us for another go-around, nice to have you back.

Our latest offerings feature four more slippery and subversive works. They haven't been excavated to make you feel good about your life, validate your existence, or put a smile on your face. This is a hard-boiled, blood-drenched fiction—untamed and unbearably suspenseful.

It is a slice of real life that will keep you up late nights, and chill you to the bone.

This time we offer you an inside look at the numbers racket, the dramatic rise of an unlikely drug kingpin, an anguished novelist's final revenge, and a middle-class family whose love for each other has turned to hate—until their home is invaded by a couple of bungling black nationalists.

Don't bother looking for role models; you won't find them. Old School heroes are a tortured and tormented breed—alienated, existential, and disaffected men for whom success is measured in terms of survival and escape is just a pipe dream. On the fringe of so-called respectable society, they may win, they may lose, but at least they go down swinging.

But for all their creeping menace and crashing violence, we think you'll agree that these are landmark works told with terrible honesty and explosive brillance. Adventurous, ambitious, and aggressively undogmatic, these premature postmodernists weren't afraid to gamble for high stakes.

What was their reward? Obscurity. Poverty. Rejection. But for what it's worth, they also gained the self-knowledge that they hadn't minced words or sold out their genius. And that's why we're celebrating them.

Lost since their original publication, they've been dead and bur-

D0864130

ied—impenetrable as a tomb and inaccessible as a dream. Here in the Old School, they are born again.

So if you think you're ready, pull up a stool, have a round on the house, and read your way into oblivion.

See you next time.

The End of a Primitive

OLD SCHOOL BOOKS

Edited by Marc Gerald and Samuel Blumenfeld

The End of a Primitive

CHESTER HIMES

Old School Books

W · W · Norton & Company
New York · London

*The text of this book is composed in Sabon, with the display set in Stacatto 555
and Futura.*
Composition by Crane Typesetting Service, Inc.
Manufacturing by Courier Companies, Inc.
Book design by Jack Meserole.

Library of Congress Cataloging-in-Publication Data
Himes, Chester B., 1909–
      The end of a primitive / by Chester Himes.
          p.   cm.—(Old school books)
      Originally published in a different form under the title: The primitive. This
edition restores the work in the form the author intended, and includes his introduc-
tion, not previously published.
      ISBN 0-393-31540-1 (pbk.)
      I. Himes, Chester B., 1909–   Primitive. II. Title. III. Series.
PS3515.I713E53   1997
813'.54—dc20   96-9795
                                                                              CIP

W. W. Norton & Company, Inc., 500 Fifth Avenue, New York, N.Y. 10110
                    http://web.wwnorton.com

W. W. Norton & Company Ltd., 10 Coptic Street, London WC1A 1PU

1   2   3   4   5   6   7   8   9   0

CHESTER HIMES

WHEN CHESTER HIMES sat down to write *The End of a Primitive* in 1954, his fortunes were at an all-time low. After the triumphant success of his first novel, *If He Hollers, Let Him Go,* in 1942, his follow-up, *Lonely Crusade,* had brought him scathing reviews from all quarters—*Ebony* to the *Daily Worker*—and his next two novels, *The Third Generation* and *Cast the First Stone,* had been rejected out-of-hand by his publisher. Little wonder everything—the streets, the sky, the night, the tormented couple themselves—are so dark in this, his most powerful, personal, and revealing novel.

But if the early 1950s were a disastrous time for Himes, he might have been used to it already. He'd enjoyed more than his fill of bad luck.

Born in Jefferson City, Missouri, in 1909, Himes had a love-hate relationship with his poet-mother, and suffered from lifelong guilt from having blinded his brother while playing with fireworks.

Expelled from Ohio State University in 1927 over a prank, he took up with a band of roughnecks in Cleveland. A year later he was sentenced to twenty years in prison for a jewel heist. Bad timing. While in confinement at the Ohio State Penitentiary, a prison fire killed 300 inmates. In the smoldering ashes, Himes, inspired by the

Black Mask writings of Dashiell Hammett and by the grim events he'd witnessed, bought himself a Remington typewriter and began hammering out stories of his own.

Better received in France than in his native America, Himes set sail to Paris in the spring of 1953. Shortly before leaving, he optimistically told his good friend Richard Wright, "I have been studying le francaise, and soon je le parlai suffsamment pour me faire comprendre par d'autres."

His optimism was short-lived. Torn between unbridled joy at being in a country where skin color was less of an issue, and depressed by financial worries and his increasingly stormy relationship with Wright, Himes began to work on *The End of a Primitive*. It was a novel he would continue to work on through his journeys to the South of France, London, and Majorca.

Shortly before his death in 1984, Himes gave this remarkable plot summary of his novel to Michael Fabre (see *Conversations with Chester Himes,* University of Mississippi, 1995): "I put a sexually frustrated American woman and a racially-frustrated black American male together for a weekend in a New York apartment, and allowed them to soak in American bourbon. I got the result I was looking for: a nightmare of drunkenness, unbridled sexuality, and in the end, tragedy."

His editor William Targ, then at the World Publishing Company, agreed. "The manuscript appears to me as a night of Walpurgis, a nightmare of alcohol, frantic and deviant sex, scatology, nymphomania and many other things." An incensed Himes fired back, "What can one expect from a culture as chaotic as ours?" In the end, the work was rejected.

To eat and make rent, Himes sold his typewriter. A year would pass before *The End of a Primitive* was finally accepted by the New American Library.

The following year, Himes, at the suggestion of editor Marcel Duhmel of Gallimard's prestigious La Serie Noire crime line, began work on what would become a turning point in his career—his Harlem Domestic series, featuring Ed Coffin and Gravedigger Jones. Although Himes often spoke of these crime novels as if they were throwaways, they would finally begin to garner him praise in his native country.

In later years, Himes would remark that *The End of a Primitive* was a transition between his earlier protest novels and his Harlem detective series, and that it was his favorite of all his books. "I put a lot of myself in Jesse Robinson," Himes told Michael Fabre in 1983. "I probably said everything I wanted to say in that novel. . . . It was an attempt, and I believe a successful one, to depict the repressive influences in our time."

Until now, America has had to make do with a significantly abridged version of *The End of a Primitive*. "They [Himes's publisher] found the novel too daring, too risky, too obscene and they cut quite a bit out of it without my permission."

Rest assured, we haven't changed a single comma from his original manuscript.

INTRODUCTION

I WROTE *The End of a Primitive* in 1953 and 1954 while living with an American white woman in Majorca who had a husband and four daughters far away in Central Europe. I began to write it as a reaction to the American editorial rejections of the book I had coauthored with this white woman. American editors, knowing I was the coauthor of the book, *The Golden Chalice*, rejected it with such hypocrisy and malice I became furious. They would not publish a book that might have become a bestseller because I coauthored it with an American white woman while living with her and enjoying her sexually, so I decided to write a book about an American black living with a white woman under similar circumstances in New York which would be an affront and challenge to all white American editors.

But strangely enough I was cleansed of envy and hate by writing about white Americans with satire and scorn. And the catharsis was all the more effective because at the same time, I was enjoying the white woman sexually. Naturally I incorporated all of my own emotions into the book to demonstrate how a black American rids himself of fear, but in the book it cost the black protagonist his life. Which is its theme, rid yourself of fear, if you are a black man, and die. My white woman thought the book was hilarious for which I am grateful.

Writing this book not only purged me but made me strong. Forever afterwards, I have been shocked by the absurdity of racism. How more absurd could two people be than me and my white woman? My mind became free and highly creative and in the following eight years I wrote twelve books on the absurdity of racism and its effects on both black and white people. First I wrote *A Case of Rape* about the two of us, then *Pinktoes* about intellectual blacks and whites in the vicinity of New York, and ten detective stories about the blacks of Harlem and their white acquaintances in an atmosphere of sensuality and crime created by racism in reverse. And the only thing that stopped me from writing more about the innumerable instances of racism was a series of strokes.

But I paid for writing *The End of a Primitive,* I paid my dues as the brothers say.

The French, who published it first, referred to the book as "sadism and buffoonery."

Victor Weybright, who bought *The End of a Primitive* for New American Library, and I went to New York to get permission to submit it to the hardcover publishers. Some editors thought it classical, most thought it despicable. There were many furious controversies about its value. To my knowledge, it caused three fistfights between white editors and several long estrangements. And in the end New American Library had to publish it with the title changed to *The Primitive.* At New American Library five copy editors employing different colored ink went through it with a fine-tooth comb and deleted what was thought to be objectionable, and made many changes even as ridiculous as the residence of a rich white Bostonian homosexual from the unfashionable West Side (where no upper class Bostonian homosexual ever deigns to live) to the respectable East Side. And it took me weeks to restore what I could.

—Chester Himes/Moraira (Alicante) España

CHAPTER 1

THE GOLD-PLATED Swiss clock on the nightstand whirred softly, curdling the silence of the small dark room. A woman stirred tentatively on the three-quarter size bed, flung a heavy bare arm searchingly across the faded blue sheet. It encountered only emptiness. She became rigid, scarcely breathing, her nude body suddenly chilled beneath the two ample blankets, her emotions momentarily shattered by the blind panic she always experienced on awakening and finding herself alone.

When it came as her first conscious realization of the day, she found the aloneness terrifying. More than mere loneliness, for one could be lonely in the arms of a lover, by the side of a spouse, in the midst of a crowd. She had always been lonely with Ronny, throughout the ten years of their marriage. She could not recall a time when awakening by his side that she had not thought first of other things, other men. But there had been the security of his presence, his being there, his heart pulse at her side, assuring her that she was not alone, that her desires and emotions, her living and breathing, were joined with another's, linked in a chain of the larger whole, if only temporarily, before his first cross babyish mewling cut them in two, if only by the nearness of his flesh, shaped and molded into that ofttimes repulsive thing called *man*.

Aloneness was her greatest fear, had always been her greatest fear; greater than her fear of becoming an alcoholic, or a slut, the lesser two but mere eruptions from the sickness of aloneness. Even as a child in North Dakota, a lonely child ostracized by her German heritage during the years following the First World War, she had feared aloneness. Her mother was of sturdy Norwegian peasant stock, but her father was the last soured dregs of a line of German nobility, embittered by the German defeat, castrated by his isolation, a broken, lonely man, sitting despised and aloof in the back room of the local bootleggers, drinking himself into oblivion. She couldn't think of her father without crying. He was the epitome of defeat. Not defeated like a man in battle, but like a woman defeated by her sex, by the outraged indignity of childbearing, of monthly periods, long hair, skirts, and sitting down to pee. Like a prostitute she'd seen once in a Third Avenue bar crying over a jukebox song: "It makes no difference now . . ." His defeat had filled their home with a dark despair in which she had grown up always on the verge of terror, sometimes within the terror, never far away. Once, during her first year in school, she had come home to find her mother gone. Three young boys, playing hookey from school, had been buried alive in a water-soaked cave at the outskirts of town. One of them had lived next door and there had been many strange cars and trucks parked on the street, alarming her before she'd reached her house. She had called to her mother on entering and had raced from room to room, screaming, the terror pursuing her in the empty house, finally engulfing her in a black void that was like death. On returning from next door, her mother had found her in a faint. But she had never forgotten the terror of the empty house, the feeling of complete aloneness somehow coming from her father too in a way she couldn't understand.

Now it was more. Now, fifteen years after she had married Ronny to escape the despair that had settled in her home, aloneness in bed on awakening was an indication of her failure as a woman. To have lived for thirty-seven years in this world, five of those years in New York City, eleven in Chicago; to have slept with countless men—once she had counted up to one hundred and eighty-seven—most of whom had respected her, many of whom had loved her, felt some manner of affection for her—and now to find herself alone, unloved, even the link with the larger whole broken, gone completely; it was almost like defeat. How many times during the five years since she had divorced Ronny had she awakened alone? she wondered vaguely. Too many! Too, too many! And not because she played hard to get. She was easy—too easy, she knew—but she couldn't help it; she hardly ever did it now for any other reason than to keep them near. God, what sons of bitches some of them had turned out to be!

But at this moment of awakening, before her mind had restored its defenses, regained its equanimity, phrased its justifications, hardened its antagonisms, erected its rationalizations; at this moment of emotional helplessness when the mind is not fully detached from the body, when thoughts are still vaguely orgastic, to a large degree physiological, sleep-stupid and defenseless; when the feminine mind suffers its one brief period of honesty, she could not blame all on the men. That was for a time later in the day. Night was the time for crying, and day for lying; but morning was the time of fear.

It was a terrible thing to face this fear each day at the moment of awakening, to face another empty day which could only be filled by one's self. In her apartment, situated as it was on the first floor rear, entombed by the concrete cliffs of other buildings, as remote from the sounds of voices and traffic on the street as the crown of Everest, a veritable dungeon where the light of day penetrated only for a few brief hours in the late afternoon when she was seldom there, this sense of being alone was almost complete; not only shut off from people, from others of the species, but shut off from time, from seasons, from distance, from life—all life, dog life, cat life, cockroach life—shut off from eternity. It was like waking in a grave.

For a time she lay unmoving, rigid, fighting off the panic. Slowly her thoughts took nebulous shape in the form of memory and the events of the night before returned like sequences of a dream. Bill had dropped by for a moment before dinner to bring some illustrated maps of Italy, Sicily, and Majorca. She was planning to tour Europe during the coming summer and he was trying to be helpful; he had studied architecture in Rome two years before and was consequently an authority on Europe. Bill was the helpful type—tall, skinny, redheaded, freckled, ugly, perseveringly cheerful, and sexless as cold boiled potatoes.

They had become engrossed in an exchange of accounts of their great adventures. He had lived in a miserable *pensione* near a noisome area of moldy ruins, unable to speak the language, repulsed by the filth, and had made no acquaintances and had been unhappy all the time. While for her part she had spent three weeks in Paris,

1 5

three years previous, in an attempt at reconciliation with her husband, which had turned into a nightmare of wet-nursing him through a siege of disgusting drunkenness and at the same time trying to sleep with whoever became available in protest. He had cried long and hard over their "ruined" lives; he had vowed tearfully he wanted to marry her again. She would have married him again at any time if she could have found some means of keeping him erect long enough. But she decided it wasn't worth it. He had been drunk from the moment she arrived until she left; perhaps from fear of having to sleep with her again. He couldn't get over the fact she had divorced him to marry a black man. She hadn't married the black man, but that was beside the point. Perhaps he was afraid if he slept with her again it would bring on a recurrence of his homosexual urges which he had spent ten thousand dollars to get rid of by psychoanalysis. It couldn't have been just because of the black man, because he'd known of her sleeping with blacks while they were still married and together, and all he'd done in the end was join the army as a buck private when he could have had a commission for the asking. God knows he loved blacks as much as anyone; his love for them had impelled him, a Mississippi boy, to devote the ten best years of his life working on their behalf, ten frustrated and guilt-ridden and cuckolded years in what he had once called in postmortem regret "the bright, shining world of race relations!" For ten years he had been a Negrophile, an extreme Negrophile, enjoying the beds of his black colleagues' wives without any condescension whatsoever. But much of it had gone after the analysis. He had been analyzed to rid himself of a homosexual bent so he could sire an heir, and it had turned out that afterwards he loved blacks less. That always struck him as being very strange. He had discussed it at great length with her.

But she didn't hint of this to Bill. He respected her, so she didn't dare risk hurting him. He thought that she was pure. Perhaps not *pure*—but not *easy*! She had such a highly respectable job he couldn't possibly have thought otherwise, being the very nice young man that he was, the type that believes the job makes the lady. Perhaps *chaste* would be a better word. Well, why not? she asked herself. She'd never felt completely like a slut at any time. Besides it was nice to have one man think of her like that.

At ten o'clock, realizing he had kept her from dinner, he had invited her to a supper club. But she'd declined. That would have been the bitter end, going out to dinner at some night club with Bill and coming home to sleep alone.

Then, as Bill was leaving, Harold had staggered in, drunk as usual. A frown came into her thoughts. She wasn't ashamed of Harold—she wasn't ashamed of any of her black friends, what few she had left. Besides which, Harold was an impressive looking man when sober. And once she had respected him more than any man she'd ever known, really worshipped him. Anyway, Bill had met him there before. But why the hell did he have to come crawling around to her place every time he got helplessly drunk?

Suddenly she recalled having loaned him another twenty-five dollars. "Oh shit!" she said aloud. It gave her a perverse satisfaction to pronounce the word. She was really through with him this time, she firmly resolved. She had sat drinking with him, trying to comfort him—he'd been hurt and dejected as usual—and had forgotten to eat. After he had borrowed the money she had become so enraged she had put him out of her apartment, despite the fact that by then he was barely able to stand and had begun weeping sloppily over his cruel fate. "You make more money than I do, and besides you're fifteen years older, you son of a bitch!" she'd condemned him bitterly.

Now, in the recollection of it, of all those great things he had been to her during her first year at the university—he'd been a great man on the campus in those days, one who was going great places; he hadn't seen her, a little country girl—of all those "bright, shining years" of which he'd been a part, nothing was real any longer. It was this moment she feared the most. The unreality. The years of dust. The blubbering self-pity of men. . . . Ronny crying in her room at the Commodore Hotel that winter when she'd divorced him and come to New York to marry Ted. . . . "Don't marry a nigger, Kriss. . . . Don't kill me, Kriss . . . I know I've been a bastard, but don't break me. . . . I'm from Mississippi. . . ." Herself replying with sensual cruelty, "Go back to Mississippi then, you son of a bitch, and sleep with all those black women you're always boasting of having grown up on. You don't know how to have a white woman. . . ." His tears wetting her new nylons. "Please don't, Kriss! I'll get analyzed. I'll give you a baby. . . ." Her final stab, "Give yourself a baby, you louse; you've tried hard enough!"

"What an awful rotten life!" she thought. "I'm a good girl, really." In some manner the strange thought brought a sharp vivid memory of Willard, the year he was such a star on the football team, and the two abortions at sixteen which had prevented her from ever bearing children.

"I must call mother tonight," she told herself firmly, groping blindly for this one last hold to reality.

She glanced at the luminous dial of the clock. It was ten after eight. Abruptly she sat up, her bare feet groping for her golden mules. Absently she cupped her breasts in her hands, gently squeezing them, relieved by the slight pain. Her nude body, heavy with years, was Buddhistic in vague dejection. Her mind was flat, stale, stupid, but she didn't have a hangover. Tim, her doctor, had advised her to drink only the best of whisky because it contained less fossil oil. She paid six dollars and forty-two cents a fifth for her Scotch, and averaged six bottles weekly. But no matter how much she drank, she never suffered from hangovers. On the physical side, she was disgustingly healthy.

It was just these awful depressions on awakening.

Now she stood up and went into the breakfast nook and switched on the lights of the sitting room. The entrance hall of her small, three-room apartment angled like a short-handled crank, encasing two deep storage closets in the angle at front, and widening beyond the kitchen door into the breakfast nook containing a blond oak table shaped like a heart, on which reposed two watery highball glasses on silver coasters and a flat silver ashtray with several squashed butts. Here the hall angled once more, ending at the full-length mirror on the closet door, across which faced the doors of the bedroom and the bath. The far corner of the breakfast nook was cut diagonally by an archway opening onto the sunken sitting room, one step lower than the rest of the compact, well-designed flat.

18

It was a modern room with a stunning decor, the facing walls done in soft pastel shades of gray and pink, the floor in rose colored carpet, and the far wall with its two windows looking down on a concrete well completely covered by floor-length drapes of a deep maroon color.

Along the gray wall ran a waist-high, handsome, highly polished blond oak storage cabinet, above which hung a large, rectangular charcoal drawing of three antelopes in flight. Centered against the maroon drapes was a blond television set on a three-legged stand, atop which stood a slender female nude carved from caramel colored wood. The pink wall held a small blond oak writing desk with a tubular chair padded in foam rubber and covered by removable terrycloth slips of dove gray. On that wall were three paintings, a large oil of a small Indian girl sitting disconsolately on a curb, vaguely reminiscent of the famous painting of the papoose by Diego Rivera; a smaller water color in abstract design, which might have been a portrait of the inflamed lungs of an alligator that died of pneumonia in the upper reaches of the Nile one cold and stormy winter; and a dark somewhat menacing drawing in pastel of a Polynesian woman with large bare breasts and large round eyes. The sofa set against the bedroom wall as if in ill repute, its upholstery a somewhat faded grayish-green, like an elderly but undefeated matron among a bevy of cover girls, gone but not forgetting. Beside it stood a set of glass-top coffee stands that fitted one atop another, on which sat another watery highball glass in a silver coaster and a large, lovely foam-glass ashtray filled with lipsticked cigarette butts. Just inside the archway, at the corner of the storage cabinet, was Kriss's favorite chair, a wrought-iron, three-legged straight-backed thing with a large opening between the seat and the high small back ostensibly to trap the behinds of well-cushioned females, as was once suggested in a *New Yorker* magazine cartoon.

Sometimes this room gave Kriss pleasure, and she loved to show it off. The paintings had been done by artists who'd received fellowships from the Chicago Foundation, and were adjudged good and valuable by those who knew such things. But now, as she crossed to switch on the television set, it had a morning-after look which fed her general depression.

She had a strong body, revealed sympathetically by the table lamp. It was fantastically well-preserved for her age and the abuses to which she had subjected it. Her full breasts had fallen but slightly and were still firm, and she had handsome shoulders, peppered with tiny red pimples, but voluptuous as a Botticelli painting. Her legs were long and gorgeously shaped with beautiful knees, but her stomach was bloated and those old demon rubber tires had begun forming above her hips. Her skin was very fair, the faint hairs on her arms and at the base of her spine golden in the slanting light, the longer hair on her mound and that on her head, cut short in the modern businesswoman's fashion, was of a light translucent brown, verging on gold. Her face had the high cheekbones and flat planes of Mongolian ancestry, contradicted by a short, straight, tiny nose, and huge, light blue, slightly glassy, almost bulging eyes, slanting upward at the outer edges. A famous writer and critic of New York City, an old man famous for flowery phrases, once described her as handsome as four peacocks. But he had seen her only when she was dressed. Now as she bent over the set in the somewhat awkward and unflattering position of a can-can dancer *sans costume* stooping to peer through the monocle of an inebriated Englishman, the thirty-seven year accumulation of *derrière* belonging to the one hundred and thirty-six pound body commanding fullest attention, she looked extremely naked and shockingly obscene.

Just at that moment the light appeared on the twenty-inch screen and the close-up of a man's face, blooming with the bright wide smile of a bleached skull, and wreathed in that dreadful early morning cheerfulness of this telatomic age which inspires old-fashioned die-hards suffering from old-fashioned hangovers to rush into their kitchens and cut their throats. The happy, smiling eyes, crinkled about the corners with inner joy and healthy living, stared knowingly at her anatomy, causing her to feel suddenly indecent and very unhealthy.

"Oh!" she exclaimed, involuntarily shielding herself with her hands.

She had turned the volume too high and a booming jovial voice issued from the smiling lips of the happy face: "*Are you overweight?*

Are you overwrought? Do you suffer from morning depression? Do you have a stale brown taste of biliousness on arising?"

This boisterous catechism bursting upon her mood of morbid introspection rattled her. She did what she always did when rattled; she giggled.

"THEN THIS IS WHAT YOU NEED!" the loud voice informed her.

"What?" she asked the happy face, her quick, spontaneous wit coming to her rescue.

The face instantly disappeared and in its place appeared a giant's hand holding a giant bottle with the label forward. "THIS!"

"Oh, shit!" she said disgustedly.

The face disappeared. *"Yes! This enervating laxative, charged with vitamins, also contains chlorophyll. Not only does it urge nature about its business, but it also provides a pickup after a sleepless night. It sends you cheerfully to work with a clean body, an alert mind, and a sweet breath!"*

Kriss turned the volume down, her giggle turning to a chuckle. There was a corny humor in the situation—she'd have to tell Dorothy about it—but she was still a little disconcerted. It was the first time she'd ever tuned in during the commercial and caught Gloucester's close-up almost nesting in her thighs. She knew it was foolish but she felt embarrassed, which inspired the impulse to do something naughty, some kind of striptease dance or shake her behind. However, she mustered her respectability and began to walk away from the set with becoming dignity. But she felt Gloucester's appraising eyes on her bare rear, and looked over her shoulder, wondering the while how many broad beams and rare nudes paraded each morning before his amused, straightforward television gaze. The laughing face of a pet chimpanzee now appeared on the screen, the little beastie jumping up and down in such glee that impulsively she hastened from its view and stumbled over the three-cornered chair, falling against the glass-topped coffee tables, and upsetting the glass ashtray over her prized pink carpet.

She had to laugh. Mattie, her black cleaning woman who came in three days each week, would swear that she'd been drunk. Now she felt a little drunk. Briskly she set herself to her morning routine.

21

She got her copy of the *New York Herald-Tribune* from the mat outside her door, first peeping through the Judas window to make certain the coast was clear; put on water to boil for coffee; lingered for a moment to watch the antics on the television screen; then devoted the customary five minutes to bodily functions, glancing at the lead stories the while. Vaguely the television voice penetrated her consciousness, "casting" the morning news, which, in modern usage is the province of the "newscaster." The headlines from both sources were the same: TRUMAN SEIZES STEEL INDUSTRY; the same names cropped up: John L. Lewis, Dean Acheson, General Dwight D. Eisenhower, Mayor William O'Dwyer, Queen Juliana, and Prince Bernard; NATO was praised with faint damning; the State Department was damned with faint praise; the Soviet Union was damned outright; nothing was praised outright; McCarthy had found two thousand communists hiding among the President's bright print sport shirts; all five-star generals had decided to run for President, but MacArthur, who had become a six-star general since his recall from Korea, had the jump on the others, due no doubt to the extra star which the Truman Democrats hinted he had pinned on his tunic himself without the proper authority; everyone had agreed "It was time for a change," but no one was clear as to what was to be changed from what to what other than Republicans who were insistent that Democrats be changed to Republicans; Supreme Court Justice William O. Douglas urged a "peasants' revolution" to end economic slavery in backward areas; a Harvard professor suggested that it was a "peasants' revolution" that had started all the trouble in the first place, but he had been quickly convicted as a communist spy by McCarthy and when last seen was rapidly disappearing beneath the ledge of a twelfth story window from which he had recently jumped; the U.N. forces in Korea had killed seven thousand Chinese communists the day before, but the war still dragged on, due no doubt to the fact, as a Columbia University professor pointed out, that seventeen thousand Chinese communists had been born during the night.

After digesting this news, Kriss showered, brushed her teeth, put on a fresh girdle, taking the stocking fasteners from the soiled one in the garment bag inside her closet door where she put her soiled underwear and stockings for the maid to wash, the soiled linen in the hamper in the bath going out to the laundry. Now she felt sufficiently presentable to brave the television eyes. From the middle drawer of her storage cabinet she selected a pair of nylons from a loose pile, first inspecting them for runs. Then she went to the kitchen, poured the boiling water into the drip coffee pot, inserted two slices of expensive white bread into the automatic toaster, and returned to her dressing, pausing for a moment before the closet mirror. In the nylons her legs were slim and svelte, nowadays the only pleasure derived from her reflection. Her hips were held reasonably flat and hard by the girdle but, to her infinite disgust, that old demon bicycle tire went leering around her middle. She'd have to begin dieting, she resolved for the thousandth time. Although it really wasn't her food, she amended; it was too much drinking. Well, she could stop that too. It was time she stopped, before she became one of those big baywindowed mannish women whom she so despised. But she shouldn't complain too much about her weight: now, when she became slim, her breasts drooped. She'd never had to wear a brassiere; it was one of her great prides. Her slips sufficed to hold her full firm breasts somewhat steady, which was all that was necessary.

She selected a red dress from the two racks of dresses in the closet, one third of which were red. She liked herself in red; it went with her fair skin, blue eyes, and tawny hair. Besides which, it made her feel daring. She couldn't get along in the world without feeling daring.

From alongside a bottle of red and yellow capsules of barbiturates in her medicine cabinet, she took down a bottle of bluish-gray tablets, a patented drug relatively new on the market. They were made from a combination of dexedrine and amylobarbitone, and the directions on the label stated: "Indicated in states of mental and emotional distress." The first time she had read that statement she had told herself, "That's me. That's me all the time." Now, after swallowing one with a little water, she shook a couple of dozen into a lacquered snuffbox to take to the office; her store there had run out.

Then, bringing her toast and coffee, she sat on a stool at the end of the table so she could see the television, ate one-half of a piece of toast, and drank two cups of coffee sweetened with saccharine tablets. On the television screen, Gloucester was interviewing the chimpanzee.

"Who do you think will get the Republican nomination for President?" he asked.

"Five-star General of the Army, Dwight D. Eisenhower, will be nominated on the first ballot," the chimpanzee promptly replied.

"And are you sure it won't be Senator Taft?" Gloucester, who was a loyal Taft supporter, prompted the chimp.

"No, not even for Vice President," the chimpanzee asserted positively. "All Bob Taft will get will be a big hug from Eisenhower when the General rushes across the street directly following his nomination to congratulate Taft on losing and calling for party unity. Senator Richard M. Nixon of California will be nominated for Vice President, and on September 28, 1952, he will go on television—the same as you and I—defend a political fund placed at his disposal by innocent and patriotic businessmen of California, most of whom have somehow become involved in the real estate business and are hamstrung in their desire to invest in low rental properties by the Democratic administration's rent control program which, paradoxically, precipitates high rent. Mr Nixon will also bare his financial status to the complete satisfaction of the Republicans and the complete dissatisfaction of the Democrats, after which he will hasten to the special campaign train of Republican presidential nominee General of the Army, Eisenhower, to pose for a newsreel parody of the Jerry Lewis–Dean Martin comedy, *That's My Boy*.

"What do you think of General Eisenhower's chances of being elected?" Gloucester asked condescendingly.

"On November 4, 1952, Republican nominee for President, five-star General of the Army, Dwight D. Eisenhower, will be elected President of the United States by an overwhelming landslide of 442 electoral votes and a popular vote of 33,938,285, the largest popular vote in the history of *your* Republic, thereby giving Senator McCarthy a mandate to rid the nation of its mentality," the chimpanzee stated with extreme boredom. After all, this would bear no effect on chimpanzees—chimpanzees didn't think. "Does that answer your questions?" he asked shortly, anxious to collect payment for his appearance.

Kriss stared at the chimpanzee in horror. "How can it say such things—and Roosevelt dead but seven years!" she thought indignantly.

The pill worked rapidly on an empty stomach. The tremendous physical stimulation provided by the five milligrams of dexedrine was levelled off at peak efficiency by the counteropiate of thirty-two milligrams of amylobarbitone, holding the brain, which had been sharpened and alerted to almost supernatural brilliancy by the caffeine contained in two cups of strong black coffee, to an almost unbearable lucidity, like Hemingway writing a novel. By the time she had combed her short, curled hair, powdered her face smoothly white, painted her lips becomingly red, applied a light sheen of vaseline to her upper eyelids, and adorned herself with appropriate jewelry: two hollow gold matching serpentine bracelets on her right wrist; a gold wrist watch with leather band on her left wrist; a leaf-shaped gold pin containing a dark blue stone at her left breast; a gold rope-shaped necklace; two gold-plated, snap-on earrings; along with her wedding and engagement rings which she still wore for the same reason she still kept her married name, she felt capable and serene and alert and very secure. She loved her little pills for the security they gave her. Thus bedecked and ornamented to the wildest fancy of any savage, emotionally fortified by the latest in patent drugs, faintly amused by the early morning television antics of MCs and chimpanzees, her wits made keen by the essence of twenty-five milligrams of good, pure, American coffee, she felt herself an efficient executive, ready to face the day.

Now she could afford to think about Dave Levine. He hadn't called her again, the son of a bitch! She had tried hard to marry Dave, and had almost gotten him, but his mother who was very orthodox, and incidentally held the purse strings even though Dave maintained an apartment in Manhattan, had put her foot down. Since then she had hated him, but she couldn't bear the humiliation of his breaking off before she did. "The Jewish son of a bitch!" she thought, trying vainly to arouse some inner racial prejudice to support her ego. But she didn't have any racial prejudice, really, and most of the people whom she had ever deeply admired had been Jews and a few blacks, so it didn't work. The tragedy was that she loved Dave's warm, friendly, compassionate mother more than she had ever loved Dave, whose chief influence over her had been to make her feel inferior. "The chiseler! He's practically lived off me this past year," she told herself, trying another tactic to prod her anger. But her clean cool thoughts would not accept the lie. She wished, wryly, that it was true, so that when he called next time she could say, "Get out of my house, you bastard! Get out of my life! You've done nothing but sponge off me ever since you knew me. Go back and marry that girl in the Bronx, Susan or Vivien or whatever her name is!" She knew very well the girl's name; it was Denise Rose; and she was a damn pretty girl whose parents had money; and she had graduated from Smith and traveled extensively in Europe, read good books and dabbled in art as a pastime, now wanted to get married like herself and bear her husband some fine sons, one to take over the business, another to study law at Harvard, a girl to marry one of their good friends. Secretly Kriss felt that Dave was a damn fool not to have married her a long time ago.

"The Brooks Brothers ass!" she thought, going quickly to turn off the television set. On the way out she made a quick cursory examination of the contents of her pocket book. She had three twenties, two tens, a five, and three ones, in a green billfold. She'd stop by Best & Co. at noon and pay her bill. In the change pocket were coins for carfare. The remaining contents consisted of the lacquered snuff box of pills; an enameled lipstick case of saccharine tablets; a dollar lipstick of Chinese Red; a large, flat, round, gold inlaid, plastic compact; a long, flat, magnificent, solid-gold cigarette case given to her for a birthday present the year before by Fuller, and incidentally a letter from Fuller that had come to the office the day before, stating that he was making a quick hop to Los Angeles on business; a gold-plated Dunhill cigarette lighter given to her for a Christmas present by Dave; a ninety-eight cents ballpoint pen from a Whelan's drugstore; a book of special account checks from a midtown Manhattan & Company branch bank; two clean initialed linen handkerchiefs; a half-filled package of Chesterfield cigarettes from which she smoked unless she wished to make an impression with the solid case—but she never smoked before lunch; the three keys necessary to get into her apartment, another key to the side entrance of her office building, two small flat keys to the large Hartman suitcases in her storage closets which she had not used since her trip to Europe, all held securely in a snapbutton red leather key case; and a small, red leather-bound address book, containing the addresses of nine couples, six single women, and two men, there being nothing to indicate whether single or married. One was a Jim Saxton from Dallas, Texas; the other a Kenneth McCrary from Hollywood, California. It was a neat, orderly, and comparatively uncluttered pocket book.

From one of the front closets devoted to coats she selected a soft plaid of medium weight and neutral shade. She pulled on black cotton gloves, picked up her purse and the morning paper, took a last sip of the now tepid coffee, leaving a smudge of lipstick on the cup, put out the lights behind her, and started to work. It was then exactly nine o'clock, at which time she was due in her office. But she'd gotten into such a habit of being late it was now practically impossible for her to be on time. "I'd better buck up," she cautioned herself. Sooner or later her boss, Kirby, would get on her tail—in a nice way, of course; he was really a very nice guy—but she wouldn't like it. She was extremely sensitive to reprimands, although, unlike many businesswomen who cry and sulk on such occasions, she became unreasonably furious.

On opening the door into the corridor, she met Mattie about to enter. Mattie was a very dark-complexioned woman who never wore makeup nor gave any other indication of an interest in her personal appearance. Her face always looked unwashed, her short, kinky hair uncombed, her old tattered garments as mussed as if she had slept in them. She weighed over two hundred pounds, but was as solid as a rock.

At the sight of Kriss her face lit with her professional grin, showing a row of sizeable pale yellow teeth with amalgam fillings here and there. "Mawnin' Miz Cummons." She seemed to have some manner of psychological block against pronouncing the name, *Cummings,* although once Kriss had heard her say distinctly, "Mister Drummings." However, Kriss had no way of knowing that the gentleman to whom she referred was named *Drummond*.

Kriss grinned back at her, giving the little amused chuckle that made her so well-liked. "I'm late again, Mattie. It seems as if I just can't get off in time."

"Y'all needs tuh be ma'd, Miz Cummons. Dass wut y'all needs," Mattie replied with easy familiarity. What she didn't know about Kriss's sex life, she had guessed. "Den y'all woud'n have tuh git up attall."

Kriss was never quite certain during these exchanges whether Mattie was slyly poking fun or stating a profound conviction. She chuckled uncomfortably and hastened down the corridor, her hard heel taps echoing about her.

Outside she was greeted by a bright April morning. Her apartment building, an eight-storied, light brick structure erected during the middle nineteen-thirties, faced south on 21st Street, between Third Avenue and the south end of Lexington at Gramercy Park. To one side was an old blackened church: to the other a renovated brick residence, converted into apartments, with big, pleasant, modern windows catching the morning sun.

It was a pleasant street, she thought, as she walked briskly along in the sunshine. Expensive, sophisticated. To her left the old Irving Hotel, facing the Park; to her right a modern, yellow brick, high-rent apartment house with beautiful windows, all lit at night, revealing the many wondrous decors. Down here it was so rich and luxurious with a quiet, expensive exclusiveness. Rich in tradition, also. She loved it here. She loved New York. But she loved it here far more than any other place she had ever lived in New York. It made her feel confident and exclusive. Her telephone exchange was *Gramercy*—"Right up the street, a few doors from Gramercy Park," she always said when directing friends to her address; never, "Right down the street a few doors from Third Avenue." But she liked that part of Third Avenue, too; there were wonderful stores in that section.

The street had emptied since the eight-thirty rush; only the service people and executives hailing taxis from the stand facing Lexington were about at this late hour. A few nurses already had their

28

charges in the park. "I must remember to get a key," she reminded herself. It was a private park enclosed by a high, iron fence, and the gates were kept locked. But the neighborhood residents could rent a key for twelve dollars annually—or was it twenty?—by applying to the Gramercy Park Association. The trees were already beginning to green, and red and yellow tulips were blooming in the well-tended plots. Although what she'd do with a key, frankly she didn't know. No one she knew would be found dead spooning on a hard bench in a dark chilly park when there was her beautifully furnished apartment so near, equipped with television and bed. After a moment she thought, "*Spooning*? What an ancient word for it!"

She walked erectly, with long quick steps, but it was a feminine walk and very attractive. Most of the service people along the way knew her by sight. She always looked at them directly. "You're late again, Miss," a taxi driver said. She grinned. Another said, "Maybe she knows the boss." The first one replied, "Maybe she is the boss." She passed on without commenting. "Probably means I sleep with the boss," she thought; then, smiling sensually, "Wouldn't mind if I did." Across the street the doorman of the Gramercy Park Hotel saluted briskly. She gave him a smile. Dave had taken her there to dinner several times, and at other times she had dropped in the bar alone. It was a pleasant bar, dark and intimate, but with that complete safety of high-class American bars. A woman was as safe there as at home in bed—safer, really, New York being what it is.

She continued down 21st Street to Fourth Avenue, turned north to the subway entrance at 22nd Street. There was a smile on her lips. She felt very happy. Passersby, even the surly printers and warehousemen of the neighborhood, noticed her happiness and smiled at her. She smiled in return, suddenly recalling the Harlem saying she'd often heard at Maud's:

I'd rather be a doggy lamp post in New York City
Than Governor General of the state of Mississippi.

CHAPTER 2

*H*E HAD DREAMED fitfully.

At first he had dreamed he was skating somewhere in a crowd and had broken through the ice. "Help! Help!" he had called as the icy current tugged at him. He had a thin grip on the broken edge of ice but he couldn't swim and the cold water tore at him, trying to pull him under. "Help! Help!" he had called again, desperately, as he felt his grip loosen. But none of the other skaters, all of whom were couples, boys and girls, men and women, looked in his direction or gave any indication that they had heard his cries. They skated about the hole, smiling and chatting, engrossed in each other. "Jesus Christ! They don't even see me!" he thought as his grip broke and he went down beneath the icy water, clutched in an ice cold fear.

He awakened and went to the dresser and poured a water glass full of gin. The faint glow of the city night came through the two side windows, silhouetting his nude body in the dim mirror. His hand trembled and his teeth chattered against the glass as he forced the gin down his throat. He held his mouth open, gasping until he got his breath, then he went back to bed.

"That ought to knock me out," he thought.

But he dreamed again.

He dreamed he was at a banquet, sitting near the end of the table where two very pretty young blonde women sat side by side. But there was an empty space between his seat and the end which hindered him from speaking to them. Then the man on his right stood up and moved because he didn't like his neighbor on the other side, and that left him sitting at the banquet table between the two empty spaces. He felt suddenly isolated. He was vaguely aware that he was the only black at the banquet, but that didn't have anything to do with the feeling of isolation until a very well-dressed, very handsome, very assured black magazine editor, whom he knew quite well, passed by without speaking and took a place at the head of the table. Then he thought, "Jesus Christ!—Even that son of a bitch ignores me!" But when the banquet was over and the guests began to leave, a black woman with a putty-coloured complexion, short straightened hair, and several strange embossed scars down her cheeks, but very well-dressed in a rose-beige evening gown and a black satin cape, stopped for a moment beside his chair and smiled at him. "Don't worry," she said. "You'll get one to go. Just keep on trying." He felt so grateful he wanted to kiss her hand, but she had gone on down the stairs and he saw her getting into an expensive foreign car with the magazine editor who had ignored him.

"Jesse Robinson!" he muttered in his sleep. His voice was so vicious it made the name a curse. "You goddam bastard! You goddam fool!" he ground out between clenched teeth. His body threshed about in a wild fury; his right fist lashed out in a rage. Then a blinding flash exploded in his brain like a flash of lightning and he cried, "Unhn!" His body became still but he began to grind his teeth like the muted sound of rats gnawing.

Then he dreamed he went down the stairs from the banquet room to a small parking lot where many cars were jammed together, trying to get away. There was no order and the cars were running into one another denting fenders and locking bumpers. In the center of the parking lot was a big bus, and a short squat man stood at one side leisurely washing it. Suddenly there was a commotion and a big wild-eyed man came around from behind the bus and began cursing the short squat man in a loud, uncontrolled voice. "I'll kick out your teeth!" he shouted. A crowd of men were standing about and someone said, "He's drunk." The short squat man backed away and several of the bystanders tried to restrain the big wild drunken man. But he broke loose from them and kicked viciously at the short squat man's face. His foot missed by inches but his shoe flew off from the force of the kick and went over the heads of the crowd and out of sight like a mightily powered line drive clearing the bleachers in Yankee Stadium. The big wild man was so enraged that he had missed, he wound up with his right fist and hit the short squat man in the mouth, despite the fact that six or seven men were trying to restrain him. Then he wound up his left fist and hit him again. Everyone thought it was time for the short squat man to run. But instead he ducked down and hit the big wild drunken man in the stomach with a long looping right as hard as he could. "Oof!" the breath went out of the big man as he doubled forward. But he straightened up instantly, more enraged than ever, looking to see where the short squat man had gone. Now was really the time to run! everyone thought. But the short squat man had got behind the big wild man and he picked up a heavy oak chair and hit him across the back of the head as hard as he could hit. "Jesus Christ!" the big wild drunken man howled painfully like a wounded dog and fell stretched out as if dead on his back.

Jesse laughed in his sleep and muttered, "Damn right!"

Then he dreamed the sweetest dream. He was seventeen years old and he was wrestling playfully on a bed with the prettiest girl he'd ever seen, trying to kiss her. She had a coffee-cream complexion and short black curls and her eyes flashed laughingly as she struggled to get loose from him. She had a strong slender body, hard and round, and she wore a middy blouse and skirt. She gave a quick turn and was free, her body extended away from him, tensed for flight. But instead of escaping she lay passively on her back, her hair spread out on the white counterpane, and he bent forward tenderly, looking into her dark laughing eyes, and kissed her from an upside down position. He knew it was the first time she had been kissed, and it was also the first time he had kissed a girl. He felt a sweet, nameless sensation spread all over him.

He opened his eyes wide. The sweet sensation was still with him and he lay unmoving, scarcely breathing, trying to hold it a little longer. But immediately his mind began analyzing it, dissecting it, breaking it up, pulling it down, twisting it this way and then the other. It was sweet because it was so pure. Never in all of his life had he felt a pure sex feeling—not even with his wife. But *pure* wasn't just the word. His thoughts began leafing through the dictionary of his mind: *good,* look under *good*; pleasant, virtuous, admirable. How about *clean*? *nice*? *good*?—there's that goddamned *good* again. There must be some goddamned word!

Sex in his mind had always been something a little soiled, a little weird, perhaps somewhat sordid too. Not in a bad sense always, but always a little tainted by his Protestant upbringing, his grotesque memory, his strange imagination. But this sex feeling in his dream had been completely undefiled. Perhaps the way two virgins felt. He'd never had a virgin; perhaps he'd never been a virgin, either.

Leroy's laugh came through his closed door and he heard the nasty little dogs racing over the hall floor. . . . "Now Napoleon, behave yourself. You come back here and get into your collar, you bad little thing." It was a man's falsetto voice affecting a womanish air. "Goddamned homos," he thought. "The dogs too."

All the sweetness went and the loneliness closed in. He was lying diagonally across the wide, old-fashioned, dilapidated, mahogany bed, and had to roll over to reach the night table where his cigarettes lay. "There's nothing lonelier than a double bed," he thought, putting a paper match to his cigarette, and with the first inhalation the dizziness came. He was still too drunk for a hangover but his head felt unset and his body unjointed and everything had a double-edged, distorted look like a four color advertisement with each color slightly out of line.

However, his brain was sharp. For the past five years it had never let him down. It was always packed with some definite emotion, defined in intellectual terms; futile rages, tearing frustrations, moods of black despair, fits of suicidal depressions—all in terms of cause and effect, of racial impact and "sociological import"— intellectual horseshit—but nagging as an unsolved problem, slugging it out in his mind, like desperate warriors. No matter how much he drank, whatever he did to deaden his thoughts, there was this part of his mind that never became numb, never relaxed. It was always tense, hypersensitive, uncertain, probing—*there must be some goddamned reason for this, for that*. It had started with the publication of his second book, five years before. . . . *Some goddamned reason for all the hate, the animosity, the gratuitous ill will*—for all the processed American idiocy, ripened artificially like canned cheese.

The night before he'd wandered from bar to bar, trying to find a safe-looking pickup. At the Ebony up the street, on Amsterdam, he'd tried to make the hostess, a show-girl type, what the guys used to call a "Brown-skin Model." The joint had been practically empty and she had come and sat with him at the bar. He recalled trying to kiss her, and her asking him to go with her the next day out to a used car lot near Atlantic Beach, across the street from Cab Calloway's roadhouse, where she was to pick up a new Cadillac she had ordered; and him telling her he'd like to but he had to go down to the 57th Street dock where he was picking up a new ocean liner he'd ordered; and her getting angry and telling him to go to hell; and him saying he wished she'd got angry before drinking seven Scotch highballs at his expense.

"Everybody's lonely in this goddamn city," he thought bitterly.

He'd come home and begun drinking gin and reading Gorki's *Bystander,* hoping the combination would render him unconscious. But the story came and went as he read on into the early hours, confusing itself with stories of his own imagining, until he'd become entombed in a completely new and frightening world. And still his thoughts had kept on churning, turning back to one passage and another, here and there snagged by a line like one's clothes in a bramble thicket: "To love, to love! Life is so frightful—it is torment if one doesn't love! . . . An habitual—just grasp this!—an habitual lack of desire on the part of others to look into your soul kindly, tenderly. . . . You must learn this: all women are incurably sick with loneliness. This is the cause of all that is incomprehensible to you men—unexpected infidelities, and everything. None of you seeks, none of you thirsts for such intimacy with a human being as we do . . ." And always they came back to the passage describing the drowning of Boris, Clim's friend, and the line: "Clim heard someone in the crowd question gravely, doubtfully: *'But was there really a boy? Perhaps there was no boy at all!'*"

—Jesse Robinson.

—mmmm . . . Jack Robinson . . . James Robinson . . . Jeff Robinson . . . *Jim*—we have no Jesse Robinson listed here.

—J-E-S-S-E . . . Jesse . . . You *must* have me on the list . . .

—mmmm . . . *Jeff . . . Jim . . .*

34

—But I lived in the world for forty-one years . . .

—mmmm . . .

—I was a writer! I wrote two books—about blacks.

—mmmm . . .

—I was an American—a black American . . . I wrote about the black problem in America. . . .

—Ah yes! A very grave problem. We are very much concerned about the black problem. . . .

—Then certainly you've heard about me. I wrote two books about the black problem. It was all in the newspapers, in the book review sections. They reviewed my books. One of them said—I remember quite well: Robinson writes like a Dark Avenging Angel with his pen dipped in gall. . . . You must have heard of me!

—*Jesse* Robinson. . . . Let's see . . . *Jeff* . . . *Jim* . . . Funny . . . Are you absolutely sure there was a *Jesse* Robinson? . . . Perhaps there was no *Jesse* Robinson at all!

"Just think: half the men and women in the whole world in these few moments are loving one another, even as you and I are . . . My dearest, my unexpected one . . ."

—Perhaps there was no *Jesse* Robinson at all! . . .

"Or magnanimity, of compassion toward a woman, in a word! . . ."

—Lawd! There ain't nobody in this coffin!

—Ain't Jesse Robinson—

Nobody!

—But Jesse Robinson—

—Who's Jesse Robinson?

—He de one wu't died uf lonesomeness. Say fust time in hist'ry uh nigger die frum lonesomeness. In all de newspapers. . . .

—But ain't nobody in dis coffin!

—Lemme see . . . mmmm . . . empty as a minister's plate! . . . But whar de body of Jesse Robinson?

—Now you is askin' me. . . . Ah doan b'lieve dare evah wuz uh Jesse Robinson tuh bagin wid! . . .

Abruptly he opened his eyes. The cigarette butt was burning his fingers and he mashed it out in the cheap glass ashtray atop a battered, ancient, mahogany radio cabinet that served as a night table. Beyond the ashtray was a half-emptied package of Camel cigarettes, a half-eaten, twenty-five cent bar of milk chocolate, a half-emptied, pint-sized carton of milk, a small white enameled alarm clock with a broken crystal, and a milk-stained water glass smelling of gin. All were clustered like a repulsive brood of hybrids about a pumpkin-sized spherical bottle containing a green solution, which comprised the base of a night lamp which had a large, faded pink shade that sat loosely on a frame made for something else. Inside the cabinet, behind the closed doors, were his stacks of unpublished manuscripts, carbon copies, old papers and letters which he always kept nearby, carting them from place to place, hanging on to them year after year, to remind himself that—no matter what he did for a living—he was a writer by profession.

According to the cracked face of the clock, it was ten minutes after eight. The sun was over East River at about 125th Street, beyond the flats of Harlem and south of the Triborough Bridge, but in a direct line with Flushing, L.I. Sunlight slanted through the open venetian blinds, making thin stairways of light and shadow on the pale green of the opposite wall, and underneath the blinds, where they failed to reach the window sills by a matter of over two feet, a solid block of light fell obliquely across the hideous green, red and yellow cover of the couch.

His windows, facing south, were on the fifth floor, overlooking 142nd Street between Convent and Amsterdam Avenues, midway in that stone ridge, probably from the ice age, that runs up the western shore of Manhattan Island from 135th Street to the Cloisters. He could not see the Hudson River because at this point Amsterdam Avenue was higher and Broadway was in between, but over the rooftops of the houses across the street he could see the stone arch of the entrance to City College, the towers of Riverside Drive Cathedral higher toward the right, and on clear days the spire of the Empire State Building down at 34th Street and 5th Avenue. He was never impressed by the view. He liked best the fact that no one from across the street could look in through his windows. For many times in the night he walked about in the nude with his lights on and the blinds open.

He got up and surveyed his nude body in the mirror. It was a trim, muscular body, the color of Manila paper, with the broad-shouldered proportions of a pugilist. From the neck down he could have been anywhere from twenty-five to thirty. Only his face ever showed his age, now it was swollen from heavy drinking and had the smooth, dead, dull-eyed look of a Harlem pimp. The bright windows in the background impaired his reflection, so he leaned forward and stared at his image close-up. "Jesse Robinson," he said aloud. It was a reflex comment of a man whose name has been so beaten and battered it's out on its feet. "I oughta just tricked with the bitch." He didn't realize he said the latter aloud. He had been talking aloud to himself for a long time now without knowing it. "Anyway—" Whatever it was he intended to say, he forgot before he had said it.

Across the top of the dresser was a remnant of dark upholstery fabric, raveled at both ends, and littered with toilet articles—combs and brushes, a bar of green soap in a yellow saucer, three tooth-brushes in a dirty glass, a rusty safety razor in a plastic case—a huge, vicious-looking, pearl handle clasp knife made in Denmark, a bottle of iodine, a tin of bandages, an empty hair tonic bottle, an empty sparkling water bottle, a gin bottle with three fingers of gin, a dirty drinking glass, a brown sack containing three raw eggs, and a number of half-used folders of paper matches.

He fingered his chin, decided he needed a shave. Then, sticking out his lower lip, he blew his breath into his nostrils to see if it smelled bad. "Not my breath," he said. Pouring the remainder of the gin into the water glass, he broke in two raw eggs and filled it with milk. He drank it down without pausing for breath, swallowing the eggs whole, his hand trembling slightly. Then he broke off a piece of the milk chocolate bar and munched it absently. He believed this diet of gin, eggs, milk, and chocolate gave him great sexual potency. Although what he needed with sexual potency he didn't know. Here it was the beginning of April and he hadn't slept with a woman since before Christmas, although he knew none of his acquaintances would believe it. "Just loading my gun, that's all," he said. The thought amused him. Laughter blew from his nose. "Better not let the birdmen know," he thought. "They won't be able to keep out of range."

Suddenly he caught a whiff of some foul scent. "Dog piss!" he said. He got down on his hands and knees and sniffed about the legs of the dresser, about the bottom of his wardrobe trunk in the corner, about the legs of the ancient radio cabinet. The dust made him sneeze. "For what I pay for this goddamned room I ought to get it cleaned up once in a while," he said. He thought he heard a voice ask, "What did you say?" To which he replied shortly, "I wasn't talking to you."

Finally he located the area of the scent in the dark brown stains on the polished oak floor about the legs at the foot of his bed. It was definitely the scent of dog urine. "Dirty little bastards! I'll poison 'em!" he muttered angrily, getting to his feet. Then he thought, half-amused, "Everybody else has pissed on me; why not Leroy's dogs?" His mind kept fiddling with the thought, "It's only us dogs, boss." He didn't like that particularly and tried again, "There's nothing too good to go to the dogs." But that sounded too much like a wise saying. Scratching his pubic hair he exhausted the thought with "What's that you say, boy? . . . All I say, boss, is more lamp posts more dogs grow."

For a moment he stood absently looking at his toes. "Even black feet are white on the bottom," he said. On the side of the bed was a very old, frayed, rust-colored Persian rug, but its coloring was still rich and bright. "Wonder where they get all this strange junk in this house?" he said. "No doubt Leroy's. His white folks' throw-aways. Wonder how—" Leaving the thought unfinished, he put on a pair of faded flannel pyjamas that were draped across the back of a chair, stepped into a pair of white rubber bath slippers with red rubber soles, slipped on a dark blue rayon robe, greasy about the collar and cuffs, and went out to the toilet.

The apartment was located in the rear corner of a large apartment house with the three front rooms, including his own, overlooking 142nd Street, while the kitchen, bath, and back bedroom on the other side faced across a narrow air well toward the blackish brick walls and incredibly dirty windows, always closed, of a small Catholic Convent.

The two front bedrooms, his and the corner one, Leroy's opened onto short hallways, not more than a step in length, that led to a large square back hall, which was separated from the small sitting room at front by a glass partition. But the sitting-room blinds were always closed, throwing the hall in deep shadow. Jesse never left his room without mixed feelings of awe, admiration, and laughter, inspired by the fantastic furnishings crammed so thickly into every nook and corner that the mere act of crossing the hall to the john became a perilous journey, never to be taken lightly, and not to be ventured upon whatsoever when one was drunk and lacked full command of one's senses.

In the narrow passage just to the left of his door stood the wooden cabinet of a Grandfather clock, over six feet tall, which he had dubbed the "mummy's coffin," its dark dulled finish blending with the surrounding gloom to form a perfect hazard located with uncanny skill and foresight to bump the heads of any who dared venture in that direction in the dark. He had yet to avoid it when either going or returning from the john at night; for to the right was a huge pot of imitation evergreens sitting on a wobbly tripod that had to be skirted, and beyond the clock cabinet, placed, strategically, directly in front of the glass partition, stood a cracked, white marble statue of a half-nude woman resting precariously atop a small round stand with rickety iron legs. The entrance to Leroy's bedroom was rendered reasonably secure by two small bare tables arranged like a tank-trap in the Siegfried line. Beside the plastic evergreens was another table on which stood a huge, gilt clock that never ran and an empty glass fishbowl; beyond which was an old-fashioned writing desk and a rusty umbrella rack, the two of them efficiently blocking the entrance to the long narrow hallway, always pitch dark, through which one passed to reach the distant outside exit to the corridor—if you didn't break your hip against the one, you tripped over the other and knocked out your teeth against an ancient iron footscraper located in the dark at just the exact distance to catch you in the mouth should you fall on your face.

Against the back wall of the hall stood a chest of drawers, atop which sat a glass-enclosed bookcase crammed with dusty, hand-me-down books, dusty stacks of sheet music, broken victrola records, and a scatter of whisky glasses; it in turn served as a perch for a stuffed owl which appeared so shockingly lifelike in such natural surroundings Jesse often wondered how the birdmen would dare venture from their nests.

On the other side of the hall was a huge black marble-topped dining-room table, leaning heavily against the wall for support, and serving as a zoo parade for a strange menagerie ranging from a large beribboned Teddy bear to a set of three wise monkeys carved from a peach seed. "Leroy's Ark," Jesse called it.

Although the sitting room was much smaller than either bedroom, it contained an armchair, a settee, a sculpted head in white marble atop a tall, mahogany column, a combination radio, phonograph and television set with a twenty-one inch screen that was larger than the family Renault, a Baby Grand piano complete with piano stool, and a magnificent coffee table, the top of which was a removable, hand-carved circular brass tray about a yard in diameter. A tall man with long arms on the settee could easily, without moving, play the piano with his toes, operate the phonograph with his left hand while mixing drinks with his right and spit in the eye of any face which appeared on the television screen without having to turn his head—which Jesse considered a great advantage.

When Jesse stepped into the hall he noticed that Leroy's bedroom door was open, and the young man, Pal, who slept with Leroy, was sitting on the edge of the rumpled bed, clad in green-and-white striped pajamas, telephoning. "That's when my love came down," he confessed, laughing uproariously, but broke off upon sight of Jesse and looked embarrassed. He nodded and Jesse said, "Good morning." He was about twenty-eight, Jessie guessed; a well-built virile-looking young man with a sepia complexion and kinky hair clipped short; and he had a warm smile and dull doe eyes quite suitable for his role. "*Fau-nesse*," Jesse thought, "Suffragette casualty," as he maneuvered himself through the narrow treacherous pass between the marble-top table and the bookcase to the short side hall that led to the kitchen on the left, the bath straight ahead, and Mr Ward's back bedroom to the right.

Mr Ward's door was closed, as was customary, and there was no way of telling whether he was in or out; he had worked in the post office for close to twenty years and took advantage of his sick-leave, seniority and other accrued benefits to stay home whenever

40

he pleased. Mr Ward was a short, dark, heavyset, partially-bald man with marbled eyes. "Image of God," Jesse thought, half-amused. "Genesis 1:27." Then, "If it'd been me, however, I wouldn't have admitted it."

He stepped inside the kitchen with the intention of making coffee. But sight of the devastation discouraged him. Garbage spread out from a pile beside the dumbwaiter, empty beer tins, crab shells, chicken bones, gin bottles, broken glass, and what closely resembled dried vomit, beneath which the garbage pail was completely inundated. The breakfast table was covered with dirty egg-stained dishes, coffee cups, and scraps of bread, the spoils of breakfast; the sink was stacked with dirty dishes, the ravages of last night's feast. Atop the oven of an incredibly filthy gas range in the corner were piled helter-skelter a variety of blackened kitchen utensils and several coffee percolators, including his own, which still contained the coffee grounds and dregs of aged coffee. On the stove's warmer were cups of runny fat, greasy boxes of matches, a jar of salt, a tin of pepper, and a saucepan partly filled with burnt rice. The burners held a dishpan filled with cold boiled bluepoint crabs, their bluish shells resembling unevenly tempered metal. Underneath the stove was the dog bed, lined with filthy rags and surrounded by layers of newspapers which were stained in several places where the dogs had peed.

Looking at the mess with disgust, Jesse recalled hearing one of the boys say girlishly the night before, "I feel so *unnecessary*!" He thought, "Damn right! Unnecessary and unexpurgated too!" But he lingered for a moment longer because the kitchen always fascinated him.

In the recess beside the dumbwaiter stood a huge refrigerator, above which, extending along both inside walls to the sealed door that had once connected Leroy's bedroom, was a glass-enclosed china cabinet, beneath which was a wooden kitchen cabinet with many drawers. This cabinet was crammed to overflowing with glass and chinaware of a great variety of texture, size and design: individual glasses of innumerable shapes, ranging from exquisite, long-stemmed crystal wine glasses, delicate cutglass goblets, to the cheap gaudy ten-cent store tumblers and "shot" glasses of the kind used in cheap bars; several cocktail sets in stainless steel, colored glass and yellow plastic; a huge variety of pitchers, platters, serving dishes, stacks of plates, saucers, cups, finger bowls, egg cups, soup bowls, and beer mugs in the shape of miniature chamber pots, each and every one of different quality and design. Below, atop the kitchen cabinet, was an open tray of "company" silver, a few pieces of sterling, but most silverplate, worn along the edges and in the bowls of the spoons, no two pieces matching; and to one side a glass pitcher crammed with utensils of a dullish metal resembling pewter and others stamped with the names of chain restaurants and cheap hotels. "Too late to fire me now, boy," Jesse said. "I got mine already."

Among other items contributory to a varied cuisine and good housekeeping were: two containers of eggs with different trademarks; two tins of coffee of different brands; a battered tin bread box half-filled with four partly used loaves of white bread, each of a different brand; an unopened box of cube sugar, its surface covered with dust, and two paper cartons of granulated sugar; three partly-filled bottles of cheap, popular whiskys of different brands; one empty and one full gin bottle; two empty siphons; two containers of Pepsi-Cola, one with two empties and one with three; an electric iron sans cord with a rusty plate; three boxes of soap powder, two opened; a batch of policy slips neatly filed on a nail driven through a board; a jar of pickles, two rolls of toilet paper, and a paper sack of strange roots. "Double or nothing," Jesse thought.

Beside the sealed door was a broom closet containing a two-foot stack of old newspapers, atop which was a two-foot stack of old paper bags; a lopsided broom; an old raincoat; an old sports jacket; a white rubber apron; a pair of black rubber hip boots; a soiled white chef's cap; a section of rubber hose; an assorted collection of twine; the electric iron cord; two leather belts; a broken fly swatter; three worn dog leashes; a hammer, screwdriver, handsaw, empty bottles, old shoes, dust rags, and a section of vacuum cleaner tubing. Whenever the door was opened, things began falling out. "Pandora's got nothing on you boys," Jesse muttered.

He opened the refrigerator to look for his milk, then stood back and stared. The top shelf was crammed with tins of beer; on the second shelf were butter, eggs, two bottles of milk, a bottle of grape juice, three bottles of Coca-Cola, and a quart of orange pop. His container of milk was gone, however. On the shelf beneath were the carcass of a roasted turkey, half of a layer cake with white frosting, a dish of boiled okra, a plate of fried chicken, and a quart bottle of ginger ale. The bottom shelf held one-half of a baked ham, a platter piled high with a gray concoction that closely resembled granulated putty—a speciality of Leroy's made of boiled corn meal and okra—three-quarters of a sweet potato pie, two boiled pig's feet, and a dish of stewed prunes. In the glass meat tray beneath the freezer were a number of whole fish, probably porgies. "What, no chitterlings?" Jesse said, then, "Never mind the wings, Lawd, just set out the victuals. Leave them fly who been resting all their lives."

As he started to take a swig from one of the whiskey bottles he heard the outside door open and the dogs yelping, and hastened into the bathroom. The toilet bowl was clogged and filled with excrement. "No wonder!" he said.

The window was raised and while urinating he looked absently toward the windows of the convent. The window opposite on the floor beneath opened from the toilet or bath. Once he had seen it cracked from the top. He wondered if the nuns knew what sort of neighbors they had across the way. He heard Leroy entering the kitchen, talking to the dogs in his high whining voice. "Now you let Nero alone, Napoleon. You know he hasn't got any teeth. Bad dog! Bad dog! I'm gonna have to whip yo' little ass if you don't behave." He heard the rattle of the chain as Leroy hung it carelessly over the doorknob.

He waited for a moment, hoping Leroy would leave so he wouldn't have to speak to him, but hearing him fiddling about the sink, grumbling to himself, "Now I got to wash all these dishes. They must think I'm their mother." He slipped into the hall, hoping to pass unnoticed, but Leroy saw him and greeted brightly, "Good morning, Mr. Robinson. I thought you were out."

"Good morning, Mr. Martin. No, I came in late." He'd always made a particular point of addressing *Mister* Martin and *Mister*

Ward with strict formality to avoid any familiarity; the other one he called Pal because it was the only name he knew.

Leroy was a big black man, over six feet tall, with a bulging belly and huge horny hands. He had removed his coat and hat and was now clad in a soiled white shirt with rolled sleeves and black, chauffeur uniform trousers, baggy and shiny, unbuttoned at the top so his belly could overflow. His eyes popped slightly from his flat round face, giving him a look of perpetual surprise, which went admirably with his surroundings. But whenever he looked at Jesse his lids lowered lecherously and his smile widened hungrily, giving to his startled face an expression of a murderer confronting his victim. However, it was intended to be a coquettish look, at once admiring, indulgent, respectful and desirous, by which he hoped to overcome Jesse's reserve.

"Won't you have some coffee? I've just made some fresh coffee." He bustled up a cup and saucer like an eager widow.

"No, thanks, I'm going back to sleep. Coffee keeps me awake."

Leroy looked crestfallen. "Whenever I ask you to have a bite to eat you always say you're just going out or you've just eaten or you're just going to sleep," he complained. "One of these days I'm gonna quit asking you."

"Why the hell don't you," Jesse thought, but instead he smiled and said, "You always ask me at the wrong time, Mr. Martin. This is my drinking day."

He tried to hurry on before Leroy could reply, but the little dog, Napoleon, who had been waiting his opportunity, charged him, barking furiously, and began nipping at his heels. Both dogs were blond Pomeranians, thoroughbreds with recorded pedigrees, the best of their species. Napoleon had been sired by Nero, who now lay quietly in his dog bed, old, shaggy and stinky, toothless and almost blind. They had been given to Leroy by a former employer, a wealthy dress manufacturer, who had taken up Doberman Pinschers at the death of his wife, to whom the Pomeranians had actually belonged. At the last moment Mr. Fishbein had relented his long cherished resolve to have the Dobermans chew them up, and had given them to his black chauffeur instead. Whether he appreciated the irony of his decision, no one ever knew. They were very valuable dogs, or at least had been during the life of Mrs. Fishbein. And Leroy was quite fond of them, partly because he knew of their former value, partly because they were such sissy dogs. But Jesse despised them, despised the breed. Although of the two, he liked Nero the better because Nero was soon going to die, which is what Jesse was convinced all Pomeranians should do. So when this little bastard came nipping at his heels his impulse was to give him a swift kick in the ribs, which he always did when no one was about.

But now Leroy called sharply, "Napoleon! Napoleon! You nasty thing! You come back here and let Mr. Robinson alone." he raised his lidded, lecherous look to Jesse's face. "He likes you," he said with double entendre; "Those are just little love bites. He takes after his papa."

"Oh, we understand one another," Jesse said, hastening back to his room.

He stripped nude and began dressing. "Need a damn chastity belt to step out this door," he muttered. He'd gotten on his blue-gray slacks, undershirt and shoes, when someone knocked. "Come in."

Leroy entered with a tray. "Ohhhh, Mr. Robinson! You told me you were going to bed," he said accusingly.

"I changed my mind," Jesse said shortly, but softened the brusque reply by adding, "I remembered several things I had to do."

"I brought you a little snack so you wouldn't have to go to bed hungry," Leroy said, placing the tray on the dresser and stealing a look at Jesse's seminude torso.

There was a plate of turkey sandwiches, a half bottle of whiskey, the cold bottle of ginger ale from the refrigerator, a glass, mixer, bowl of ice, and a slice of cake on the tray.

"I'm no frog, you snake," Jesse thought but, seeing the whiskey, relented. "That looks mighty good. Maybe I ought to go to bed at that."

Leroy's expression didn't change, but he gave the impression of rubbing his hands together. "You know what they say; let your conscience be your guide." He was looking at Jesse's shoulder as if he might take a bite out of it.

"I don't have much choice this morning," Jesse said quickly, putting on his shirt. "If that son of a bitch makes a pass at me I'll cut his throat," he thought. "But I will have a drink," he added.

"Oh, help yourself," Leroy said, trying to keep the disappointment from his voice. "I made it for *you*."

"I suppose you made the liquor, too," Jesse thought. He took a stiff drink straight and when Leroy turned to leave, stopped him. "Oh, just a moment, Mr. Martin. I want to show you where the dogs've been using my bed for a tree."

Leroy looked, then sniffed. "The nasty things! I'll bet it was Napoleon, the nasty thing! I'll bring him in here and put his nose in it and whip his little ass."

"No need of that. I just wanted to show it to you. My door'll have to stay shut." He didn't have a key to his room and what he meant was he wished they'd close the door when they entered it during his absence to look through his things. Leroy understood perfectly what he meant. "The little dog didn't mean any harm. When you gotta go, you gotta go, even if you are a dog."

Leroy laughed but caught himself just as he was about to slap Jesse on the shoulder, shake himself and shriek, "There's nothing for it but to *go*!" Instead he said, almost gruffly from having to exercise so much control, "I'll clean it up for you while you're out, Mr. Robinson," and hurriedly left the room.

"Jesus Christ, how'd I get mixed up with these birdmen?" Jesse asked himself. However, it hadn't been as involved as he wanted to make out. Three weeks before, directly after he'd gotten the five hundred dollar option on his new novel, he'd quit his porter's job in White Plains and had come to New York to look for a room.

Finding rooms for its itinerant population is one of Harlem's major businesses. One half of the population, at least a good two hundred thousand, live in rented rooms. They are never satisfied and move often. Or their landlords put them out. The rooming agent finds them another room, for which they pay a fee of five or ten dollars, depending on what kind of clothes they wear, cars they drive, or money they flash.

Jesse had consulted a woman agent selected at random from the classified advertisements in a Harlem weekly newspaper. She had sent him to see a woman, a Mrs. Susie Braithewaite, on the floor above him, who had registered a room with her agency. She hadn't really had a vacancy. The room was rented for a good price, fifteen dollars weekly, to a bartender who only used it during his days off and one or two nights in between, which Mr. Braithewaite thought was a "good deal." But Susie didn't like the fact that the bartender brought white girls there; and if he didn't bring them they came anyway and stood out in the hall where they could be seen by the other respectable Negro housewives, and rang her bell until someone answered. Who, of course, would not be the bartender; for unless he expected them he would have another white girl in his room, and two white girls at the same time always complicated matters. So she had decided to put the bartender out.

She hadn't apprised her husband of her intention until Jesse called for an interview, then she had telephoned him at the cleaners where he worked as a presser. He had said, "Hell no!" being a sensible man and realizing in the long run money was worth more than respectability. Besides which, the bartender threw some fine white girls his way every now and then—which was what his wife suspected.

But she was attracted to Jesse on sight and didn't want him to get away. She was one of those brownskinned women who look as if they might be voracious in bed. She was about twenty-five, Jesse guessed, with the strong solid body of a girl athlete, the bosom of a wet nurse, and the big, high, ball-bearing hips of a miller. She ran the tip of her red tongue slowly across her wide full cushiony sensuous lips, making them wetly red, and looked him straight in the eyes with her own glassy speckled bedroom eyes. He stared back, feeling all of himself run down to one point, too weak to move, knowing his eyes were begging *now! yes now! please now! it's got to be now! oh now! the rust is all dissolved. . . .* and hers replying *not now! you know it can't be now! but soon! just wait! can't you wait? it can't be all that loaded. . . .*

So she'd gotten him this room on the floor below with Mr. Martin. He should have recognized Mr. Martin as a Panette on sight. But you can't expect a man in that state to be very observant. He'd paid his rent and moved in before he'd realized the setup. Of course he could have moved after the first week. But it wasn't worth the trouble.

"What the hell I care what people think!" he said defiantly, tying a Duke of Kent knot in his dark red tie.

"I really ought to shave," he said as he pulled on a gray, cable-knit sweater. "I wish that punk would get a job and get the hell away from here sometimes." From a curtained alcove along the wall toward the sitting room which served as a clothes closet, he took down a gray tweed sport coat, brushed the dust from his dark brown suede shoes, and poured himself another drink. He was beginning to feel a light glow. "Not bad for an old man," he said, looking at himself in the mirror. His hair was cut too short, but that couldn't be helped. He'd gone to a barber in White Plains who kept getting one side shorter than the other until he'd almost cut it all off, like the story of how the dining-room table became a flying saucer. "Good thing I didn't get a shave there," he thought. "Look like hell with my teeth sticking out my jaws." He put on a welt-edge, snap-brim, dark brown hat, taking care to have it straight. The hat emphasized his tan skin and semicaucasian features, hiding his kinky hair. He poured himself another drink, then, noticing that the bottle was almost empty, poured the remainder into his glass, gulped it down and made a face. "Can't keep this up, son!" he told himself. He felt very gay, on the verge of laughter. "Long as his ass will lass. So, lass ass! Or should I say, ass, lass!"

He found himself staggering slightly as he opened the door to the hall. A ball of tan hair, barking furiously, charged from the dark cave beneath the marble-top table as if to nip him on the shin bone. But a voice of concern called quickly from the dark sitting room, "Napoleon! Napoleon! You behave yourself!"

Jesse glanced into the sitting room. Mr. Ward sat in the armchair watching a morning television program. He was clad in an old ragged and faded cotton robe, and on the brass coffee stand there was a bottle of whiskey and a half-filled highball glass.

"Good morning, Mr. Robinson." His greeting was polite, respectful and impersonal.

"Good morning, Mr. Ward."

The door to Leroy's bedroom was closed. Jesse switched on the

48

lights and went cautiously down the long narrow hall toward the front door. He had once counted seven tables in this hall, in addition to much more incredible junk. Halfway down he turned on another light so he could see to get out.

The door was bolted at the top and at the bottom and there were three locks. From the center lock a long heavy steel bar extended on a slant to an anchor in the floor. To unlock it, the top end was slipped from its socket in the lock, and passed upright through a bracket as the door opened inward. "Fort Knox!" Jesse muttered, manipulating the locks and bolts. He heard Mr. Ward call, "I'll turn out the lights, Mr. Robinson."

"Thanks, Mr. Ward," he called back.

Outside the door in the tiled corridor there was an iron and rubber door mat, welded to a short chain, the chain locked to a bolt, the bolt embedded in concrete in the floor. He had to lock all three locks again with separate keys. "I don't believe these people trust each other," he said.

A tall thin black and very old West Indian woman had just come from the apartment next door. She looked at him critically and disapprovingly. A couple emerged from an apartment farther down and looked at him curiously. The superintendent came from the elevator and looked at him interestedly. The super spoke. "What say, sport." He looked as if they had a secret, but he wasn't going to tell. "Can't say," Jesse replied. "All said." The super grinned knowingly. "Keep 'em guessing, sport."

Jesse was smiling to himself when he got in the elevator. "They all think I'm one of the boys," he thought. It tickled him. He noticed a very good-looking girl in the corner of the elevator, probably a student or a model, staring at him. He winked at her. She kept staring without any change of expression and when the elevator stopped on the ground floor, she hurried off like a very independent and competent young miss on her way to business—whatever her business might be—her high, hard heels tapping rhythmically on the tiles, her tall lithe body tripping down the steps, swinging through the outer glass door. "You were born on the wrong side of the genitals, son," he told himself, half-amused.

It was a bright sunshiny April morning. He stood in front of the apartment for a moment, looking up and down the street. That part of Convent Avenue, from City College to 145th Street, was very attractive and clean, with its well-kept, picturesque old houses and stone and brick-faced apartment buildings among the most desirable residences in Harlem. Parking was restricted, and the black, slightly slanting macadam was lined with trees beginning to green. It was very pleasant standing there in the sun, watching the stream of students pass, the lovely young girls and the bright young men, as they came up from the Independent Subway at the corner of St. Nicholas and 145th Street. "From little icons big skyscrapers grow. Heaven's the next floor, please," he thought.

Now that he was dressed and outdoors, he didn't know where to go. He didn't know anyone he could visit at that hour." At any hour!" he said aloud. Two men passing looked at him. He looked away. He wasn't hungry yet. The thought of braving a lonely breakfast in some cheap Harlem hashjoint repelled him. The bars weren't open yet.

He decided to go down to 42nd Street and see what was showing at the cheap movie houses between Eighth Avenue and Times Square. They opened at eight. "Good thing you like movies, son," he thought. "Otherwise you'd believe all that crap about your country you experience every day."

He started down the slope toward 145th Street. "I go down but it's uptown," he thought. Everyone else was going the other way. He went down the street walking against the crowd. He staggered a little, but didn't feel drunk. Millions of thoughts were churning into grotesque patterns in the back of his head, crowding out the gaiety.

CHAPTER 3

KRISS ALIGHTED FROM the IRT local at 59th Street and Lexington Avenue, turned west at 60th Street, and walked north on Madison Avenue.

For more than twenty years this strip of Madison Avenue had been relinquished by the city fathers to old ladies of the *Arsenic and Old Lace* variety as a reservation in which to walk their cats and dogs. Then came the apocalyptic day when the quiet, genteel atmosphere of the reservation was shattered by house wreckers and steam shovels excavating for the foundation of the new, modern, aluminium building which, later, was to house the Ford Foundation. The old ladies freshened their arsenic and ventured forth, but the lower-class laborers didn't drink tea. So the elderly females were forced to dally behind blackened curtains and had to learn to exercise their dogs and cats early in the morning and late in the afternoon when the danger of their being squashed into Harlem hamburger was minimized.

They considered the clean, shining, bright building a profanation, a veritable tower of Babel, in which, as events have proved, they were not so far wrong. They sharpened their tealeaves and bided their time.

But when the old stone Godwin Mansion was given over to the India Institute, and the reservation was invaded by its rabble of employees, Jews from Brooklyn, Italians from the Bronx, Irish from Hell's Kitchen, blacks from Harlem, foreign Americans from such outlandish places as Akron Ohio, Gary Indiana, Tulsa Oklahoma, that was the bitter end. Now the old ladies walk their cats and dogs with veiled eyes and closed ears, seeing only the glory of the past and hearing only the quiet gentility of remembrance, the faint shape of bitterness in the puckers of their old lips, perhaps of sadness, of sorrow that they should have lived to see the day.

Kriss liked the old ladies. She always smiled at them and sometimes spoke. She would stop to rub the arched back of a sleek fat spoiled blue Persian cat, cooing with genuine admiration, "Oh, isn't he lovely! He's the loveliest thing!" Or she would grin sympathetically at some old blind Scottie that had mistaken a gentleman's leg for a lamp post and was about to make a faux pas; and would be seized by an almost incontrollable impulse to say, "No, no, darling, that's a man's leg," and guide it gently to the proper edifice.

The old ladies liked her. "She is the only real gentlelady of the lot," they had informed themselves. "It's too bad she had to associate with such trash, poor thing."

But there were no old ladies about this morning and Kriss had to be content with the greetings of a few old fat pigeons that moved aside grudgingly to let her pass.

It was twenty minutes after nine when she ascended the worn stone stairs and entered the Godwin mansion. By this time the employees were all at their places and the huge reception hall with its marble fountain, the focal point of prework congregation, was deserted. Water no longer cascaded from the four mouths of the marble Brahma in timeless, uncreated, immaterial and illitimable streams upon the bevy of frolicking cherubins in the empty basin, but the four faces of the supreme soul looked down upon all who entered with benign intelligence and bliss. Kriss had once flirted with the Brahmanic concept, years before when she was a freshman at Chicago University and had tried sleeping with a Hindu; and many times of late, when passing beneath the four faces of this bastard monstrosity, she had the strange feeling that perhaps after all life was but a dream.

The mansion, built in the shape of a U about an inner court devoted to a formal garden, was a weird combination of Renaissance architecture, Indian impressionism, English pretentiousness, adapted to the basic idea of American plumbing, lighting, and comfort. It gave a fairly accurate reflection of the personality of old Marcus Cornelius Godwin who had erected it. By incorporating in both England and the United States, M. Cornelius Godwin had taken a fabulous fortune out of India during the nineteenth century and had died in 1905 at the age of eighty-nine an avowed Brahman—although this latter had not been taken seriously by his family who

5 2

had given him a decent Episcopalian burial. Old Godwin had loved India but had been greatly impressed by the cold-blooded commercialism and upper-class idolatry of the British aristocracy. However, in his later years he had discovered, somewhat to his chagrin, that he had lost his enthusiasm for monocles, ice-cold castles, the correct thing, and conversations conducted in a smaller vocabulary then that employed by an English-speaking Zulu. So, in the 1880s he had built this monstrosity to pass his declining years in both style and comfort. It was not comfortable in the modern connotation of the word, but it had been warm, heated by a steam furnace that consumed in the winter an average of two tons of coal a day, and it had been lived-in despite the rococo decor, the gilded mirrors at every turn apprising him of approaching death, the lifesize angels in full flight about the ceilings of the rooms ready to bear him off at a moment's notice, the English drawing room with its leaded windows looking out on Madison Avenue, a concession to his youthful awe of titles. He had entertained many of the great and famous there, distant neighbors from Fifth Avenue, old cronies from Gramercy Park. There was a full-length portrait of the old boy on the landing facing the double stairway.

Most of the employees poked fun at the stern, bewhiskered visage of the erect, somewhat soldierly old pirate, dubbing it the "Face on the Gold Room Floor." But Kriss revered the venerable old man and when no one was about, ofttimes stood for minutes before his portrait. He reminded her of her great-grandfather, whom she vaguely remembered seeing when she was five or six. He had the same stern look and a great white forest of whiskers, and his eyes were the ice cold blue of the Godwin in the portrait. Her mother had always maintained that her great-grandfather was a bona fide German count, but as a little girl Kriss had thought of him as God.

However, this morning she didn't pass the portrait but continued quickly along a side hall toward the elevator.

There were four floors given over to the Institute personnel, including the basement. The main floor with its formal garden was unused, being maintained as a museum. And the servants' quarters

5 3

in the rear of the right wing were closed and empty, except for a suite occupied by the superintendent.

Kriss's office was on the third floor, in what had once been a guest bedroom, but was now partitioned into three small offices, of which hers was the center. Along the inner wall a corridor had been fashioned by enclosing the cubicles with a glass and wallboard screen, such as might be found in banks. There was no privacy, and audibility between the three offices were unencumbered by the thin partitions.

On her way past, Kriss smiled and said hello to Dorothy Stone, Kirby's secretary, who had the office to her left. Dorothy gave her a scintillating smile in return, looking as if she had scads of things to talk about. But Kriss didn't stop. Dot's personality was not the type to start the day off right.

From beyond, in the far office, came the rapid clatter of an old upright typewriter. Benny Field, the accountant, was hard at work. Kriss didn't disturb him.

Her office was furnished with a glass-top desk on which lay several stacks of typed pages, her telephone, an inkwell, an empty porcelain vase, and a small bright glass globe of the world; a metal typewriter stand holding a new plastic-covered upright typewriter; a new desk chair and two leather upholstered straight-back chairs, leftovers from the original furnishings. On the deep window edge at her back, a pigeon had built a nest and was now sitting on four eggs. Kriss made a soft clucking sound and the pigeon looked at her indignantly. She gave a little girl's laugh—her private laugh reserved for animals, children, and television comedians. "Go on," she whispered. "I don't want to sit on your old eggs." The pigeon stirred nervously. "Now you know how I felt when you used to stand there and stare at me by the hour," Kriss said, then hung her coat on the tree in the corner, and sat at her desk. She looked at the stacks of summaries before her, some to be proofread before mailing, others to be corrected and retyped. One stack was more or less just data to be correlated, organized and summarized. Across her desk passed the entire program of the Institute.

The Institute had its origin in a foundation left by Godwin for the purpose of bringing ambitious Indian students to the United

States to study. For more than twenty-five years it had been directed by a small staff of elderly women, retired school teachers and the like, who had played nursemaids to a small select group of high-caste Hindus through the Ivy League universities. But following the war, during India's crusade for independence, it had assumed a startling stature as a source of reference and a point of contact, not only in the field of education, but for the federal government, private enterprise, and all other major foundations as well. So the trustees had reorganized, and expanded the personnel to over two hundred. Having soon outgrown the modest fund of eleven million dollars left by M. Cornelius Godwin, the new India Institute was subsidized by more than a dozen other foundations and indirectly by the Federal Government. M. Cornelius Godwin III, seeing it slip away from the family name, donated the use of the family mansion, and proposed to the trustees that it be changed to Godwin Institute or Godwin Foundation or even Godwin India Institute. But by then nine-tenths of the funds for its operation came from other sources and they could not very well do this.

Kriss had started four-and-a-half years ago at a salary of fifty dollars a week, when the staff had been comparatively small. Now her salary was six thousand dollars a year and she had the title of assistant director. She wrote the summaries of the Institute projects which were sent, as prospectuses, to all of the subsidizing foundations and to the U.S. State Department. They were subject of course to approval by the directors, there being a director for each of the four major divisions of the Institute's program, a director of personnel, and *the* director, Kirby Reynolds. As a consequence she sat in on all policy meetings. She was important, well-liked and permanently situated.

And yet she had liked her temporary job at the Chicago Foundation far more. This morning, as every morning, on facing the dull tedious work, she remembered her office in the old mansion in Chicago overlooking the spacious grounds that had formed a circle of exclusiveness, the leisurely, personalized routine, the president's morning kiss—of course, after she had begun sleeping with him—lunch on the terrace, bridge in the card room before dinner, conversation and drinking afterward, always the visitors, good-looking

5 5

black professionals, artists, writers, college deans, and presidents, the excitement of choosing the one she wanted for the night, which was the only reason she ever had to return to her apartment at all in those days. The memory lasted but a moment, but left a definite block. She was still alert, still eager, still confident, but her mind didn't want to engage in the task before her.

For fifteen minutes she read the morning paper, after which she sorted her work, called her secretary from the floor below and gave her the pages to be typed, and rapidly read the completed summaries for typographical errors. She was an expert proofreader with a complete command of punctuation and grammatical construction, and in addition a very excellent writer of clear, explanatory prose. Her sentences were always concise and to the point, never ambiguous, and were phrased with amazing simplicity and conclusiveness and in perfect logical sequence. No man would ever believe a woman wrote such prose until taken into her office and confronted with the fact. Then they wanted to date her.

At ten o'clock she began composing in longhand and continued without interruption for an hour, by which time she had written nine pages.

Anne Sayers, her assistant, came in to ask if she wanted coffee.

"Yes, dear, thank you," she replied without looking up.

Anne was a huge young woman, over six feet tall, with a round pleasant face, a mop of tan curls, and was smart as a whip. She compiled the data for the summaries, checked the facts and figures with the sources. Her office was similar to Kriss's but was located in the wing overlooking the court. There were only women in that section and something like a boarding school atmosphere prevailed. Anne had a sideboard in her office where she kept tea, coffee, tea biscuits, cocktail crackers, jars of cheeses, tins of hors d'oeuvres, and usually a bottle of claret and a bottle of sherry; and, of course, cups and saucers, sugar and—if she thought to bring it—cream, an electric coffee pot, a cocktail service, and a set of silverware. Kriss's only concession to office refreshment was a silver flask of Scotch she kept in her desk drawer; but coffee was always welcome at this time. With it she could take another pill.

A few minutes later Anne returned with a flaming face. "God-dammit!" she choked furiously.

Kriss looked up in surprise. "Why—what's the trouble, Anne?"

"That damned Watson again!"

Watson was the personnel director. He disapproved of the girls making coffee and toast in the big pleasant bathroom across the corridor, and had wanted to post a notice forbidding it, but Kirby had said no. So he had initiated a campaign which couldn't be refuted. Every day at eleven, when the girls began making tea and toast and coffee, he had to answer the call of nature. He would stand patiently beside the door, merely waiting his turn, until the girls cleared out, then he would enter and lock the door. They despised him.

"Seems he could shit somewhere else while we're making coffee!" Anne flared.

"He's a son of a bitch if ever there was one," Kriss murmured consolingly.

"I'm going to curse that man yet," Anne declared.

Dorothy heard them talking about Watson and came from next door. "Kirby says he's going to have a toilet installed in Watson's office," she said, grinning at Kriss.

"Well, I'm going back and knock," Anne said defiantly. "He's had time enough."

Kriss chuckled. "He's not a duck, dear."

Anne had to laugh. When she left, Dorothy came around the desk and looked over Kriss's shoulder. But instead of commenting on the work, she tenderly fingered Kriss's curls and said, "Your hair always looks so fresh."

Kriss was slightly embarrassed. She didn't like women to touch her. But Dorothy was different. She knew that Dorothy had a crush on her that amounted almost to worship. Dot was forever complimenting her on her dress, her carriage, her poise, telling her how pretty she was, how brilliant everyone considered her. Every now and then she wondered if Dot were a lesbian. She was disconcertingly affectionate, and awfully jealous. Whenever another woman came to Kriss's office—even Anne, who was as soft as butter about men—Dot would find some excuse to come in too. But she liked

Dot. And it paid to be nice to her. As Kirby's confidential secretary she had inside information about everything that went on at the executive level—and she told Kriss everything she wanted to know, in strictest confidence of course. Besides which, Kriss felt sorry for her. She was such a shy woman and so sensitive, so easily hurt; really a virgin at heart despite the fact she was almost as old as Kriss. She had such an enormous capacity for emotion; she wanted to be loved violently, but was petrified with fear by the very thought of it. Kriss often wondered if Dot had ever slept with a man. Probably so! She'd never heard of the stone lions roaring when Dot passed the library at 42nd and Fifth, which they did whenever a virgin passed.

"It's just my country look," Kriss giggled. "That's a very pretty blouse, baby."

"Oh, this old thing!" It was a soft white nylon of a mannish cut, worn with a large black bow. "You've seen it before."

Kriss wished that Dot would wear things that were more feminine. It would do her good. "Quit despising yourself," Kriss wanted to say. Dot's air of wistful self-deprecation always slightly angered her. She quickly changed the conversation from clothes.

"Watson's going to keep on until Anne sits on him someday," she said. "And he doesn't know how much Anne weighs."

"Oh, that reminds me of a joke I want to tell you. Mrs. Donahue told it to me last night." She grinned. "I don't know where she hears such things."

Kriss knew Mrs. Donahue, the eighty-two-year-old semi-invalid with whom Dorothy lived, and she knew why the old lady told Dorothy those Rabelaisian jokes—she thought her prim genteel roomer much too respectable for her own good. So did Kriss. She gave Dorothy a wicked grin. "Tell me, baby."

Anne came in at that moment with the coffee and Dorothy hesitated. She couldn't bear to be intimate with another woman. But when Kriss urged, "Go on, Dot, tell Anne, too," she began. "Well—" then looked at Anne and blurted, "I got this from my landlady."

Anne flung her a quick look and continued serving the coffee.

"She knows, dear," Kriss said, but the sarcasm was lost on Dorothy.

"Well—there was a Texan wandering about the city wearing a ten gallon hat—"

Now Anne looked solidly at Dorothy, but bit back the words, "You don't say?" Instead she put her sting into the anonymous Texan. "With water on the brain."

Kriss chuckled. "No doubt, dear, but not ten gallons!"

"Just like a Texan. Always exaggerating."

"Do you want to hear this story or not?" Dorothy complained jealously.

"Let Dot tell her story," Kriss said.

"Well, this Texan ran into an actor on Broadway dressed like a Quaker. He'd never seen a Quaker before. So he went up to the actor and said, 'Talk some Quaker for me, will you, Friend.' The Quaker smiled indulgently and tried to pass, but the Texan took hold of his arm 'Oh, come on, partner, talk some Quaker for me. Ah never heard nobody talk Quaker.' The actor tried to disengage his arm, but the Texan held him firmly. 'Ah tell you what I'll do, Friend. If you talk some Quaker for me, I'll buy you the best feed they can throw together at 21.' When the Texan said that, the actor turned slowly and looked him straight in the eye. 'Fuck thee!' he said."

Kriss laughed with childish glee. "Someone should tell that to Watson. The last part, I mean."

Even Anne giggled. "I'll tell him," she said. "You just wait. And I won't say *thee,* either!"

Dorothy glanced at her watch. "Oh, I've got to run; Kirby wants me before lunch." She gave Kriss a beseeching smile. "What I wanted was to ask you to go with me to the Museum of Modern Art this evening. It's the opening of the Monet exhibition." Through the corners of her eyes Kriss noticed Anne flick a glance at her as she began stacking the dirty cups and saucers. Once they had discussed Dorothy's passion for art exhibitions, but now she felt a faint disloyalty for having done so.

"I'm so tired, baby. Can't we go some other time," she begged off.

Anne carted off the coffee service with no comment.

"Oh, Kriss—" She'd promised herself not to feel badly if Kriss couldn't go, but she couldn't keep the disappointment from her voice.

Kriss felt sorry for her. "Oh, baby, I'm just so tired." Then, relenting, she said, "Why don't you come and have dinner with me tonight."

"But—but—" She couldn't bring herself to ask.

"He won't be there tonight," Kriss assured her. "Nor any other night," she thought bitterly.

Now Dorothy was happy. She looked like a girl who'd been asked on a date. "All right. But you let me do everything. Promise?"

Kriss wondered again if Dorothy understood her own emotions. Probably not, she thought. A veil lowered over her eyes. "I promise," she said, chuckling mechanically. If I find myself in bed with Dot, that'll be the bitter end, she thought. Anyway, I'd like a virgin, she added mentally, chuckling to herself. "Make it around seven-thirty."

"All right, then, at seven-thirty."

Immediately after Dorothy left, she regretted asking her. But at least Dot would be better than being alone, she confessed. Anything was better than being alone. Although she'd never come to the stage of letting herself be picked up. . . . "You son of a bitch!" she thought with sudden venom, but whether her venom was directed toward Ronny or Ted or Dave or anyone else in particular, she didn't even know herself.

CHAPTER 4

JESSE CAME UP from the subway through the arcade with its tobacco shops, barber shops, shoeshine parlors, notion stores, florists, lunch counters, turkish baths, to the north side of 42nd Street, next to the corner drugstore. "This is what they mean by the underworld," he had thought in passing, and now he viewed the upper side with equal distaste.

From where he stood at the corner of Eighth Avenue—a pesthole of petty thugs where a man could buy a gun, hot or cold, for fifteen dollars up—down to the tricornered, old stone *Times* building in the narrow angle where Broadway crossed Seventh Avenue, was a block of infinite change. Once in the lives of very old men it had been a mudhole; then had come an era of fashion, of furred and diamonded women with their potbellied escorts alighting from lacquered carriages beneath the glittering marquees of plush modern playhouses. Now it was descending into a mudhole again, but of a different kind. The once famous playhouses, lumped together on both sides of the street, were now crummy second-and-third-run movie theaters, contesting with the cheap appeal of a penny arcade with its shooting galleries, mechanical games, flea circus, thimble arena where Jack Johnson had done a daily stint of boxing in his waning years. And in between there were the numerous jewelry stores with fake auctions every night, beer joints, cafeterias, sporting goods stores, shoe stores, shoe repair and valet shops, book stores that dealt principally in pornography, second-class hotels and filthy rooming houses.

"Poor man's Broadway," Jesse thought sourly, as his searching gaze flitted from the lighted movie signs to the passing faces: then his mind began improving on the commonplace phrase, "Melting pot. . . . already melted—rusting now. . . . last chance. . . . I can get it for you hot—hotter than you think, bud. . . . this side of paradise—way this side. . . ." His eyes rested on a black couple, the man tall and strutting in a cream colored suit, a yam-colored woman with a hundred pounds of hams. . . . "Nigger Haven too. . . ."

Ahead of him a short swarthy man in a striped blue suit backed angrily from a narrow-fronted hash joint, shouting belligerently, "You come out here, you bastard, I'll show you!" A big blond buck, Swedish-looking, dressed in a white apron, a white shirt with the sleeves rolled up, obviously the counterman, charged onto the sidewalk. His face was red with rage. "Don't you call me no bastard,

61

you son of a bitch!" The short swarthy man stood his ground defiantly. "Don't you call me no son of a bitch, you bastard! You're out here on the street now and I'll knock you on your ass!" Whereupon the big blond counterman knocked him down with one wild swing. The short swarthy man staggered to his feet and lurched about dizzily in a fighting stance. "You ain't got no counter now to protect you," he said. Whereupon the big blond buck swung wildly and knocked him down again. Jesse recalled his dream where the short squat man had brained the big wild man with a heavy oak chair, and said, half-laughing, "Law of averages."

A cop ambled up lazily and broke it up. "Go on, go on, get on back tuh work 'fore I lock you up!" he said to the counterman, giving him a push, then he turned to the short swarthy man, "Why-oncha pick on somebody yo' own size?" A snigger ran through the crowd. "He slipped up on me," the short man defended his prowess. "Go on, go on," the cop said. "I can tell you never wuz a boy scout."

"Never was a boy, son," Jesse thought. "Where'd you study psychiatry?"

Further on, a book store claimed his vagrant attention. He stopped for a moment, searching among the titles for those of his own two books. There were several books by black writers, but not his. "If you ever find someone who's read your books you'll drop dead," he told himself. His gaze picked out the title, *Lost Horizon*. "Good and lost right here," he thought. Then he recalled an editor who'd rejected his second book, complaining, "Why do you fellows always write this kind of thing? Some of you have real talent. Why don't you try writing about people, just *people*." He had countered, "White people, you mean?" The editor had reddened. "No, I don't mean *white* people. I mean *people!* Like Maugham and Hilton write about, for instance." He laughed at the recollection and his bitterness left. "I should have told him I don't want no Eskimos, and that's all the *people* they left. Don't even know no ape-men, I should have told him, and no apes either, for that matter—although he probably wouldn't have believed that, close as he thinks I am to Africa." The thought kept tickling him as he ambled along, unmindful of the gay who trailed him on the leeside. "My folks didn't do right by me," he said aloud suddenly. "They shouldn't have got themselves caught."

Suddenly he turned and retraced his steps to another small bookstore that had just registered on his mind, disconcerting the gay. He stared at the titles without really seeing them, a sort of reflex gesture. "What I really ought to have told the son of a bitch," he thought, "is why don't you read the Old Testament, son? Or even Rabelais for that matter. That's the way I should have started the damn book." He blew laughter from his nostrils. "The nigger woke, sat up, scratched at the lice, stood up, farted, pissed, crapped, gargled, harked, spat, sat down, ate a dishpan of stewed chitterlings, drank a gallon of lightning, hated the white folks for an hour, went out and stole some chickens, raped a white woman, got lynched by a mob, scratched his kinky head and said, Boss, Ah's tahd uh gittin' lynched. Ah's so weary kain keep mah eyes open, and the Boss said, Go on home an' sleep, nigger, that's all you niggers is good for. So he went back to his shanty, stealing a watermelon on the way, ate the watermelon rind and all, lay down on his pallet, blinked, yawned, and went to sleep hating the white folks." "We can't print this crap," the editor would have said.

"Why not?" he would have asked.

"It's too bitter. People are fed up with this kind of protest."

"What is protest but satire?"

"Satire? Satire must be witty, ironic, sarcastic; it must appeal to the intelligent. This crap is pornography."

"Depends on where you think a man's brains are."

"What does?" a falsetto voice squeaked at his side.

For the first time he noticed the gay. He was big, blond and well-dressed, had a pleasant face but greedy blue eyes.

Jesse turned and walked on without replying. In front of him two painted showgirls flanking a tall, woozy westerner, came from the Hotel Dixie and crossed toward a waiting taxi. He caught a whiff of Lanvin's My Sin and found himself looking at their slender nyloned legs, long-eyed and woman-hungry. For an instant he stopped and considered turning back to 8th Avenue and heading uptown. There were always cruising whores in that section from 42nd Street through Jacob's Beach, even this early in the morning.

63

But he put it from his mind. He'd always been afraid of disease, syphilis in particular. Not so much for his own sake, but he'd been afraid of infecting his wife. "Wouldn't believe that about a nigger, would you?" he thought. Although once he'd taken on all comers who were thought to be healthy.

For a moment his thoughts went back to that time in 1944, when all the liberals were trying desperately to elect Roosevelt for a fourth term against strong fascist opposition and the CIO's Political Action Committee had been all the rage—"Clear it with Sidney"— Sidney Hillman and the boys. He always thought of that time at least once a day. Not so much with regret as with wonder. Greatest time in the history of the Republic for interracial lovemaking. "Nothing like politics for getting white ass. Black ass either, for that matter. Better than Spanish fly. Although the black ass don't need a crusade" he amended. "Just some good white boy who wants it." And after a moment he said aloud, "Old Jimmy. Wonder if he ever got enough." Jimmy had been a lieutenant in the navy then, handsome chap in his whites. Hollywood scenario writer now; he'd seen a first-run, Class-A picture a few weeks ago Jimmy had done the scenario for. Cleo, the wife of a black newspaper editor, had been nuts about him. "This is Cleo, Jimmy, she'll screw hanging from a chandelier," had been the way Maud had introduced them. For a moment his thoughts lingered pleasantly on Maud.

"What a bitch!" he thought. "A great woman, really. Greater than anybody'll ever know!" Many times he'd considered writing a novel about her. But he'd never been able to get the handle to the story. "Great whore! Madame, actually. Worked with her tools. That whore did everything. Besides which she was a cheat, liar, thief, master of intrigue, without conscience or scruples, and respectable too. That was the lick—the respectability." He felt a cynical amusement. "Son, that's the trick. Here's a whore who's friend of the mighty, lunches with the Mayor's wife, entertains the rich, the very rich, the Rockefellers, on all kinds of interracial committees, a great Negro social leader. While you, you son of a bitch, with your so-called integrity, are just a pest and a nuisance."

Suddenly he was at the curb of Seventh Avenue. Opposite was the *Times* building; across 42nd a restaurant with tables out of doors. Uptown to his left was another small theater that specialized in weird off-trail films, displaying a huge poster of a leopard-skinned wild man bearing off a half-clad blonde. "That's what you should be, son," he told himself. "Then you could just grab a piece of ass and run and all they'd do would just be to make a film of it." Beyond was the glittering front of the Astor Hotel, looking onto the chasm of Times Square; the bottom of the V where the canteen had been, now a recruiting center; and on the other side the old stone profile of Hotel Claridge which had once housed the Hall of Science on the second floor behind the Camel Cigarette sign where he had worked as a porter. He thought of the narrow marble stairway he'd had to scrub five times a day. "I wonder who's scrubbing you now," he thought to the tune of the popular song. But the Hall of Science was gone, defunct, no more, and the Great White Way looked cheap and naked and repulsive in the bright morning sunlight, like a striptease on awakening, fumbling about a small dingy hotel room in a soiled kimono, fixing her morning needle.

He now felt only a deep-welling loneliness. "You dood it yourself, son," he said, "You thought you were being noble," and turned in at the first theater without looking to see what was showing. An automatic middle-aged blonde stopped tallying her change long enough to push an automatic key for his automatic ticket and he went through a long narrow mirrored foyer garnished with scenes from coming attractions into the dim musty interior. He turned to the right and climbed the dusty worn carpeted stairs which smelled strongly of stale urine to the balcony which smelled strongly of stale people. He went down the perilous stairs to the front row and took a seat between a young white man in a sweater and a sleeping black, one seat removed from each. Suddenly he felt exhausted.

"You think too much, son," he told himself. "Your heads for knots, not thoughts." And then, "Besides which, it's un-American."

Kriss remained at her desk until six o'clock to finish the report on the Reverend John Saxton project for an Indian Protestant school, then took the Madison Avenue bus home. As a rule she enjoyed this ride down the gray-stone, gleaming-glass canyon, past the window-lighted chain of women's shops, the shiny bustling entrance to the

C.B.S. building, the brittle pyramids of the ad writers, the gloomy old mansion of Random House, turning at 42nd through the tide of day's end traffic over to Grand Central, down lower Park Avenue until it changed its name to Fourth, and over to Lexington at 24th Street. It ran a crooked line through the city's heart, from the high brass notes of the hucksters to the low muted scale of Gramercy Park, and on nights when she'd known Dave was coming she could hear the heart beat. She loved the city and all who inhabited it, but never when alone; in aloneness it was a prison. Now the tired faces against the city lights were like mirrors of her mind. She dreaded her empty apartment almost to fear.

At 23rd Street she walked over to Third Avenue and down, stopping at her favorite delicatessen and greengrocers to buy a small barbecued chicken, frozen peas, whipped potatoes, and a salad. When she turned the key in her lock she felt ready to expire. Her mind felt dead, her body dry as straw, a desert waste. She went straight to the kitchen, deposited her purse and purchases on the sideboard, melted loose two ice cubes, and mixed a stiff Scotch and soda. Only after she'd taken a long cool soothing swallow did she feel slightly human again. She hung up her coat and took the drink on a silver coaster to the sitting room, eased her tired bottom into the straight-backed three-legged chair which rested her, and opened last week's *New Yorker* magazine.

It was always at this time, the butt-end of a hard day, that thoughts of Ronny invaded her mind, and *The New Yorker* lay neglected on her lap. Now, before the drink began taking hold, she recalled the happy things, nights talking until daylight before an open fire, their drunken wit, picking their friends to pieces . . . "If Hal could lift his brains three feet, get them back into his head, he'd be a great man." And her secret sensual smile, that cream-fed look of unfaithful woman that no painter on earth has ever caught—because she knew more about Hal's brains than he. . . . "If you ever married again, Kriss, I'll give you a reference; I can say I was never bored." Now smiling at the memory of the compliment, not secretly, but lost beyond the moment in time and place.

It was after her second drink she thought, "You son of a bitch, you ruined me!" Which in great part was true, if you care to think of this thirty-seven-year-old, six-thousand-dollar-a-year, junior executive, brilliant, healthy, handsome-as-four-peacocks, sexy and highly respectable woman as *ruined*. She couldn't bear children. But that might have been all for the good. Besides which, Ronny was not the cause of that.

What she meant at such times was that he had ruined her chances for happiness. Being a homosexual, he had always slept with her in a panic of guilt, and knowing he gave her no satisfaction intensified his guilt which, when fed with drink, caused him to run to anyone who would have him. Then, afterwards, he felt impelled to tearfully confess all his infidelities. On their honeymoon to Georgia he slept with the Southern belle whose virginity he had revered until she'd jilted him to marry a less reverent policeman; and with his mother's mulatto cook and her octoroon daughter in Mississippi; and with Kriss's maiden aunt in North Dakota; and with every tramp that came along when they had returned to Chicago, tearfully confessing all these indiscretions as soon as they had happened. She often wondered at the Divine compensation that made this man so intelligent and scholarly, really brilliant, on the one hand, and such a louse on the other.

Her first infidelities had been a shield against the pity of their friends. Then when she'd learned he was a homosexual too, her promiscuity became a social amenity. . . . She smiled maliciously, remembering how she'd picked them out before his eyes. She had a blues record she would play, "It's Waiting For You Baby," and she would dance to it with the object of her desire. At that time she had thought, the thought giving her as much pleasure as the act, that she was deceiving him. But now in melancholy retrospect she realized that he'd not only known but had condoned. . . .

"It's a queer existence, being married to a homosexual," she thought. One had to be sister and mother and father confessor, nursemaid and housekeeper, and on drunken occasions, whore, too; but never wife.

It was after the third drink she thought it might have been pleasant being a lesbian. "So many of them are," she thought, suddenly recalling the little Spanish girl who'd been her secretary in Chicago for a short time. She'd been a nuisance at the time, more like a lady's maid, fluffing her hair, straightening her dress, eternally finding some excuse to touch her. A year later she'd run into her in Washington, D.C., and had invited her to the hotel for a drink for old times sake. She was a beautiful girl, small, dark and velvet-eyed. After the second drink it had just sort of happened. Now the memory of it brought that secret, sensual smile again, but lit with a candle of real humor. If you don't know what to do in such cases, you just do what comes natural. Being the larger of the two, she felt she should assume the masculine role even though she lacked the equipment. But it had come off. "Something those b.d. niggers ought to learn about a woman's body," she thought maliciously. And it had been rather pleasant, a painful, straining ecstasy, like forcing oneself to swoon, which even now came up in the vagrant thoughts that varied and seasoned her sex acts.

While she was sipping her fourth drink the telephone rang. She went into the bedroom to answer it. "Mrs. Cummings speaking."

There was a little catch on the other end, not quite a laugh, nor a sigh; a sort of blowing from the mouth and nostrils all the vanities behind which we hide ourselves. And she knew, with suddenly diffused emotions, even before she heard the soft slurred voice with its faint, almost indistinguishable lisp, that it would say, "Hello, Kriss-baby, this is Jesse." In the following instant it all came back: Chicago and Maud and that divine weekend that Fern had later destroyed with all those lies about herself and Jesse in New York. She'd come closest to loving him of any of them since Willard—except Ted, of course.

"I really loved Ted," she told herself. But it had gone into contempt, and he had married some Negro woman in Los Angeles. She had never felt contempt for Jesse, although she didn't know why. He was a contemptible son of a bitch if there ever was one, and she wished she felt it now as she said with cold venom, "Have you murdered your wife?" He laughed and his tension relaxed.

Jesse had been waiting in his room since three o'clock to call her. The idea had come upon him in the movie that morning but he'd decided against calling her in her office. It had been over three years since he had seen her and he didn't know what kind of reception to expect. The last time he'd seen her had been disastrous. On his way home he'd picked up a bottle of gin, and had forced himself to wait until six-thirty. Then he'd decided to go downstairs and use the public telephone because the two extensions in the apartment were in the bedrooms of Leroy and Mr. Ward, and he didn't want to be overheard. Kriss was unpredictable, she might say, "Go to hell!" and hang up, and he didn't want to be seen with his mouth hanging open holding a dead receiver.

There was an old-fashioned pay phone on the whitewashed wall of the basement hallway, where he put in his call, and while he was waiting for an answer two pretty school-age girls came from the green door of the super's flat, and looked him over as they passed. He whistled a bar of "If I Had You" and they went into the elevator giggling, and he experienced the sudden blind panic of being lost in a world he no longer understood, a feeling which had been seizing him of late.

"You damned fool, what are you doing this for?" he asked himself, the whole tide of all his disappointments and frustrations washing up and over him; and when he heard her voice his heart caught. He knew then he didn't feel a thing for her; he just wanted to sleep with a white woman again. But after he had laughed it was all right. "I love you, Kriss, baby," he murmured. "You say the nicest things."

She didn't answer but he could hear her purring on the other end, and he knew she was wearing that secret, sensual look she always wore when her men came back to her.

"I've sold a book," he said. "I'd like to take you out to dinner."

"Are you living in the city now?"

"I just came back a week ago. I have a room up on Convent."

There was a pause and she asked, "Is your wife with you?"

The thought occurred to him suddenly that he'd never heard her call Becky's name. "We're separated," he said. "I haven't seen her now in almost a year."

She was silent for a moment, then asked, "When's your book to be published?"

"Well, it's not exactly sold, really. Hobson just took an option on it. They want to cut it."

"What's the title?"

"*I Was Looking For A Street.*"

"I hope it's nothing like that last thing you wrote," she said viciously. "I'm tired of listening to you blacks whining. I've got enough worries of my own."

He laughed deprecatingly. "This has no protest, baby. I've made a separate peace."

Although she didn't answer immediately, he knew by her silence she considered that a special concession to herself. "I have engagements for tonight and tomorrow night, but I have Thursday night free."

He tried to keep the disappointment from his voice. "What time shall I call for you?"

"Seven-thirty. You have my address?"

"I have the one in the directory."

"All right, I'll expect you at seven-thirty." She sounded brusque.

"Until then, Kriss baby. Do nothing I wouldn't do."

"That's practically nothing," she said viciously and hung up.

Slowly he walked toward the elevator. "Son, eat your crow and like it," he said, and after a moment added, "Crow eat crow—*kismet.*" At that instant the elevator door opened and the super emerged, lugging a short stepladder. He looked about and seeing no one besides Jesse appeared startled. "I thought I heard you talking."

Jesse grinned, unaware that he had spoken aloud. "They got you hearing things," he said.

"Else got you talking to yourself."

"Won't be long."

"Don't make it too long," the super said with an insinuating air.

Jesse closed the elevator door. "This world," he said. "What would man do without sin?"

Kriss went into the kitchen, mixed her fifth highball, and took it back to the living room. Then she switched on the television to catch *The Goldberg Family* that came on at seven, but the program was just coming to the end. "Damn Jesse to hell!" she muttered in a sudden rage. "Son of a bitch!" *The Goldberg Family* was her favorite program. Furiously she wished that he'd grown old and ugly. "Hungry niggers!" But unconsciously she amended it: "Hungry for some you-know-what." Suddenly she giggled. For an instant she regretted not having him come straight down. But Dot would be hurt and sullen.

There was nothing on the television she wanted to see, so she went to the kitchen with the intention of unwrapping the frozen whipped potatoes to thaw. But on noticing, with mild surprise, that her glass, which she carried in her hand, was empty, she forgot the potatoes and was mixing her sixth highball when the doorbell rang. She went quickly to the door and opened it, not staggering but walking differently, like balancing on her pelvic arch in a way that made her girdle feel tight.

"Come in, Dot baby," she said, giggling guiltily. "I'm a little tight."

CHAPTER 5

JESSE WAS DRESSED by six o'clock to give himself time to stop by the Chinese bar for a few gin-and-beers to get himself relaxed and in the mood. Kriss couldn't abide a tense and silent escort; she wanted her black men to be entertaining, ardent, even frantic.

"What the hell else would she want a nigger for?" he thought, half-amused. "Not for his family tree—just one limb of it." And there were occasions when in the company of white women he was assailed by the futility of his position and plunged in a mood of black despair, during which he couldn't say a word, couldn't smile, lost his desire, and withdrew in sullen silence. Should that happen,

Kriss would be furious, he knew; probably kick him out of her house.

He had put on his new Oxford-blue flannel suit, bought the week before at a pawnshop on Columbus Avenue that offered factory rejects and slightly shopworn dummy models at half price. It was a beautiful suit of soft imported fabric, and with it he wore plain black English-made shoes from Wanamaker's spring shoe sale, a buttoned-down white Oxford-cloth shirt, and a heavy silk grey and white tie of abstract design, both of which had come from Gimbel's bargain basement.

"All you need now is an umbrella, a bowler hat, a mutton chop, a glass of claret, lank hair and a white skin, and you'd be on your way to civilize the world, son," he told himself disparagingly, then added, half-amused, "You've got the right inclination anyway."

He glanced outside at the weather. A slight drizzle was falling. He put on his hat and a faded trench coat that Kriss had admired seven years ago when it was new and they were new to each other, tucked a bottle of bourbon under his arm, wondering suddenly what it was he wanted downtown that wasn't uptown in abundance.

He found her name, *Mrs. Kristine W. Cummings,* beneath the letter slot in the vestibule and pressed the bell beside it. After a moment Kriss pressed the button beside the house phone in her back hallway, releasing the lock on the outside door. He entered quickly and hastened down the tiled corridor, grateful to find it empty, and at the back turned left to the door of her apartment.

She opened the door before he rang again, and for an imperceptible moment they stared at one another, their smiles of greeting frozen in slight shock. Clad in a simple sleeveless black cocktail dress with a low square-cut neck, ornamented by a heavy silver necklace and a pair of magnificent silver bracelets, she was a very handsome woman. But she wasn't the woman he remembered; he found no hint of the daredevil girl whom he'd once liked; instead he saw what appeared in flash judgment to be an assured, humorless, slightly dull woman wrapped in an impregnable respectability.

For her part she saw in him nothing of the irresponsible woman hunter with the ready grin and brilliant eyes with whom she had spent those three exquisite days, both nude every minute, taking him on the couch, on the bearskin rug before the fire, standing beneath the shower, while eating in the kitchen, candidly discussing lovers each had known and had sworn to never know again, his frantic sexuality like an aphrodisiac flame; nor anything of the repulsive drunk who had so infuriated her four years later, who at least had possessed a certain bitter effervescence that had made him interesting. This man before her, in the old trench coat she recognized immediately, was dead; hurt had settled so deep inside of him it had become a part of his metabolism. Not that he had changed so greatly in outward appearance—not nearly as much as she had hoped. Outwardly he looked much the same, the youthful contours of his face, the athletic figure, thinner perhaps, although his head seemed much smaller with his hair cut so short and thinning too, like an onion head—she liked men with hair, lots of hair, even though it was woolly. It was inside of him the light had gone out.

But both recovered instantaneously.

"I'm fat," she greeted, grinning tentatively, and he noticed about her bright blue eyes a faint border of red, as if she had been crying recently.

"I'm thin," he said, returning her grin. And now somewhat lamely, since she no longer seemed the type who would appreciate it, he added, "I brought bourbon instead of flowers."

For the first time she grinned a little like old times, "We'll drink our flowers."

He went into the sitting room while she mixed the drinks, Scotch for herself and bourbon for him, and when she brought them in he said with genuine admiration, "You have a beautiful place, Kriss. It's really lovely." And then added, looking her over frankly, "You know, you're beautiful too."

She sat on her favorite three-legged chair, pleased for the moment by his flattery. "My assistant, Anne, helped with the decor. She's studying interior decorating and the store gave her a discount."

"Are you still at the same job?"

"I'm still with the Institute." Then, her voice filling with pride, "But I'm a big girl now, I'm an assistant director." There was vindictiveness in it too, and he wondered vaguely what had happened to her.

"Do you ever see Maud?"

"I saw her during the Christmas season at a party at Ed Jones's. She tried to ignore me at first but when she saw how nice Ed and everyone else were to me she came over and started gushing, trying to make as if she hadn't seen me. She'd heard I had something to do with sending the personnel to India and she wants to use me again. I was cold as ice. . . ."

"How is Ed?" he asked politely. "Not that I give a goddamn," he thought. Ed Jones was a very successful black artist who ran a private art school.

"Fine. I love Julia, she's so sweet and real."

"She's a nice girl," he said, although he'd never met her, but he felt it necessary to be agreeable.

"I was frightened to death when I walked into that party," Kriss confessed. "It was the first time in years I'd been to a party full of blacks and I didn't know what sort of stories Maud had put out about me. But Ed was very nice and I knew most of the people there. Then Dinky Bloom said, 'Oh, Kriss is one of us anyway. She's been around niggers so long she's rubbed off enough black to be half nigger herself.'" She smiled her secret sensuous smile, thinking of the implications of the statement.

He was thinking the same thing, half-amused, but didn't pursue it. "What happened between you and Maud? I haven't seen them since we had that falling out."

"God, that woman hurt me!" the hurt coming through in her voice. "I lived with them when I first came to New York."

"I didn't know."

"I practically paid their rent and liquor bill. I had that little sitting room where you stayed, and when they entertained—which was practically every night, serving my liquor—I couldn't go to bed until all the guests left, although Joe would go into his room and go to bed and leave his company sitting up. And I had to get up before any of them. Then when I broke off with Ted, Maud practically threw me out. And we'd been just like sisters for years."

"I know," he said, thinking, "Lovers, baby, not sisters. Maud never liked anybody she couldn't sleep with—man or woman—I know the bitch." After a moment he asked, "Why should she care? It was none of her business, was it?"

"Oh, she wanted me to marry Ted so she could sleep with him when Joe and I were at work."

He picked up his empty glass and when she went to the kitchen to make fresh drinks, he followed her, wondering whether he should kiss her then or wait. She didn't appear to be in a kissing mood so he said, "This is a nice kitchen, everything's arranged so well." And when they went back to the sitting room he said, "I really like your place." This time she didn't respond and he looked at her thinking, "The hell of it is, son, you don't remember a damn thing about that weekend; you were blotto all the time and afterwards never remembered a thing past the moment when you first kissed her."

But aloud he asked, "What happened to you and Ted? The last time—in fact the only time—I ever saw you two together was at a party in Brooklyn. I think that was the only time I ever saw Ted— the only time I remember. He was a good-looking boy though, as I remember."

"He was good in bed, too," she said, smiling reminiscently, and he felt suddenly inadequate.

"Well," he said, "What more do you want?"

"I practically supported the son of a bitch," she said with sudden venom. "He was always running after cheap white people, thinking they were going to make him rich. He thought I didn't know anything and I was supporting him."

"What's he doing now?"

"I hope he's dead."

"You probably wish I was dead too," he thought. In the silence that followed, realizing their need of each other, both now ostracized from the only exciting life they had ever known, both starved for sexual fulfilment, lost and lonely, outcasts drifting together long after the passion had passed, faced with a night of sleeping together which at that moment neither desired, they hated each other.

She glanced at her watch and said, hurtingly, "Shall we go now, or do we drink our dinner."

He bit back the impulse to say, "Go to hell," telling himself,

"I'm going to have you, whether you like it or not." Then managed a thin smile, saying instead, "It wouldn't be the first time."

"If you intend to get drunk you can get out right now," she said viciously.

"I intend to take you to dinner," he said evenly.

"The last time I saw you, you were nasty drunk. Filthy! God, you were nasty. And I wanted you so."

He gave her a bewildered look. "What did I do? The last I remember is vomiting all over Don's white davenport."

"God, Ralph was mad. If you hadn't been so drunk he would have beaten you."

He felt acutely embarrassed. "I don't blame him."

"And I would have helped him."

"But what did I do to you?"

"Jesse! If you ever. . . ."

He had taken Roy by that afternoon for Don to see some of his etchings. That had been the summer following his visit to the big deluxe artists' colony called Skiddoo, and he'd been sick—sick in the head. That place had made him sick like nothing else in all his life—or perhaps he'd been sick when he went up there. Perhaps it was the book that had made him sick—that second book—and perhaps all Skiddoo did was bring it out. Some day he'd have to sit down and discover why he had hated Skiddoo and all the artists there. But Roy had been the exception; he'd liked Roy and had hoped Don would buy some of his war etchings to put him on his feet. Instead of buying the etchings, Don had taken their visit as an excuse to throw a party. By six o'clock a dozen or so persons were grouped about the big circular cocktail table in the sitting room and Don was serving one pitcher after another of a strong gin drink he called a gimlet. The last thing Jesse remembered before throwing up all over the sofa was baiting a woman named Muriel Slater whom he despised. On entering she had dismissed Roy's etchings and, seating herself in the centre of the floor, had taken off her shoes and launched into a loud discussion about a big black actor with whom she'd been sleeping off and on for years. She was one of those hard, brassy, over-ripened blondes, always loud-and-wrong. During the last Roosevelt campaign, when the communists and blacks had been working together again for Roosevelt's election, she'd been employed as a party-giver by the Central Committee of the Communist Party; and after the publication of Jesse's anticommunistic book she, as had all of his communist acquaintances and most of his Negro friends, quit speaking to him. He remembered saying to her, "Muriel baby, I know you have a beautiful, clean mind and a pure, unsullied soul, but your feet are dirty. Look at them. Really dirty, and not nearly so beautiful as your mind. Don't you feel embarrassed on climbing into bed with some strange man with your dirty feet?" He remembered her fury, and although he couldn't remember when Kriss had arrived, he remembered winking at her then taking another drink, and the next thing he remembered was vomiting on the sofa. . . .

"What did I say to you?"

"Jesse! If you ever—"

"Just tell me what I said."

"You wanted me to go to bed with you in one of Don's rooms." He didn't remember that at all. "I told you I couldn't do that. I never took anyone to bed when I roomed there, and I'd had my own apartment on 10th Street for over a month. But when I asked you to come to my apartment you got nasty. God, you were nasty!"

"What did I say to you?"

"I won't repeat what you said. I've never had anyone in all my life say the nasty things to me that you did. If I'd been a man I would have hit you in the face." He shook his head. "I was sick. That summer I was really sick." And to himself, "Sicker than you thought, son."

"I don't want to ever see you like that again."

"I've gotten over it. I've made a separate peace. I mean it."

She stood up. "We'd better go; it's getting late."

"Do you have any place in mind?"

"Oh, anywhere we can get served quickly. I don't feel up to a lot of bother."

"How about Nick's?"

"That's all right. We can have steaks."

They were tense and silent in the taxi as it skirted the quiet darkness of Gramercy Park, past the old stone mansions with their brass knockers and foot-scrapers and shining carriage lamps, and turned south on Irving Place. He glanced in passing at the front of the picturesque bar where it was said O. Henry spent many brooding hours, and he thought, "Son, you and me both." And a moment later, as they came into 14th Stret facing Luchow's, his thoughts went back to the moronic editor.

"Should have told him: 'And had I known any ape-men, bub, they would have been the progeny of ape-men and not of English peers, me being the type of ungrateful, unpatriotic, bitter-minded, sordid-souled, pessimistic son of a bitch who can only think of ape-men as half ape and half men.' Which will never do at all, son. . . . *never do at all*!" he said the last aloud without realizing it, and Kriss gave him an irritated look.

"What?"

He looked at her perplexed. "What what?"

"You said, 'never do at all!' What will never do at all?"

"Oh!" He threw her a look and told the first lie that came to mind, "I was thinking of the way you said I acted at Don's. I must have been really sick."

"Jesse! If you ever get that drunk again I'll never speak to you as long as I live," she threatened in a tight furious voice. "I swear it!"

She was in a blind rage with herself for seeing him again even now, for her sexual need of him. If she could sleep with him and immediately afterward have him beheaded, then she could enjoy his company. But now he would sleep with her and go away feeling good because he had slept with a white woman, and she might not see him again until he wanted another one. "Niggers! Niggers! Niggers!" she thought in her blind rage.

"Don't worry, baby, I won't," he muttered, impotently furious at being forced to repeat a vow he'd already made out of genuine shame.

She noticed a woman walking a poodle along Union Square. "At least they're better than dogs," she thought with such an overwhelming surge of venomous glee that her rage abated and she turned toward him, smiling maliciously, wishing he could read her mind.

But he didn't notice. Now as the taxi turned south on Seventh Avenue, from delayed reaction, he suddenly thought of Luchow's. "That's where I should have taken her." And he wondered why he had chosen Nick's. "Association of ideas, no doubt," he thought, and then, "Damn son, what goes on in your brain!"

His last visit to Nick's had been tragic. That had also been in that period following his visit to Skiddoo. He'd taken his wife to a dinner at Paul's—one of the other writers who'd been to Skiddoo—one hot July Sunday afternoon; or rather to a dinner in the Greenwich Village flat of the little tramp, Kathy, whom Paul had lived with—and off, too—that summer.

Roy had come too, bringing a very dignified and respectable looking woman whom he had introduced as Estelle. She had looked as out of place as Becky in that dirty two-room flat.

Paul had been well along the way when they arrived, receiving them dressed in a spotty tee-shirt that looked as if it might have served duty as a cleaning rag, and incredibly filthy white duck pants, the seat of which was absolutely black. And Kathy wore a soiled and rumpled sun-back playsuit that appeared to have made several tours of Coney Island since its previous laundering: the both of them giving the impression by their unkempt hair and red-smeared lips of having just arisen from bed.

The dinner, sent up from the corner delicatessen, had consisted of greenish-tinted slices of hard-boiled eggs, curled and fragrant slices of bologna sausage, withered slices of tomatoes dressed with dabs of yellow paste, and watery cabbage slaw; and had been served on an egg-and-wine-stained, repulsively filthy paper table covering. However, Paul had provided eight quarts of domestic ale and a gallon of California sherry, and since Roy's ladyfriend drank only a very little sherry, and Kathy no more than a quart of ale, there had been plenty left for the three escapees from Skiddoo, wine and ale being a combination they'd found to be satisfactorily potent during their sojourn there.

Becky had drunk against despair.

When the sherry was finished, Paul and Kathy had begun slobbering over each other in a manner that presaged violent passionate action at any moment. Fearful of this action taking place right there on the floor, which would have been nothing new for Greenwich Village, and having no curiosity about the sex habits of psychotic writers, Estelle had quietly departed. And an hour later, never having remembered what took place in the interim, Jesse had found himself standing at the bar in Nick's with Becky between himself and Roy, ordering three bottles of ale, and the bartender had charged him seventy cents for each. He had thought nothing of it until the woman at his left asked, "How much did he charge you for your ale?"

He looked at her, trying to get her face into focus. "Seventy cents. Why?"

"We had ale just before you came in and he only charged us thirty-five cents," she informed him.

He didn't remember what happened immediately following. The next thing he remembered he was shouting at the top of his voice, "What the hell kind of goddamned shit is this! You're not in Georgia, goddamit, this is New York City!" And the headwaiter and another waiter were standing beside him and the bartender across from him, and all of them were trying to explain at once that after eleven o'clock, when the orchestra played, all prices were doubled. But he didn't hear their explanations. Deep inside of his muddled thoughts he felt he'd been victimized because he was black, and he was asserting his rights. "I'm not sitting at a goddamned table!" he kept shouting, letting them know he knew the score. "We're standing at this goddamned bar, and you charged everybody else here thirty-five cents—"

"I can't stand it!" Becky had screamed suddenly, and had run outside, crying hysterically. "I can't stand it anymore. I can't! I can't!"

Caught first in bewilderment, like finding oneself naked in Times Square, there followed a sudden hurt that went down through his body like the shock of death. "Becky baby! Becky! Wait, baby!" he had called thickly, his brain instantly sober, but his body still drunk as he had run staggering after her. "What's the matter, baby? Wait, baby!"

Turning quickly to escape him, she had run out into the middle of Seventh Avenue before an oncoming car, hoping to be killed.

The squealing of the suddenly applied brakes and her sudden

action threw him into panic. On catching her, he had clutched her about the waist, and had tried to drag her back to safety. But at his touch she'd gone crazy, fighting him in hysterical frenzy. In the struggle they had fallen to the street, rolling and threshing on the brick pavement as two persons fighting desperately. Not realizing what had happened, Roy had run after them and tried to separate them. Nick's and the nearby bars had emptied their patrons into the street to watch the nigger fighting his woman, and there had been several hundred persons crowded along the curbs while he and Becky had threshed in the street.

Finally a policeman had come and yanked him to his feet.

"I don't want her to get hurt!" he had shouted at the cop and had tried to push him away.

The cop had twisted his arm behind his back and Roy had helped Becky to her feet. Because of the gaping crowd and Becky's hysteria, the policeman had let them take a taxi to the station.

Roy had been released but he and Becky had spent the night in jail.

That had been the most awful thing that had ever happened to Roy, and the day after the hearing he had revealed himself to Jesse as a homosexual, making a grand slam of all the white men Jesse had met that summer, which he always thought of afterward as the Summer of the Da Da Dee, a nameless tune, he had shouted through the nights at Skiddoo, coming back to the estate from the cheap bars in the early hours of morning, weary and bedraggled and blotto. Its basic theme was the melody of a popular song on the jukebox in his favorite downtown bar, sung by Ella Fitzgerald, with words that went, *I'll get by as long as I have you. . . .* but he had never known this. It was just a sound that had kept him going the four miles down the dark and sleeping elm-lined highway back to the quiet splendor of Skiddoo when he had felt more like just lying in the gutter and never getting up. . . .

And why, after that, he chose to come back to Nick's with Kriss—"Customary!" he thought grimly, as they alighted from the taxi. "They always return to the scene—what kind of detective stories have you been reading, you don't know that?"

They were taken to a booth along the wall up front, to one side of the Dixieland Band. The place looked completely different from his memory of it, and now he could not conceive of why he had caused such a row. Everything seemed perfectly normal.

He thought of a boy he knew in Harlem who said he smoked marijuana because it made him feel so normal. "You know one thing, Jess, only time I ever feel normal is when I'm high."

She had been thinking, "God damn Dave to hell!" The last time she'd been there, he had taken her, and she had felt the envy of the other women. Now she felt their indifference, bringing a sense of shame, and in a roundabout way she was enraged with Jesse by hating Dave. If Jesse were big and black like Charlie Thompson, the union official with whom she'd spent a weekend in Cleveland, clinging possessively to his arm as they walked down Euclid, she could have felt a daredevil defiance. Or, if he were gorgeous like Ted, she wouldn't even have to look to see how they were taking it; she could just relax and feel hated. All of them had wanted Ted, his thick black curly hair and smooth moustache; he'd even slept with Lady—what was her name?—Lady—anyway, some relation of the Duke's—all during the war when he was stationed in London with the Red Cross. They'd often talked about it, and he'd often said to flatter her, "She was a Lady but you're a woman, sugar."

Silently she watched Jesse give their order. . . .

"No, both rare."

". . . to drink, sir?"

". . . for me, Scotch for the lady. With soda."

Their voices drifted in and out of her consciousness. She wondered what she'd ever seen in him that had once attracted her.

"You look sad, Kriss baby," he observed.

For the first time she thawed a little, pleased that he had noticed it.

"Wan, really," he continued, "But it gives you an interesting look. Are you grieving for your love?"

She grinned suddenly. "When I first went to the university I used to pray to become sick so I'd get thin and pale and interesting looking. I was disgustingly healthy and North Dakota stuck out all over me. I used to dream of having tuberculosis and looking like Camille."

He smiled. "Transparent." It was a term blacks applied to blondes which she had learned while at the Foundation, and when he added, "You're transparent anyway, baby," she gave him her sensual bedroom smile.

Through the corner of her eye she noticed the blonde he'd been staring at giving him a long appraising look and she began to feel a spread of warmth displacing her lethargy. He could be cute, she thought.

Seeing the change in her, he continued in the same vein, trying to get her in the mood, "Like gossamer. If it wasn't for the table I'd kiss you." Letting his desire flood from beneath lowered lashes into her bright blue staring eyes. "Like pink champagne."

But the waiter served their steaks and broke it off. He ordered more drinks and asked curiously, "Do you ever hear from Ronny, Kriss?" and her melting mood froze again.

"He writes me every month. He's in Austria—with the State Department."

"I know. I heard he was married again."

"He has a son now."

"He has?" To himself he thought, "He must have given birth to it."

A slow blush mounted to her face. "He's cured now."

"Really? What's his wife like? Do you know her?"

"I've never seen her, but Arty knew her in Chicago. He tells everyone she's a cheap edition of me."

"I think I saw her at a party once at Harold's," he said, his interest straying. "He'd brought her. If she's the same girl." While talking, his gaze had wandered toward the blonde at the other table and locked for a moment with hers.

Noticing, Kriss said, "Let's go!" in a way that sounded like a curse.

They rode in silence to her apartment, and when she'd unlocked her door, she turned on him in fury, her eyes wide and icy with repressed rage, and said brutally, "Jesse! I don't want you to come in unless you're really free of your wife. I am sick and tired of having you niggers' wives hating me." She was paying him for looking at the blonde.

But he didn't realize it. Accepting her statement at face value, he said flatly, "I am really free of her," adding to himself, "There's a limit—even a nigger limit, bitch!"

"If you're lying to me I'll kill you," she said gratingly.

Relaxing, he said, half-amused, "You'd have to bury me, baby, I'm not insured."

She relaxed too, and, entering her front hall, permitted him to enter too. After hanging up their coats they went into the kitchen and he stood by silently while she mixed highballs with four fingers of whiskey in each. To get the mood rolling, one way or another, he said, "I've always wanted you, Kriss baby, even when I couldn't have you—but if you want me to go. . . ."

She turned suddenly and embraced him, kissing him hard, her body feeling big and unwieldly in his arms. Their eyes locked for a moment, and then she thought with a sudden icy chill of how she had once felt about him and broke from his embrace.

Glancing at her watch, she said brusquely, "It's time for Barry Gray," and hurried to the sitting room, while he followed with the drinks. A thin, good-looking, aquiline-featured man came on the screen and the voice began saying something about Negroes.

She sat in her three-legged chair, listening as if to God, and he sat on the sofa and gulped his highball silently. "Big Talk, Small Do—Indians," he thought and stood up to get another drink. Kriss gave him her glass too.

He made them stronger than before, kissing her hair as he placed hers on her coaster. Resuming his seat he stared at her profile, ignoring the television, and for the first time noticed the seams in her fleshy neck. The next thing he noticed his glass was empty and a film was showing. He got up to mix more drinks for them both and found both bottles nearly empty. "I must be getting drunk," he thought, as he bumped against the wall when returning to the sitting room, then, half-amused, "Power of suggestion."

He did not remember reaching the sitting room. His next conscious action was of walking nude from the living room to the bedroom and finding her nude body inert on the faded blue sheet, eyes closed. He stood looking down at it until vague wisps of desire were transmitted from his brain, then he heard his voice saying with a slightly shocked note, "Damn, you're white!"

She opened her eyes and looked at him with the last flicker of sensual pleasure. "I am about as white as one can be," she said distinctly.

For a long time their senses were dulled almost to insensibility with drunkenness. Her first reaction was memory:

He had come into her office in Chicago shortly before noon, wearing the same trench coat, new then and somehow dashing, and a double-breasted business suit with handstitched lapels. His hair was long and heavily greased with an interesting kinkiness, and she had noticed instantly his long girlish eyelashes and beautiful eyes. He didn't look at all like the type of young black writer who'd been given fellowships, neither hungry nor scholarly nor intellectual nor "called." More like a good lover with that air of frantic sexuality scarcely contained beneath his respectful manner. So she had taken him to the executives' luncheon to meet the president and other officials, and afterwards she'd had him wait in her office while she finished some reports. He had sat in one of the straight-backed uncomfortable chairs, looking at her all the while with restrained and polite desire until she couldn't stand the warmth. She'd suggested that he go and do whatever he had to do and come to her apartment at six for dinner. Ronny had been in the army then—overseas at that. He had brought bourbon, like this time, and she'd made her special goulash. Afterwards they'd sat on the sofa in her pleasant sitting room, drinking slowly, and he had told her all about himself; she refusing to answer the intermittent ringing of the telephone. All that time sitting at opposite ends of the sofa, turned toward each other, her legs tucked beneath her and one of his beneath himself. Then he had said, "I think I'm going to kiss you," and her face took on a melting look as she offered him her mouth and he had moved close to her and that first kiss had been almost as penetrating as the moment of conception. He had undressed first and was in bed and—of all things—covered up when she had come naked from the bathroom, and she had seen in that first look he had of her nakedness all she'd ever wanted from a man. On the very first time they finished in a dead heat, making the night too precious for sleep. Later sitting on the sofa again, the bed now consecrated and their nakedness as natural as the night, she had read aloud the whole of *This Is My Beloved,* then afterwards on the white bearskin rug before the hearth, and in the sunrise through the French doors to the terrace they had read to each other laughingly the early love twists of John Donne.

Once they had gone together to a chicken shack in the black belt, hot fried chicken-in-the-basket. She adored every instant with his beautiful eyes only for her, and that night, with bottles from the friendly liquor store, it had been a dream of heaven. She had loved him then, and even more when next morning in the kitchen he had said, "God, I'd like to marry you." And that third morning, after he'd dressed and packed to continue on the journey to California and his wife, he had begged her humbly, "May I have you just once more," and she'd undressed him and taken him and he'd made a solemn vow to divorce his wife and come back and marry her, and she'd believed and hoped that it would be forever. "I would have married him then," she thought. And now thinking about it again, having kept it from her thoughts for many years, she closed her eyes and let unconsciousness take her.

And the next moment he was asleep, grinding his teeth like a rat gnawing wood, threshing about and striking out in unconscious fury.

CHAPTER 6

*T*HE GOLD-PLATED Swiss clock on the nightstand whirred softly, curdling the silence of the small dark room. A woman stirred tentatively on the three-quarter size bed, flung a heavy bare arm searchingly across the faded blue sheet. It encountered a nude human body, and the panic that had begun to well up inside of her abruptly subsided. Dave? she wondered, and cracked a bleary eye. On the adjacent pillow a fuzzy round object, like a frizzled coconut, black in the dim light, showed faintly in her thin scope of vision. Jesse! she remembered. She closed her eyes and, recalling his abject acceptance of her atrocious behaviour, felt pleased. "I'll make him eat roots," she resolved and silently kneed him in the back.

"Uh!" he grunted, coming awake as furiously as he'd gone to sleep. His startled gaze searched the dim, cell-like room and, finding everything strange, he felt a shattering of emotion. He was on the verge of leaping up and searching for the light of reason when his hand encountered a nude body beside him in the bed. Peering from bloodshot eyes, he recognized the matted head of Kriss. "Ready to light out and run, eh, son?" he thought, laughing at himself with self-disparagement.

She appeared to be asleep. He moved towards her. "Maybe she won't awaken," he thought hopefully. Half laughing, he recalled a burlesque skit of a guy in a hotel room eavesdropping on a honeymoon couple in the next room who were trying, unknown to him, to close an overstuffed suitcase. "No, not that way," he said as she tried to close it with her hands, "I'll put it on the floor and you get on top." The eavesdropper's ears perked up. But it still wouldn't close, so she said, "Oh shucks, it won't fit, you get on top." The eavesdropper's ears wagged in a frenzy. But still it wouldn't close, so he said, "Let's both get on top." That's where the eavesdropper broke down the adjoining door. "*This I gotta see!*" he cried . . .

But Kriss pushed him viciously and said in a cold dictatorial voice, "Jesse, I've got to go to work," adding viciously, "You don't have anything to do but hang around some Harlem bar and you can sleep all day."

"Fine," he said, and turned over as if to go back to sleep.

"You can't sleep here!" she said, trying to push him from the bed. "My maid's coming this morning to clean up," she lied, then, to infuriate him, she added, "Go back to your wife then, she'll let you sleep all day. She always has."

He found the switch for the hall light and went into the bathroom without replying. She had a glimpse of his body before he closed the door, smooth sepia skin, strong back and broad shoulders, his well-formed legs and smooth calves, almost hairless, that could have been a woman's; and she thought of other women who'd seen him naked in the morning and resented his body bitterly. "He's five years older than I am," she thought, indulging in the complicated reasoning of attributing his youthful appearance to the fact that white people, like herself, supported him so he could write a book every four or five years. "If they had to work as hard as I do, they'd all die," she concluded.

He looked at his greasy reflection in the mirror and thought, "You don't look a damn bit different, son." There were five tooth-brushes on the rack; to one side on a wall-shelf of glass a box of talcum powder, comb and brush, colognes and perfumes; beside the tub one gray and white bath towel. Inside the medicine cabinet he found two safety razors, a container of blades, many bottles labeled with a doctor's prescription, a septic pencil and a man's comb, aftershaving lotion, and the bottle of blue tablets which had the shape of dexedrine but not the color. "Man, woman, and doctor," he thought, immediately amending it to, "Statue of modern woman standing atop a drugstore, right hand lifting nude male to prophylactic couch, left hand behind back beckoning to hovering figure of doctor in background with two middle fingers crossed."

When he came from the bathroom she said, as though to a servant, "Jesse! Put on some water for coffee and make some toast." He went into the sitting room without replying and found his shorts among his other clothes heaped in a pile on the floor. She giggled luxuriously at his silent resentment. "Get the paper from outside the door and turn on the television to Gloucester," she directed.

"I've had it now, little sister, for what it was worth," he thought, disdaining to reply. After donning underwear, socks, pants, and shoes, he went to the kitchen, poured the remnants of the Scotch and bourbon into a water tumbler, ran it full of water from the tap and drank it down without stopping. On a high shelf beside the stove he noticed an unopened bottle of imported sherry and a half-filled bottle of vermouth. Looking through the refrigerator he found a remnant of grilled steak, a barbecued chicken leg, and two fried crab cakes, all of which he ate greedily without bread.

The liquor took immediate effect and he began to feel good,

bubbly with laughter inside, but slightly dazed as if everything, both mental and material, were just a wee bit out of line. "What I prescribe for the world is continuous drunkenness," he thought, amusedly, as he broke two raw eggs into his highball glass, filled it with milk and drank it down, breaking the egg yolks in his mouth by the pressure of his tongue. "Nothing like a good diet," he thought— "Man eats seed of chicken to replenish own seed to give to chick— *Robinson*."

"Jesse!" He heard Kriss call to him from the bedroom.

He felt very indulgent toward her now. Returning to the bedroom, he turned on the small night light. "Yes, baby."

"Did you do what I told you to do?" she asked, laughing up at him with childish humor and he knew then she'd done it to annoy him.

He pulled the covers from her and in the soft pink light her nude body resembled one of Van Dyck's nudes. Sitting slantwise on the bed he kissed her breasts and stomach and when trying to pull her close discovered she was ticklish. He tickled her until she was pink all over and nearly hysterical, then said, "That's what you get for being so mean," and left her to get the paper and make the coffee and toast.

She arose and turned on the television to Gloucester before taking the paper to the john to begin her morning ritual. He felt wonderful, no sex drives and almost completely senseless, which was the way he would have loved to feel forever, but he could never let a good glow be, so he went back to the kitchen and drank a water tumbler of the vermouth. It put a sharp sardonic edge on his glow and his thoughts came back, not vivid, but alive, and about ten degrees off the line of conformity.

"Want some eggs, baby?" he called, and getting no reply, went to the bathroom door, "Will you have eggs, chicken—or should I say *do* you have eggs."

"You can poach me an egg on toast." She was taking a cold water douche and brushing her teeth at the same time and her voice was muffled. "You'll find them in the icebox. I'm not laying this morning," she added with double entendre.

He was curious but he didn't go in. "Ought to do an article for

Cosmopolitan on Woman in Bathroom in Morning—no, no, Profile of Woman at Dawn, for *The New Yorker*," he was thinking, as he returned to the kitchen, fried six slices of bacon and two eggs, poached one egg in vinegared water that came out frayed and uninteresting looking, which he put on a slice of dry, unbuttered toast and served it with a cup of black coffee.

"Your breakfast is ready!" he called, then made himself four well-buttered slices of toast, brought his own bacon and eggs to the table and began eating.

He had neglected to turn up the volume of the television and was surprised to look up and find the busts of a man and a chimpanzee on the screen. "Good God! The Russians are here," he called to Kriss and she came from the john to see the excitement.

"Oy, you must hear this, he's the cutest thing," she said and hastened to turn up the sound.

"Which one?" he muttered, but she was acting so silly, backing from the room with her hands covering her loins, that he forgot the crack in his amazement. "Now I know her secret," he thought with drunken cleverness, "She's chimp-shy!"

She slipped into a robe and pulled the table in front of the archway so both of them could see, then sat on the stool beside him and said with giggling anticipation, "He says the most fantastic things."

He looked up again at the two grimacing faces and after listening for a moment realized that the man was interviewing the chimp.

"Well, what will happen after that?" Gloucester asked the chimpanzee with a condescending smirk.

"On July 1 responsible officials of the United States will charge that slave labor exists in Russia on a scope unknown in the history of man," the chimpanzee replied grinningly.

"Not a Russian after all" Jesse thought. "Not even an ape-man. Must be a man-man."

"That's no news," Gloucester protested. "You're supposed to forecast news events."

"All right then," the chimpanzee replied. "On September 8 a woman named Bella V. Dodd will testify before a Senate Internal Security subcommittee in New York City that there are fifteen hundred Communist party members teaching in schools throughout the nation. And—"

"Who cares?" Gloucester interrupted rudely. "People are always testifying—"

"Wait! Wait!" the chimpanzee said. "Following which the New York City Board of Education will declare that ex-communists who admit party membership will not lose their teaching positions if they are genuinely repentant." The chimpanzee looked at Gloucester expectantly. "Doesn't that sound like wonderful doctrine?"

"Get on with the facts and forget the doctrine," Gloucester snarled angrily.

"Just what I was saying, facts not fancy," the chimpanzee murmured slyly.

"On May 21 fascist Spain will be admitted to UNESCO. On June 2 Secretary Trygve Lie will deny that the U.N. is a communist nest. On July 13 U.S. generals on an inspection tour of Yugoslavia will endorse military aid to communist Yugoslavia. On October 14 Senator O'Conor of Maryland will urge the U.N. to dismiss Americans employed by the U.N. who refused to say whether or not they were communists. On October 15, following the reorganization of the Soviet Directorate, Stalin will say in capitalist countries, 'So-called freedom of the individual does not exist any longer.' On October 16 U.S. Secretary of State Dean Acheson will urge the U.N. to continue to fight in Korea as long as is necessary to stop aggression and restore peace and security. On October 27 communist Yugoslavia will win a seat on the Economic and Social Council of the U.N. On November 8 police will fire on black rioters in Kimberly, South Africa, killing fourteen and wounding thirty-nine. African blacks will be protesting against government segregation policies of African blacks in Africa." The chimpanzee's interest strayed; he began looking about for his bananas. "Police will shoot into a mob of ungrateful African blacks, impressing them with white man's goodwill toward African blacks who respect white man's rule in Africa," the chimpanzee concluded, yawning with an air of extreme boredom. After all, no one was shooting down chimpanzees.

"The little stinker!" Kriss said. "Imagine the U.S. giving military aid to Yugoslavia!"

"That's what I'll do!" Jesse said. "I'll write a book about chimpanzees." Then hastened to ask, "There isn't any chimpanzee problem, is there?"

"Not that I know of," Kriss said. "All of those I've seen—most at the zoo—seem well satisfied."

"I guess you're right at that," Jesse said. "I've never heard of a chimpanzee being lynched for raping a white woman and so far none have been cited as communists."

"Nooo," Kriss said thoughtfully. "But I once saw a chimpanzee in the zoo leer at me."

"Damn!" Jesse said. "That lets them out. Leering at a white woman is considered rape in some states. And if I write a love story about chimpanzees, some white woman is sure to remember how some chimpanzee leered at her and the critics will say Robinson has written another sordid protest story, why doesn't the black bastard stop and count his blessings."

"You could write about snakes," Kriss suggested. "Everybody hates snakes."

"But I don't know any snakes,' Jesse said. "I've seen some in the snakehouse in the Bronx zoo but I can't say I came to know them."

"Kathleen Windsor didn't know any dukes, either. But she didn't let that stop her," Kriss said.

"I know, but she didn't write about duking. She just went on the age-old principle that human conscience is only waist deep."

"Why don't you read her and learn then?" Kriss asked.

"But it's below the waist the color problem lies," Jesse pointed out.

"Lays!" Kriss corrected him. "It's not the *lies* but the *lays* that make the color problem."

"The *lies* make the *lays* and the *lays* make the *lies*," Jesse expounded, feeling very clever. "If there were more *lays* and less *lies* it would soon be solved, or conversely, if there were more *lies* and less *lays* it would soon be resolved."

With that profound analysis, he went into the bathroom to tie his tie. Everything seemed so extremely normal he forgot to swipe some pills as he had intended. Way in the back of his head he found

92

himself humming *da-da-dee*. The floor was listing first one way and then the other, keeping everything in normal perspective. When he finished dressing, he kissed Kriss on the neck.

"When will I see you again, baby?"

"Call me Saturday at noon," she said, smiling sweetly. She felt wonderfully sane and cheerful.

"You're going to see your love tonight?" he asked.

She smiled her secret sensual smile.

At the front door he peeped through the Judas window to see if the coast was clear. He heard footsteps and waited until he heard the outer door open and shut. Then he went hurriedly down the corridor, relaxing only when he had safely reached the street. "Not that I give a damn for myself," he thought. But he didn't know what might result from her neighbors seeing a black man coming from her apartment early in the morning.

She cared less about it than he did. But he didn't know that.

It was shortly after nine o'clock when Jesse let himself into the apartment where he lived. "I hope all these damn birdmen are at work," he thought. "Or at least visiting some other nest." He didn't turn on the light in the pitch-black hallway because he'd have to go back and turn it off after turning on the second light. As he groped his way through the treacherous tunnel, bumping into first one hazard and then another, Napoleon came tearing from the kitchen, barking furiously, and began nipping at his ankles. He aimed a vicious kick but missed him in the dark and kicked the leg of an unseen table instead, the sharp pain running up his legbone . . . "You little bastard!" he hissed. "Wait 'till I get you in the light!"

"Napoleon, now you behave yourself," came the dulcet voice of Leroy. "Don't you know Mr. Robinson yet?"

"Oh, he's not bothering me," Jesse lied, muttering under his breath, "The little sissy cur!" Aloud he continued, "He's just saying hello."

Leroy was waiting for him in the dim front hall, his big teeth grinning from his round black face, his big belly pushing the soiled white shirt down over the half-buttoned fly of his greasy black uniform pants. "I believe Napoleon likes you," he lilted coyly. "He's just flirting." He shook his finger at the pop-eyed little beast. You stop flirting with Mr. Robinson." The mop-shaped dog trotted complacently back to the kitchen where his ancient sire was dozing beneath the kitchen stove, dreaming of young lions frolicking on the African coast.

"Perfectly normal," Jesse thought. "Sane as life." He tried to get past Leroy by saying, "I've been peeping at hole cards all night. I'm beat."

But Leroy saved the choice morsel. "Your wife stopped by last night after you'd left. She wanted to get some blankets."

"Oh!" Suddenly everything went crazy, abnormal in an insane world.

"You've been holding out on me," Leroy accused coquettishly. But on seeing the bleak, drawn expression that had come over Jesse's face, he quickly dropped the levity. "Mrs. Robinson is a very fine-looking woman."

"Thanks." Leroy's face swam before his vision and he thought he was going to be sick. He staggered blindly toward his room.

"Oh, I almost forgot. She wants some sheets too," Leroy added. "And said to tell you she was getting along fine. She asked how you were getting along and I told her—"

"Thanks," Jesse cut him off, finally managing to get his room door open. "I'll get them for her sometime this morning. Thanks very much." And he closed the door in Leroy's face.

"Who times these things?" he thought, and the next moment he was lying face down across the bed crying with deep gasping sobs. "Don't let her get hurt, God. Please don't let her get hurt," he kept praying over and over until the paroxysm passed, then he stood, leaning weakly against the dresser top, and stared at his ravaged reflection.

"Jesse Robinson," he said in a voice of utter futility. "Jesse Robinson. There must be some simple thing in this goddamn life that you don't know. Some little thing. Something every other bastard born knows but you." After a moment, without being aware that he had moved, he found himself in the window looking down across the flats of Harlem. His vision encompassed a sea of rooftops from 135th Street and Eighth Avenue until it was lost in the mists of East River, like sharp-angled waves of dirty water in the early sun, moving just enough to form a blurred distortion. "Every other nigger in this whole town but you." There had been a line in a piece he'd written for a white daily newspaper years ago, which all the blacks had objected to: "*Just a pure and simple faith in the whiter folks and the days . . .* " For ten years he'd forgotten it, now it came back to mind. "Your trouble, son, you got no faith. Fine people really. Just got to believe all their lies."

The shimmering distortion of the rooftops made him nauseated. Must be the way everybody sees the world," he thought bitterly. "All nauseated! Every mother's son of them!" He sat down weakly on the horribly covered couch, bent over, swallowing down the vomit that kept ballooning into his mouth. "It's normal, though," he tried to convince himself. "Any son of a bitch who sees it otherwise is crazy. Unnauseated bastard abnormal. Put him away. Going around shouting, *Peace, it's wonderful!* Lock him up! Menace to society." Suddenly he thought of the woman editor who, upon reading the galley proofs of his first novel that had been submitted for a prize, said it made her sick at the stomach, nauseated her. "Fine lady! Perfectly normal! No cause for alarm if everybody's like her. Let the commies come, long as we got McCarthy and nauseated normal lady editors."

He felt a great need for a drink. His hands shook when he held them out and he could feel his legs trembling. He couldn't make it to the store but he could telephone for a bottle. But when he stood up he noticed by the clock on the dresser that it was only a little past nine-thirty. Stores wouldn't be open until ten. Half hour; another half hour to be delivered. "Too Late The Opiate–Race Problem." He debated whether to ask Leroy for a drink, but decided against it. "If I have to look at that bastard's greedy eyes, I'll vomit," he thought. His reflection in the mirror showed that he was fully dressed, even to his trench coat, but minus his hat. His hat was on the bed where it had fallen off while he was crying.

And suddenly it was back and he knew all his vagrant thoughts had been a shield, but to no avail. It was back and he knew he couldn't escape it, no matter how much liquor he drank. He lay down on the bed without undressing, his black shoes on the white spread, and put his hat over his face, and gave in to it, crying quietly to himself. "Jesse Robinson. How do these people do it, son? The white man is pissing on them too, and the days don't know them either. How is it they keep their wives, bring up children, get along? Why can't you believe too, son? They say after the first bite it tastes like sugar. How come you have to be the only one to act a fool? And think you're being noble, too . . ."

The winter before the one just past, the last winter he and Becky were together, they had lived in an isolated summer resort on a small island in upstate New York, where he had been employed as caretaker. The blankets and sheets she wanted were part of a shipment of rejects the proprietors had sold to them for a fraction of the list price.

It had been pleasant there among the empty houses, far from the hurts of modern city life. No condescensions and denunciations, no venomous intrigues and shattering infidelities, no black problem and bright shining world of race relations with all its attendant excitement and despair—the frantic, frenzied and ofttimes funny interracial social gatherings, the frenetic interracial sex, the abnormally sharpened wits and equally sharpened spite, the veneer of brotherhood and exchange of beautiful ideas in a ghostly garden of hope, and the unrelenting hatred of them all, white and black, if you did not agree that history was made in bed—no mean and undermining competition with your black brothers for the favors of white folks, which had always reminded him of lines from that devastating poem, "Three Ways of Hunger," by Francis Robert White:

> *Want, will assume a lost, Lysippan*
> *Animal proportion of man:*
> *Small of head and long of arm's reach,*
> *Whose knuckles break, break again*
> *In the brute contest for contested ends.*

His duties had been light, raking leaves, a few minor repairs, and nothing after the snow came in late November. The proprietors had known he was a writer, had given him the job for that reason, believing him to be honest and chiefly wanting someone to keep a close watch on the property. He and Becky had a car to use, a lovely cottage with central heating, a fireplace and plenty of wood. And there had been a little terrier, owned by one of the proprietors, that had stayed with them; and in the cellar a hogshead of homemade wine that tasted a little like muscatel but was dry and very strong which they had drunk all winter. It was full of dead gnats and had to be strained, but on occasion, to show off his ruggedness, he drank it with the dead gnats floating about in the glass. "Ah laks marinated gnats," he would say. "Marinated gnats is good." Amusing himself with this parody on a fine novel written by a fellow black author, the part of which he remembered most vividly was a bit of dialogue between the protagonists and his brother:

—Ah likes chiddlins, do you like chiddlins?
—Ah likes chiddlins.
—Chiddlins is good.
—Ah likes de big gut, do you likes de big gut?
—Ah likes de big gut.
—De big gut is good.

It was very cold that winter and the lake froze and all day long the ice fishermen sat beside their fires, tending their lines. Gradually he'd come to feel an inner peace, such as he had never known, and the sickness following the vile stoning of his second book had almost gone. He had begun his book: *I Was Looking For a Street.* In a sense, he had almost found that street.

When spring came and the summer crew came back, his job was over. He had bought a fifteen-year-old Plymouth sedan with part of the money he had saved, and they went to Bridgeport, Connecticut, and rented a room in the home of a widow who worked as a domestic. Why Bridgeport? Why not Yonkers? Or New Haven? Afterwards, he never really knew. At the time he knew that Bridgeport had a Socialist mayor, and he vaguely remembered driving through it once and it had seemed like such a pleasant town.

Each morning he drove out to Barnum Park and found a quiet

97

spot of shade beside the Sound in which to park; and sat on the back seat with his typewriter on his knees and wrote. The sounds of the lapping of the waves and the cries of the sea gulls fishing in the rocky shoals were ineffably soothing, and he was at peace with his work.

Their money ran out about the middle of July and they decided to return to New York City from whence they'd gone upstate to the resort, and she would try to get a job in the welfare department. He advertised his car for sale in the classified section of the evening daily—*First $100 gets sound-bodied Plymouth sedan containing floating-power motor.*

The day the ad ran Becky took their last twelve dollars and went to New York City to put in her application, intending to return that evening, leaving him a half-dollar for cigarettes.

At eleven-thirty that morning he contracted to sell the car to a young immigrant worker at the G. E. factory who was to return with the money shortly after he got off work at four.

At three-thirty he drove down to the corner of Fairfield Boulevard to buy cigarettes. On his return, when pulling out from the curb, his front bumper caught in the fender of a new Buick Roadmaster that was passing too close on his left, and jerked it off. The Buick was driven by a whitehaired white lady, dressed immaculately in a mauve-colored tweed suit that looked as if it might have cost more than Jesse earned from his second book on which he had worked more than a year. She was a very important person, and despite the fact she had been driving on the wrong side of a oneway street, and that her breath smelled pleasantly of excellent cocktails, she sent for a policeman and had Jesse arrested for reckless driving— not because she hated blacks or wished to humiliate or harm him in any manner; but her husband was always cautioning her to drive carefully and she intended to prove by the record that she had done so.

Watching her talk to the motorcycle policeman, Jesse thought, "Reason we're going to fight the Russians, son—to prove by the record we were right." But he wasn't worried. He hadn't seen any Russians about—not having the keen eyesight of Senator McCarthy. Nor had he broken any laws. How could they arrest him?

He found out shortly that to arrest him required very little skill. The policeman said, "Follow me," and mounted his four-cylinder steed. "Shows what an ingenious people can do," he thought sourly as he followed in his battered jalopy.

The desk sergeant set his bail at twenty-five dollars. He confessed he didn't have twenty-five dollars. "But I'm a well-known American writer," he said. "You can release me on my own recognizance."

The desk sergeant said the law didn't permit it.

"Should have told him you were a porter, son," Jesse thought. "All Americans trust black porters and black mammies—even with their children."

It was Tuesday and his landlady wouldn't be home until Thursday and he knew no one else to whom he could appeal. However, before sending him to the lockup the desk sergeant gave him permission to telephone his wife at eight o'clock, at which time he expected her home from New York City. But the guard shift changed at six and the night guard had no orders concerning him telephoning. He knew how much she would worry when he failed to come home, and as the night wore on, despair set in. "Don't let it throw you, son," he told himself. "Racial characteristic, like syphilis and servility and stealing." He recalled the bit of doggerel:

Some folks say that a nigger won't steal
But I found one in my corn field,

and began composing scenes to pass the night:

—What you doing in my cornfield, nigger?
—What cornfield, boss?
—This cornfield where you're at, nigger.
—Oh, this cornfield.
—Yes, this cornfield.
—I just come down to see what make the grass grow, boss.

At eleven o'clock the next morning he was taken to the magistrate's court. But the driver of the Buick had suffered from such severe shock she was unable to appear, and the hearing was postponed for a week. However, he was permitted to telephone. First he called his house. Receiving no reply, in desperation he telephoned

Becky's brother in Baltimore, Maryland, who promised to wire him a hundred dollars to the city jail immediately.

Becky had had to stay overnight in New York City in order to interview with the personnel director at nine o'clock that morning, and didn't get back to Bridgeport until eleven. The telephone had been ringing when she let herself into the house but had stopped by the time she answered it. She noticed the car was gone and she thought he'd sold it; but when the young man called at eleven-thirty with the money to buy it, she began to worry. She noticed then that the bed hadn't been slept in, and she was afraid he'd been hurt. She began telephoning the hospitals. It wasn't until after one o'clock that it occurred to her that he might have been arrested for some traffic violation. She called police headquarters and learned that he was being held on a charge of reckless driving.

At the same time Becky was talking to the desk officer, Jesse was being hustled into a patrol wagon along with other prisoners committed to the county prison. Since by then he hadn't made bail he could be held no longer in the municipal jail. At the county prison he was mugged, fingerprinted, given a uniform of blue denim with his number stenciled on his shirt and locked in a cell on the third tier. He kept telling himself that the money for his bail would arrive any minute, and tried desperately not to think of Becky. But gradually, as the day wore on, laughter started welling up from the depths of his despair. "You should have stayed up in that tree, son," he thought. "Not safe on the ground with lady drivers and atom bombs."

When Becky arrived at court she learned he'd been unable to raise his bail and had been committed to the county prison. First telegraphing her brother in Baltimore for twenty-five dollars, she rushed to the county prison but was informed that prisoners were not permitted visitors unless they had a pass from the court, and then only during visiting hours on Tuesdays and Thursdays. It was Wednesday. She rushed home to see if the money had come and found a wire from her brother stating that he'd already wired a hundred dollars to the city jail.

So she rushed back to the city jail to learn that the money had arrived but, the prisoner having already been committed to the county prison, it had been returned to the telegraph office. After getting a pass to see Jesse from the prosecutor, she hastened to the telegraph office to draw the money.

But the telegram was addressed to Jesse and they wouldn't give it to her. She explained that her husband was in the county prison waiting for the money to make bail. They said she'd have to obtain a statement from him, countersigned by the warden, authorizing them to pay her the money. She rushed to the county prison and luckily, got an audience with the warden. He said he was sorry, but prisoners were not permitted to receive money from the outside. And he could not permit her to visit her husband until visiting day. Then she began to cry.

By that time it was four o'clock in the afternoon and the telegraph office closed at five. In the meantime, Jesse had been marched into the mess hall for his supper of stale bread, macaroni and boiled cabbage, and marched back to his cell. "Anyway, the food is better than in Russia—they say in the newspapers," he thought half-amused.

Luckily, the warden couldn't bear to see a woman cry. This seemed to be a decent woman. He wondered how these decent colored women always got mixed up with some no-good bastard of a husband. So he relented, impressing upon her that he was breaking the prison rules, but he would see what he could do. He had a statement typed, giving her authority to draw the money, and sent it by a guard to Jesse's cell to have it signed. Then he countersigned it, and by then it was fifteen minutes to five.

She ran down the stairs and looked for a taxi. On the second street she found one and reached the telegraph office one minute before closing time. She drew the money, returned, and bailed Jesse out. When he came into the front hall where she waited, he saw at once that she'd been crying. Her body was trembling all over and her eyes looked huge and dark with pain in her small heart-shaped face.

"Let's get out of here," he said.

They went back to police headquarters where he'd parked the car. It had a red ticket on it for parking overnight. He put the ticket in his pocket, started the motor, drove back to the house.

The young man who wanted to buy the car was waiting for him on the porch. Jesse knocked twenty-five dollars off the price because of the bent bumper and crumpled fender, and the young man was satisfied.

Becky fixed a makeshift dinner and they ate silently. Afterwards he said, "Let's pack."

They had two wardrobe trunks and three suitcases, but they couldn't get in everything they owned, so they left some clothing and several paintings in the basement of their landlady's house. Then he went to the station and found a transfer man to take the trunks to the station.

At eight o'clock next morning they caught the New Haven limited to New York City. When they came out into Grand Central Station, he paused for a moment beside a wastepaper container and tore the red Bridgeport traffic violation ticket into tiny bits. His customarily voluminous thoughts composed for the occasion only two words, "Fuck you!"

And now, nine months later, lying on his bed in his rented room, drunk and fully dressed, recalling the incident, he thought, "Natural enough," and after a moment of consideration, in which he realized all this had happened in a modern, liberal, democratic American city, during the middle of the twentieth century following the birth of Christ, without any maliciousness or deliberate injustice on the part of anyone, he thought further, "Perfectly natural! Happening all the time. That proves it. No doubt right too. Right attitude on the part of everyone. Inevitable, anyway. Even mine. Flea bites you, you squash it. If flea says *Ouch!* perfectly natural. What the hell you expect a squashed flea to say—*Hallelujah?*"

For a time he thought about Becky. "Rough on her, though," he thought. He wondered why she had kept on taking it for so long—twelve years. "Love—But, Jesus Christ! I used to love God, too, but it didn't last for these past twelve years." He began crying quietly somewhere inside. "I used to love her, too. Still do, I suppose." But he had left her.

When, shortly after the Bridgeport incident, she got a state welfare job in a hospital about thirty miles from New York City, he'd put an end to the farce of playing husband. It was a live-in job with one day off a week, and they'd taken a room in the Bronx where they had planned she would come and spend her day off with him. But after a month of it he couldn't bear sitting there day after day, working on his typewriter at something no typical insecure American could bear to read, then having to face her haunted look when she came home for her few short hours of marriage.

So he'd said to her, "Becky, let's separate. If I'm ever a success, we'll come back together. But now, let's try it apart."

And now the memory of the hurt that had come into her eyes brought him to his feet. His hat with which he'd covered his face fell unnoticed to the floor. He stared at his greasy reflection in the mirror. His eyes were like red coals and his vision was fuzzy. "Jesse Robinson," he spoke to his image. "You thought you were being noble? There ain't no such thing, son. That's a confidence twist they put down to make bastards like you, who won't knuckle down and conform, voluntarily commit suicide, save them the trouble of killing you. Just a racket, son. You oughta know that by now."

But all along in the back of his mind he kept wondering why, in April with the weather getting warm and everything furnished where she worked, she wanted blankets and sheets? He had the feeling something was happening that he didn't know. There was a lump in his chest that made it hard for him to breathe and everything began going and coming. "Unnatural bastard," he said to his reflection. "*O heart, lose not thy nature* . . . Wonder where that old plagiarist stole all that crap. But it fits, though. It reckons. Maybe the old bastard was God, as Swinburne used to claim. Image anyway. Same as Mr Ward. *For who could bear the whips and scorns of time, the oppressor's wrong, the proud man's contumely, the pangs of dispiz'd love, the Law's delay, the insolence of office, and the spurns that patient merit of the unworthy takes, when he himself might his quietus make, with a bare bodkin?* Who can say that makes less sense than: *Blessed are the meek: for they shall inherit the earth. Blessed are they that hunger and thirst after righteousness for they shall be filled. Blessed are the merciful: for they shall obtain mercy.* Or that both are not equally senseless?"

It was ten minutes before ten, he noticed. "Get it my damn self," he decided. He wiped his greasy face with a bath towel, put on his sunglasses and his hat, and took off his trench coat. There was a slight smudge of lipstick on his white shirt collar, but it didn't matter.

When he left his room, through the open door of the bedroom opposite, he saw Leroy standing beside the bed, his black body clad only in a brief undershirt. "Uncouth bastard!" he thought, hastening along. Then, "That's where those old boys missed it. Those who lamented and those who railed and those like Henry James who avoided and ignored. If one of them had ever written: *Alas poor Culture, I knew him when, a fellow of infinite jest: of a most excellent fancy, he hath borne me on his back a thousand times. Here hung those lips, that I have kissed I know not how oft. But now his place hath been taken by uncouthness, a mean and sordid fellow without humor or refinement. How I despise this lowborn role. But me thinks, fair friends, that he is here to stay, a way of life, for a thousand years to come*—he might have rolled along with Homer."

Napoleon charged from the kitchen, skidding on the polished floor, barking furiously, nipping at his ankles, momentarily deflecting his train of thought; the dulcet voice of Leroy called, "Napoleon! You behave yourself and stop barking at Mr. Robinson. Mr. Robinson knows you're here."

As he groped his way down the long dark corridor, pitch black through his sunglasses, the popeyed cur yapping at his heels, he returned to his stream of thought: "Once it was only the sport of kings; then the upper middle classes, aristocrats, and nouveau riche took it up. But now the masses have it. Everybody's uncouth now. Probably a good thing, too." And after a moment, half-amused, "We niggers will at last have a chance to come into our own. We'll be the most uncouth sons of bitches of them all."

CHAPTER 7

DAVE WAS COMING for dinner and Kriss had donned her red silk Chinese Mandarin robe embellished with gold dragons, along with her pert Persian slippers of red suede handsewn with gold thread. Dave had called her at the office to say he wanted to see her and she had invited, nay, demanded, that he come to dinner. She knew he was coming, but whether he would get dinner depended on which turn her thoughts would take during the half hour before he was to arrive, not to say whether or not he would stay for dinner, a contingency the consideration of which she kept trying to float from her mind by a rapid succession of Scotch-whisky highballs.

But this possibility, verily a probability, had refused to be floated, the proof of which was the flaming ensemble she now wore. She knew this was enough to set Dave's teeth on edge. For she had cajoled him into buying the slippers to go with the robe which he afterwards had learned had been given her by Fuller Halperin—in fact, the information had come from herself: that Fuller had paid a hundred dollars for it in San Francisco and had given it to her that Christmas weekend in Washington when Dave had been under the impression she had gone to Chicago on business and had bought it in Marshall Field's basement. After all, Dave was a lawyer and wasn't expected to know merchandise. Besides which, Dave not only thought it made her look like a whore, but thought it proved the point as well. And because the sight of it on her so provoked him, she thought of it as her *muleta*.

Now she smiled maliciously as she sat in her three-legged chair, leafing through the pages of the latest *New Yorker*, enjoying the cartoons along with her fifth highball, the combination being aphrodisical in a highly intellectual way, that is to say, stimulating the purely physical sex instinct which, alas, is also embodied in cats and dogs and even blacks, by an application of subtlety, culture, and wit to the highbrowed intellectual processes and refined sensibilities of the cultivated—which of course excludes the blacks, who do not possess such attributes, and even lets out the cats and dogs, the latter, however, because they don't drink Scotch.

The maliciousness in her smile was in no way related to her enjoyment of *The New Yorker*. The maliciousness derived from consideration of the contingency that would not be floated away, and the additional reflection that Dave would want to sleep with her, because she looked like a whore; and he'd sit there looking at her in the red robe thinking of how she'd slept with this Fuller person all during the year of their "engagement" and had received gifts and money from him almost equal to her salary, which proved she was a whore. "God knows how many others she has slept with," he would think, wanting her in that way men, good and bad the world over, desire whores and promiscuous women, and despising himself because of it.

And the thought lit a rage inside of her. "You son of a bitch!" she sobbed. "You Jewish son of a bitch! I'm not good enough for you?" She began to cry, her full matronly face stretching and puckering in the ugly grimace of a little tow-headed girl called "Dutch" crying because her mother had slapped her drunken father the day he lost his grocery store in a little village in North Dakota. "You ruined me, you son of a bitch!" And in that moment of emotional torture, she couldn't have said who she meant by this last son of a bitch.

There were many such moments now, since Dave had thrown her over, when she was confused as to really who had ruined her. Just as in later years ofttimes her memory confused the great event of losing her virginity with the time she first had diphtheria. The confusion was brought about by the recollection of her uneasiness, which had been the same in both instances; now twenty-one years later this being the most that she clearly recalled of either instance.

The one time they had been skating on the millpond with the bunch. It had been a raw cold day with an icy blast coming down from Canada. But to please Willard she'd worn only her light skating suit. She'd become chilled to the bone. But Willard loved to skate and she wouldn't leave him. Although cold and miserable she had been happy to glide along holding his arm.

Finding her mother away when they'd returned home, he'd come in with her. Something in his attitude had made her know that he would ask. He'd looked at her with that appraising one-sided smile that had always made her heart turn over.

By then her throat had ached terribly and she'd felt sick enough to faint. She'd wanted nothing better than to go to bed. But she'd felt a strange uneasiness that made her stay with him. She had been afraid to disappoint him; he had so many other places to go and there had been so many other girls who'd wanted him. She'd been afraid to admit to being so sick. But the room had begun to blur. Against her will she had found herself saying, "Willard, you had better go; I'm awfully sick."

After he'd gone she had thought, "I must be really awfully sick to send him home." Then she'd stumbled up the stairs to bed.

Her mother had thought at first she had a cold. But the next day the doctor had said she had diptheria.

The other time Willard had arrived shortly after her mother had gone visiting. They'd been playing the phonograph and dancing when suddenly he'd drawn her down beside him on the sofa. She had known it was going to happen. She'd felt the same strange uneasiness she'd felt before. She'd been so afraid she'd disappoint him.

He'd put his left arm about her waist and cupped her left breast in his hand. His look, at once confident and demanding, had hypnotized her. She had felt herself melt as his lips touched hers. Then his right hand had moved over her stomach. She had raised her hips so he could slide her panties from underneath her. The hot wet flame of her passion had grown unbearable.

She had looked away from him, unable to breathe. And when she had felt his touch she had prayed, "Oh God, let him like me. Let him like me, God." Then it had been lost in the first sharp hurt, and she had gasped.

"Is this it?" she had asked herself. "Is this what they all rave about? What launched a thousand ships?" Then she had become conscious of his ecstasy, and that had been her reward. "I've given myself to him," she had thought, and it had fired her with exaltation.

There had been one other moment of panic, however. She'd been certain she would die on the spot if he hadn't liked it. But he'd put his arms about her and had drawn her close again and kissed her passionately. And she had known that he had liked her. She had been so reassured and happy she had cried, "Oh, Willard, I love you with all my heart."

And a year later she'd gone to Chicago and had become engaged to Ronny, whom at first she had despised. But the gang had decided she was the girl for him and had always paired them together. At that time she hadn't understood why she, a flaxen-haired, apple-cheeked, blue-eyed farm girl was deemed a match for this chunky, habitually boozed, over-brilliant, condescending, Yankee-hating, low-browed, blackhaired, misanthropic Mississippian, and a senior to boot. He hadn't given the impression of caring much for her either. Once when running up the stairs of International House with the gang she'd dropped her handkerchief, and he'd given it a glance and had kept on going.

"Why, Ronny!" one of the older girls had cried indignantly. "Where are your southern manners? Why didn't you pick up Kriss's handkerchief?"

He'd given Kriss an indifferent look as she came up with flaming face and had said, "She's a Northern girl, she's used to picking up her own things." She'd never forgiven him for that. But all during that first term they'd gone about together, each instinctively disliking the other, but she trying to excite him to the pitch of asking so she could let him know how much she disliked him by refusing, while he, for his part, gave no indication that he would ever ask. However, it had given her prestige to be seen with him.

A doll-like young Siamese prince with dusky velvet skin and dark doe eyes began courting her with flowers and candy and dinners in swank downtown restaurants. She'd spent a weekend with him in New York City. When Ronny had learned of that, he'd cursed her in a violent rage, calling her a "nigger lover"; in one breath asking her how she could do that to him, and in the next asking her to marry him. She hadn't understood at that time those subtleties of white supremacy that inspired this native white supremacist to seek her hand in marriage who had bedded with a black, whereas before this incident (which she recalled as being scarcely more exciting than a conducted YWCA tour) he hadn't paid much heed to her. She would have finally had her revenge, but for a letter from her mother stating that her father was ill and they could not afford to keep her there any longer. So she'd accepted his proposal and the next day they'd announced their betrothal to the gang; and the day after the gang had gotten up a party to celebrate and even then she hadn't known what they were celebrating. An apartment had been provided for the prenuptial ceremony to which they had been jovially, if somewhat forcefully, escorted after the drinking bout. But she had no objections whatsoever, by then being very curious and knowing herself to be a lovely piece—she had only Willard's word for this but somehow she knew that he was an authority. Spread across the bed she'd found a lovely sheer nightgown that showed her to advantage. But after fiddling about in the bathroom and kitchen for almost an hour without having removed his coat, insensitive to her charms which she paraded seductively in her transparent gown, he had suddenly announced, "I'm going to run to the corner drugstore and get some toothbrushes since we're going to stay all night." An hour later he had returned exhausted with two new toothbrushes to fall into a deep sleep, while she had lain awake and fuming until dawn. Thus they had sealed their engagement and had faced the world next day with shining teeth.

The week before she returned home for the summer vacation she'd written to Willard, informing him of her engagement—a tender letter of consolation and entreaty, of humble pleas for his forgiveness and poignant regret for all those things that now could never be. He replied by marrying the local girl whom she most disliked on the day of her return; and she was greeted by the sight of the wedding procession of honking cars when she alighted from the train. From the depot she telephoned first one place and then another until she got in touch with him and begged him to see her for just five minutes. He came and took her to a roadhouse and at ten o'clock that night they went to bed in one of the rooms upstairs which served such purposes and it was twelve o'clock when he took her to her parents and he went to his bride. By then knowledge of their escapade had swept the town, and when he came into the small, dark room where he and his bride were to live until they found a more suitable place, his loving bride stabbed him with a small kitchen knife and then ran into the street crying, "I've killed him! I've killed him!" It was a cheap knife, however, with a dull blade and did more damage to Kriss's mother by way of scandal, the shame penetrating her heart far deeper than the dull blade the lout's flesh it was intended to lay low.

Guilt drove Kriss back to Chicago where she suffered the remorse of the damned.

That summer she worked on a WPA research project directed by Harold Ramsey, who was then becoming impressed by his destiny as a black Sigmund Freud in the blackest of all Black Belts. It was a glorious era of research into what is termed naively by U.S. terminologists as the "Negro Problem"—as if this American dilemma of what to do with twenty million descendants of American slaves, freed from bondage as a result of a bloody civil war, and granted equality by the due process of constitutional amendment, was some riddle these poor folk had cooked up for the mortification of white intellect and could themselves solve at a moment's notice if they so desired.

Educated blacks in great numbers—montebank, dim-witted, well-meaning, opportunistic, and otherwise—accepted this challenge and set about with great zeal, augmented to a considerable degree by white folks' money, to effect the solution, *effecting* sounding more impressive than *confecting* and more conscientious than *affecting*.

Naturally Kriss was greatly impressed by Harold Ramsey, one of the brightest apostles of this noble cause; but at that time he hadn't noticed her. She would have been both delighted and honored to have married him and shared her genuine guilt with his professional torment, but unfortunately he was already married to one white woman whom he paraded about town in his big new automobile, being wined and dined, not to say consulted, by the rich and recent Negrophiles—and two white wives would have been outrageous even in Chicago.

So on the first Monday in October, shortly after the beginning of the fall term, she had married Ronny in a veritable sweat of guilt. But it had been June of the following year before she had discovered the reason his friends had boosted the marriage was that he was a homosexual.

They'd taken a three-room flat in an old converted mansion near the campus and had quickly settled down to a married life of work, study, and carousing with the other tenants, similarly settled down, a motley assortment of students, artists, writers, and other rising young geniuses and a few old relics in whom the rising powder had evidently been omitted. There had been a party in one of the joints, shifting as was customary from flat to flat as the liquor ran out, and becoming enlarged on the way—like a seeded cat trying to get home to Akron from bitter exile in Cincinnati in the allotted three-score days—with couples drifting off from time to time to answer the call of nature. At three o'clock next morning when Kriss staggered with the assistance of some unidentified male to her flat and found Ronny in bed with some tramp of an artist from upstairs, she said indignantly, "I'm not going to sleep on the sofa." Her escort said that was unnecessary as long as his double bed on the floor below remained untenanted. So at eight o'clock she returned, sleepier than before, and found that Ronny had changed bedmates for a strapping fine sailor. She was alone this time, outnumbered and outgunned, so she slept on the sofa after all.

But that night, accompanied by much crying and continuous drinking, Ronny related the grim story of his love for a football hero, bosom friend from childhood, not to mention bedmate, who had been killed on a hunting expedition the two of them had taken one summer, by a black woodsman with an axe, the black being subsequently hunted down and lynched. This by way of being more of an explanation of why he'd slept with the sailor than why he'd dedicated his life to the Negro Problem. It was a perfectly reasonable explanation for both pursuits, but at that time she didn't understand this and despised him on both accounts.

It was after that a change came into the nature of her guilt. Where before, her guilt had provoked remorse, afterward it provided a thrill. For a time following, her chief enjoyment came from feeling she was taking some man away from some lovelier and more desirable or superior woman. And she derived an evil satisfaction from what she'd done to Willard.

"The lice! All of them are lice!" she thought. Judging her by a code of morals not one of them accepted for himself. "God knows I should know!" she thought. She'd been intimate with the President of the Foundation all during the time Ronny was in the army. He had been one of the most revered and important men in his field in the world, but in her bed he had been as much of a louse as any of the others. He'd brought home a whip from Mexico to whip her with, and ofttimes after they'd attended a serious conference in which weighty problems had been discussed and analyzed he had escorted her home and whipped her unmercifully until she had yielded to his every desire. And she had weekended in the White House and had found herself in bed with a man of such international importance she had never dared mention his name, who had wanted only that she play bitch-on-heat to his role of common dog, then there had been the worn-out heir of one of the nation's most glorious mercantile names who had demanded detailed and graphic accounts of her sex acts with big black men, she having to invent these when none had occurred, then beating her until she begged for mercy, after which, catlike, he had soothed her hurts.

How could they feel she wasn't good enough for them? she thought, sobbingly. How could they? When they'd made her what she was themselves.

So she railed against the injustice of it with all the bitterness of her soul, at the same time accepting the moral judgement that she was ruined. They'd given her a drunkard for a father and a louse for her first lover, two abortions and the loss of fertility, a homosexual for a husband and a bevy of men whose lusts she had been required to satisfy because of their importance, receiving no satisfaction in return; this along with a North Dakota farm girl's strong healthy body and a hot ass, and expected her to be satisfied. Which was against all reason. But when she'd taken Negroes as lovers they'd crucified her. "Kriss is solving the Negro Problem in bed," they'd said of her, solving their own problem in her own bed along with the Negro Problem, perhaps because of it, at the same time feeling she wasn't good enough for them and treating her like dirt. They'd made her feel like dirt before she'd ever thought of sleeping with a black man; and only when sleeping with one could she feel secure in the knowledge that she wasn't dirt. Which was the same thing they had done to the blacks. So with them she never felt ruined; they never thought of her as ruined. They were ruined by being born black, ruined in the eyes of her race, and they kept laughing at the idiocy of a race that ruined their own women and threw them in bed with men of another race they'd similarly ruined. To be sure, some of the blacks with whom she'd slept had been weird enough. But no more weird than awakening to the realization that she was married to a homosexual.

They even had the effrontery to talk about their honor. "Is that what the son of a bitch is worried about—his honor?" she asked herself with venomous rage. He'd eaten her food and enjoyed her company and pleasured in her bed, never so much however as when he'd finally decided she was a whore whom he didn't have to marry; and what was more he'd taken her extra paint she'd blended especially for her own apartment to paint his own dirty flat. And this paint had been mixed by a black who had been recommended to her by black friends, and who had charged her three times what it was worth to paint her three-room flat in addition to the cost of the paint. And this son of a bitch had taken her extra paint, and now he was coming to get his watch which he had pawned to her the month before to pay his income tax, after he'd decided she wasn't good enough for him to marry.

"I'll make you crawl, you son of a bitch!" she resolved. It being Friday night she could drink herself unconscious and disgust him even more with her. Because she knew that however he felt now, once he had wanted to marry her rather desperately. Nor would she let him have his watch, even if he had the money to pay his debt. And she'd be damned if she would give him dinner. "I'll pay you out, you son of a bitch!" she resolved. She wished now that Jesse had left something, his hat or coat, which she could place in some obvious place for Dave to see.

But sight of him brought a change of mind. He was a tall, straight-limbed man, conservatively dressed in a dark gray Brooks

Brothers suit, black wingtip shoes, striped shirt, and dark tie. The absence of shoulder pads in the formfitted jacket gave him a Pall Mall look, but his face had none of the blind snobbery of those escapees from socialism. It was a long narrow face with a strong nose and splendid bones and a wide sensuous mouth. His light brown hair was parted on the side and his dark shadowed eyes were serious. At sight of her in the red silk robe his quick mind conjured up the two thoughts, "Scarlet Letter" and "Burning Bush," and his eyes softened with pity, his lips curling slightly in an indulgent smile.

"Hello, Kriss," he greeted in his deep controlled voice. "Expecting company?"

Her heart melted and she felt suddenly cheap. Each time she saw him after a short absence he impressed her anew with being so clean and handsome, what she'd always envisioned as a "Harvard man." And all at once she had a desire to please him, to be modern and restrained and prove she was a good loser; and because she knew he was courting another woman she wanted more than ever to sleep with him. Her glazed blue eyes beneath her swollen dead-white vaselined lids swam with sensuousness.

"You're company now," she murmured, preceding him to the sitting room.

Although he had keys to her apartment, to both outer and inner doors, he'd chosen to ring both bells to emphasize his position; and as he followed her down the hall, laid the three keys on the dining table.

She took her glass for a refill, and asked him, grinning mischievously "Scotch still? Or have you changed to Kummel?"

He lowered his lank frame on the sofa, ignoring the dig. "Have you seen the Monet exhibition?"

"Dot wanted me to go with her, but I was too tired," she called from the kitchen, mumbling the words in a manner she'd picked up from Maud.

"What?"

"Just a moment, dear." After mixing the drinks she put the frozen whipped potatoes out to thaw and the steak to warm, and debated for a moment whether to make him potato pancakes, which he adored. But they were too much trouble, she'd just do the green peas and salad as she'd planned, although she wished she could make him something special. She felt a warm glow of passion, recalling Maud's sage remark, "All that men like is food, drink, and women," and felt tingly to her fingertips. But when she passed the dining table and saw the three keys he had placed there surreptitiously, her mood went cold and malicious, the only hot thing left within her being rage. However, her outward appearance remained the same, she still grinned, so Dave didn't notice the change.

"Dot wanted to take me," she said, placing his drink on a silver coaster on the table beside him. "But I've seen the best of Monet in the Louvre, and besides I'm weary of Dot."

He sipped his drink and put it down, smiling at her absentmindedly. "What have you been doing lately?"

The question infuriated her, all the more because he seemed preoccupied and didn't give a damn what she'd been doing. She felt an impulse to tell him, "Just sleeping around, you son of a bitch! What do you think?" But she only giggled in a way that had always irritated him; it reminded him of the way his sister had giggled when she'd done something naughty. And then she assumed her secret sensual smile and said offhandedly,

"Oh, the usual thing. I went to a party Sunday—just a staff party at Kirby's house in Bronxville. Arty was by Monday—you've met him . . ." He nodded slightly. "He flew in from Chicago to attend a conference. And Tuesday Johnny took me to see *Guys and Dolls*—that's the third time I've seen it—you know you took me to see it the first time—and it's just as funny as ever." She giggled reminiscently. "I adore that floating crap game scene. Afterward we went to the Versailles. Then Fuller took me shopping Wednesday." She gave him a covert glance to see the effect of this thrust, but he didn't seem to be listening. "You needn't try to be so superior, you son of a bitch, I know the time when that would have killed you," she thought, viciously, continuing aloud with a sweet innocent smile, "Oh, just the usual things a bachelor girl does in New York." And after a pause, "Jesse Robinson was by last night." Something in her voice made him look up.

"Jesse Robinson?"

"Oh, that's right. You never met him. You met Harold."

"Is he a sociologist too?"

She knew he wanted to ask if he was another Negro she had slept with, and she smiled with an appearance of sensual reminiscence. "He's a novelist. But that's right, you don't read novels." She finished her drink and gave him a lidded look. "But that's not what I like him for," she added, feeling an evil delight at the dull flush that mounted his face.

He'd scarcely touched his glass but she asked sweetly, "Would you like another drink, dear?" knowing that he detested Scotch and never drank more than one highball, and that only at some social gathering. He shook his head, half-angrily. She said, "It's just as well. Jesse practically cleaned me out, although he brought a bottle of his own." She giggled, seeing his flush deepen. "All writers drink like crazy anyway."

"He had a good partner in you," he muttered.

"Partner in drink, partner in bed," she thought, smiling sensually as she said, "I almost married him once," and flounced to the kitchen to mix her drink, throwing her hips more than usual, and feeling quite giggly inside.

At last she's achieved that superior feeling she used to achieve with Ronny after she'd cuckolded him to his face and challenged him to accuse her. She felt a delicious sense of evil which tickled her all inside and the sight of the melting potatoes and blood-dripping steak tickled her all the more. "You can eat it raw, you son of a bitch!" she thought, taking a half glass of the strong Scotch neat before mixing the highball, and when she returned to Dave she staggered slightly and knew she was getting drunk. Placing her drink with elaborate care on its silver coaster atop the storage cabinet, she lowered herself as carefully into her favorite three-legged chair as amused by and interested in the spectacle of herself as any curious bystander.

"I almost married you once, too," she resumed, her sensuous smile now mixed with such maliciousness it seemed to drip with sticky venom. "Always a bedmate but never a bride."

He flushed crimson, straightening in his seat as the pins and needles pricked, but kept his low deliberate voice controlled. "I really shouldn't have called, Kriss, but I wanted to leave your keys and get my watch. I'll give you a check with whatever interest—"

"Oh, wait till after dinner, dear . . . You know you're invited to dinner?"

'Oh, I—" He was a nice man and she had cornered him. "Please be sensible, Kriss. You know that I know you're not going to prepare any dinner. You know I know you that well."

"You ought to, you son of a bitch, as long as you've slept with me," she said savagely.

He was red to the roots of his hair. "For God's sake, Kriss, can't we do a simple business transaction without a sordid fight?"

"You can because you're a gentleman." She giggled suddenly and added, "But I can't because I'm a whore. That's what you called me, remember?"

"For Christ's sake! You're throwing that up again. We were both angry and you called me far worse."

"Did your mother tell you I was a whore? Or did you find it out by yourself?"

He shrugged with disgust. "My mother likes you—"

"But I'm not Jewish. If I joined the synagogue and—" giggling "—had the Rabbi circumcise me, would I be Jewish enough for her then?"

"Let up, Kriss, let up!" he said in a low angry voice. "This isn't getting us anywhere—"

"Certainly isn't, dear—"

"—and it'd be silly to part hating one another—"

"You've always hated me!" she flared. "You hate all gentiles, you son of a bitch! You condescending son of a bitch! You think gentiles are dirt under your feet."

"—so let me give you a check for a hundred dollars and take my watch and let's call it quits. Okay?"

"What's the extra twenty-five dollars for? A tip? Or do you want to spend the night? Fuller always gives me at least a hundred dollars every time he sleeps with me." Watching the color drain from his face, she thought, "I'm a bitch!"

His long handsome face assumed an expression of infinite pity.

117

"You always hate me when you're drunk," he said as if somewhat benumbed. "Why do you always hate me when you're drunk?"

His pity struck her like a contemptuous slap, hurting far more than his hatred or an actual blow; and she blubbered senselessly, "You sonavabitch—" and if the telephone had not rung at that moment she would have cried wantonly and disgustingly like a drunken prostitute with her brain gone in liquor and disease, crying without knowing what she's crying for.

She staggered to the bedroom and for half an hour carried on a disjointed incoherent conversation with some black unionist from Washington, D.C., on his way to Detroit, staying overnight at the Commodore, who was trying to persuade her to come down and have a drink. She'd slept with him one night in a black hotel in Atlanta, Georgia, and had disliked him ever afterwards, but she kept him dallying on the phone, he saying, "What? . . . What? . . . I can't understand you . . . You sound like Maud . . . Talk a little louder . . . Are you drunk? . . ." and herself replying, "Go on buy some you bastard—" giggling in between, giving the whole performance just to keep Dave waiting.

He sat leafing through *The New Yorker,* his white face quivering now and then from the anger he could scarcely contain. He'd written her a check for seventy-nine dollars and fifty cents, giving her six percent interest on the loan, and he'd placed it on the cabinet beside her empty glass. Now he just wanted to get his watch and go.

But she ignored the check and picked up her glass and staggered toward the kitchen for a refill, all the time talking incoherently, "He wanted me to come down to the Commodore and sleep with him—said *drink* but that's the way you say it . . ." her voice fading out as she fumbled about in the kitchen, then grew in volume on her return ". . . once a black man sleeps with Kriss he never forgets. They all come back." She smiled with infinite pleasure. "Never forget. I took Ted away from—" He had stood up and began walking toward the door. "All right, go to hell then, you son of a bitch. I slept with Jesse last night!" she called as loudly as she could, but he had closed the door behind him and didn't hear her.

She looked at his check and smiled as one bemused in idiocy. The drink sobered her slightly and she dreaded being alone. Staggering to the telephone, supporting herself against the wall, she called Jesse. An extremely courteous male voice, Mr. Ward's, informed her that Jesse was out. She was overcome by such a fury, the instrument trembled in her hand. "Probably in bed with some black Harlem bitch!" she raged inwardly. "Probably with his wife . . . If I find you sleeping with your wife, I'll kill you, you son of a bitch!" she muttered. The rage passed as quickly as it had come, and she began to giggle. Groping about in the haze before her, she found the receiver and began dialing another number without being aware that Mr. Ward was still patiently waiting on the line to ask if there was a message for Jesse.

"Hello, is this the Windemere Hotel?"

"I don't understand you," Mr. Ward replied. "You were asking for Mr. Robinson."

"Robinson?" She had forgotten his existence. "Oh, *Jesse* Robinson. Damn Jesse Robinson!" And she hung up and dialed again.

Harold was as drunk as herself. "Kriss? That you, Kriss? It's a bitch, girl! It's a bitch!"

"Come over and sleep with me. I'm cold."

"You know I can't sleep with you, Kriss. I haven't slept with you since you had the clap."

"I don't want you to screw me, baby. Just keep me warm."

"Margaret is here. She wants me to screw her. We been fighting and now we got to fuck."

"Bring her along, baby. I'll give you half the bed." She giggled. "That's enough to screw on. That is if you're going to screw the old-fashioned way."

"That's the only way I do it now. My analyst said too much of that other'll make a homosexual outa one. Just old State Street grind. Not tryna win no home no more."

"Come on then and grind over here. I'll wait until you're finished."

"No, you'll never do that to me, my dear."

"What, baby?"

"I lost one woman to a dike—"

"You son of a bitch, you—"

"Call me what you please, my dear, but you like it. You're not fooling me, my dear. I—"

She tried to bang the receiver on the rack, but it missed and fell behind the nightstand, and she left it dangling on its cord and staggered into the bathroom. "Harold, what did you say that for?" she thought accusingly, now crying bitterly, unrestrainedly, tears making ugly streaks down her distorted face. "Why did you say that? Why did you say that to me?"

Desperately she fumbled in the medicine cabinet, groping for the bottle of sleeping pills which now she couldn't see. Finally her hands encountered the small glass bottle. She held it close to her eyes so she would make no mistake. It was filled to the brim with small red and yellow capsules. She pulled out the stopper and dumped them all into one hand. With the other hand she turned on the faucet of the basin and filled her plastic toothbrush glass. "Why did you *do* that to me?" she sobbed, her mind having gone to another hurt, but she didn't know what it was. "Why did you do that to *me*?" Opening her mouth wide, she threw in the capsules with one hand and raised the glass of water with the other. She choked slightly, and then got them down. She didn't know that only four capsules had gone into her mouth, the rest scattering about the floor and in the basin. She thought she had swallowed them all, and in a vague alcoholic daze, she accepted her death with the thought, "Now try to get your watch, you son of a bitch," not knowing what she meant by it, and got as far as her bed and fell face down across it.

CHAPTER 8

O N HIS RETURN from the liquor store, Jesse stopped at the super's and got the keys to the storeroom where his trunks were stored. From the steamer trunk containing leftovers from their lighthouse-keeping days, he took two blankets, four sheets, and four pillowcases for Becky. He looked at the dusty junk about him, abandoned trunks, broken furniture, wornout baby carriages and tried not to think of her.

"Don't Leroy give you bedding?" the super asked, eyeing his load.

"Oh sure, this is for a friend."

"Settin' 'em up now, eh?"

"No, just laying 'em still."

The super laughed. "You got the best go, sport. You got the combination."

"No, you the one's got the gimmick. I see you slipping here and there when you think nobody's looking."

"I'll be slipping up your way soon."

"Come get your throat cut," Jesse thought, half-amused.

Leroy was out with the dogs and he managed the dark corridor without being assaulted. On his dresser was a letter from his editor at Hobson's, asking him to call. He called from Leroy's room and the editor asked if he could come in that afternoon at three.

"Now what?" he thought, going fluttery inside as the world became distorted again. Sighing, he poured a half glass of the cheap bourbon and tossed it off, grimacing in the mirror.

He took off his coat and shirt and prepared to shave. Then, half-smiling, said, "Better wash this white stink off; no need taking any chances," and stripped. The water in that house was always scalding hot, and as he ran the huge, old-fashioned tub full to the overflow drain, he thought, "Smart super, not his coal." Then as he lay stretched out in water hot enough to scald a fowl for pickling, he laughed,

"Can't be a nigger, using the white man's coal to heat water for other niggers—to bathe in, too. Not American nigger! Must be a Mau Mau, or a Russian in disguise. Better tip off McCarthy. Russian masquerading as nigger janitor creating coal and water shortage. See the headlines: McCarthy discovers Communist cell in Harlem Basement."

Hobson's was in an old building in the twenties on Fourth Avenue. An elderly and dignified receptionist mistook him for a messenger boy when he asked to see Mr. Pope. But when he explained it was his own manuscript he wished to discuss she flushed slightly and hastened to buzz Mr. Pope. "Go to the end of this corridor and turn to the right," she directed, smiling sympathetically. "His is the last office in the corner. And he'll be waiting for you." This last to the tune of, *I'll be waiting for you, Nellie.* I don't expect him to jump out the window," he thought, and after a moment smiling inwardly, "No such luck."

James Pope was a tall thin man with graying hair and a British mustache, something of a cross between Chamberlain and Eden, dressed in baggy Brooks Brothers tweeds. He came around the desk to shake Jesse's hand, his narrow face creased in an apologetic smile.

"Welcome to the bastard's corner." He gripped Jesse's hand and released it quickly.

"Black, isn't it," Jesse thought, but said aloud, smiling, "Howya, Jim. You got us wrong. We just *love* editors."

Pope pulled up a worn leather chair. "Sit down." He went behind his desk and offered cigarettes. Jesse declined. "Can't say as I much blame them," Pope reflected. "The publishing business is lousy these days."

Jesse felt the bottom drop out of his stomach. How many times had he heard these words, always a prologue to a rejection. But he kept up his front. "We modern writers are just spoiled. In the old days a writer starved in a garret for fifty years and wrote seventy books, all masterpieces. We write one book and want to get rich. I blame it all on Margaret Mitchell."

Pope's face resumed its customary expression of shame and guilt, like that of a man who's murdered his mother and thrown her body in the well, to be forever afterwards haunted by her sweet smiling face.

"I'm afraid I have bad news for you."

Jesse just looked at him, thinking, "Whatever bad news you got for me—as if I didn't know—you're going to have to say it without me helping you. I'm one of those ungracious niggers."

"We've given your book six readings and Mr. Hobson has decided to drop the option."

Jesse had been prepared for this from the moment he'd read Pope's letter and now, before the reaction had set in, he just felt argumentative. "I thought you were going to cut it."

Pope reddened slightly. "That was my opinion. I like the book. I fought for it all the way. I think all it needs is cutting. But Hobson thinks it reads like fictional autobiography. And he doesn't like the title."

"*I Was Looking for a Street,*" Jesse quoted, turning it over in his mind. "I was looking for a street that I could understand," he thought, and for a moment he was lost in memory of the search.

"He said it sounds like a visiting fireman looking for a prostitute's address," Pope said with his apologetic smile.

Jesse laughed. "That ought to make it sell."

Pope again assumed his look of shame and guilt. "The truth is, fiction is doing very poorly. We're having our worst year for fiction."

"Why not publish it as an autobiography then?"

"It would be the same. Hobson thinks the public is fed up with protest novels. And I must say, on consideration, I agree with him."

"What's protest about this book?" Jesse argued. "If anything, it's tragedy. But no protest."

"The consensus of the readers was that it's too sordid. It's pretty strong—almost vulgar, some of it."

"Then what about Rabelais? The education of Gargantua? What's more sordid than that?"

Pope blinked in disbelief. "But surely you realize that that was satire—Rabelais was satirizing the humanist Renaissance—and certainly some of the best satire ever written . . . This—" tapping the manuscript neatly wrapped in brown paper on his desk—"is protest. It's vivid enough, but it's humorless. And there is too much bitterness and not enough just plain animal fun—"

"I wasn't writing about animals—"

"The reader is gripped in a vice of despair and bitterness from start to finish—"

"I thought some of it was funny."

"Funny!" Pope stared at him incredulously.

"That part where the parents wear evening clothes to the older son's funeral," Jesse said, watching Pope's expression and thinking, "What could be more funny than some niggers in evening clothes? I bet you laugh like hell at *Amos and Andy* on television."

Pope looked as if he'd suddenly been confronted by a snake, but was too much of a gentleman to inquire of the snake if it were poisonous.

"All right, maybe you don't think that's funny—"

"That made me cry," Pope accused solemnly.

"I suppose you think I didn't cry too when I wrote it, you son of a bitch," Jesse thought, but aloud he continued, "But how do you make out it's protest?"

Looking suddenly lost, Pope said, "You killed one son and destroyed the other, killed the father and ruined the mother . . ." and Jesse thought, "So you find some streets too that you don't understand," and then, "Yes, that makes it protest, all right. Negroes must always live happily and never die."

Aloud he argued, "What about *Hamlet*? Shakespeare destroyed everybody, ruined everybody, and killed everybody in that one."

Pope shrugged. "Shakespeare."

Jesse shrugged. "Jesus Christ. It's a good thing he isn't living now. His friends would never get a book published about him."

Pope laughed. "You're a hell of a good writer, Jesse. Why don't you write a black success novel? An inspirational story? The public is tired of the plight of the poor downtrodden Negro."

"I don't have that much imagination."

"How about yourself? You're certainly a success story. You've published twelve novels that were very well received."

"That's what I mean."

"I don't understand you."

"Damn right you don't," Jesse thought. He didn't care to remind Pope that a moment or so back he'd termed the rejected novel as autobiographical. Instead he arose and picked up the manuscript. "There's nothing more futile than arguing with a rejection."

"You don't owe us a thing," Pope said, also standing.

Jesse grinned. "If I could get five hundred dollars from every six readers, I'd soon catch up with Norman Vincent Peale."

Pope walked with him to the elevator, pressed the button, and stood with him. "For my part I liked the book, Jesse. It's a powerful piece of writing."

"Thanks."

"And please don't think of me as an enemy. Keep in touch with me, please do."

"I will, thanks."

"I'm going to be in Breadloaf the month of August. I'd like very much to have you come up and spend a weekend with me."

Jesse gave him a quick curious look. "Thanks."

The elevator door opened. They shook hands again.

"Good luck with the manuscript," Pope said.

"Thanks."

There were two women and three men beside the operator in the elevator, but already Jesse's thoughts had turned inward and he didn't see them. "Jesse Robinson," he said distinctly. One of the women gave a slight start and everyone turned to look at him. "What did you think, son," he went on, "They'd shave you for nothing and give you a drink." The two women moved to the far corner of the elevator and looked straight ahead. The men stared at him curiously. But he was not aware. He smiled. "The ass," he said.

Jesse put the manuscript on the dresser amidst the other junk and poured a half glass of the cheap bourbon. He tossed it off and grimaced in the mirror. "You were looking for a street, eh, son?" he said. "But all you found was a blind alley." He had eaten a substantial lunch of two fried pork chops, fried potatoes, and what went for apple pie in a "Home Cooking" lunch counter on Amsterdam Avenue, but found himself hungry again. He was out of raw eggs and the milk had soured, so he munched a chocolate bar absently and poured another drink, thinking, "When in doubt, get

pié-eyed." And then, "Be nonchalant, drink a bottle of bourbon."
And after another moment, "You hired out for it, son. Nobody
made you. You were the best porter that Briggs & Sons ever had;
old man Briggs said so himself . . ." His thoughts wandered off and
he stood for a moment with his right thumb dug into his right
cheek, stroking his upper lip with his index finger, his mind a
vacuum.

Then he looked at his special account bank book and discovered
that he had $198.47 left from the $500.00. He felt a slight shock.
"Oh, how the lucre fugit," he thought, and recited aloud a half-
remembered jinglet from his childhood:

> *Oh how de ham do smell*
> *Oh how de boarders yell*
> *W'en dey hears dat dinner bell*

He laughed silently and said, "Damn right." And the next thing he
was conscious of was walking south on Convent toward the arch
of City College. His mind drew a blank for the elapsed two hours
and now it was six-thirty of a soft April evening. Students were
coming in a stream up toward the 145th Street entrance to the
subway. He went down the other way, walking against the crowd.
He staggered a little but didn't feel drunk. Although he didn't know
when he'd left the house nor where he'd intended going, it didn't
worry him. He was accustomed to these blanks of memory, and as
far as he knew nothing dreadful had ever happened to him during
one of them. At the moment he didn't remember the rejection, but
felt strangely depressed for some unattributable reason, and in the
back of his mind began silently singing his private dirge, *da-da-dee:*

<pre>
                                        di
          dee   dee
  da   da-da-da   deeeeeee   da
da-da   dee   dee-dee
                        da   dee-dee   do
          do   da
                                              doooooo
</pre>

At 140th Street he turned down the steep incline toward St. Nicholas Avenue. To his befuddled senses the slope seemed quite level but his body tended to fall face-forward and he began to run to keep up with his head which seemed some distance out in front of him. As he passed the church at the corner of Hamilton Avenue, he thought half-amusedly, "Open de door, brethren, ol' devil's chasin' me; I'm gonna pop in, once more around the block . . ."

The next he knew he was sitting alone in Frank's restaurant, eating apple pie a la mode and a heavyset dark brother sitting opposite a buxom dark sister in the booth opposite him, said with a tolerant grin, "That's an interesting theory, young man—seems to me as if I've heard it before—but I don't believe we'll solve this problem by making an all-Negro state. Who're we gonna be working for? Now my idea is what we need are more Negro-owned factories. Now the Negroes who got money ought to build factories to hire the Negroes who ain't; that's what the white folks do and that's why they got everything. Now take Joe Louis and all the money he had . . ." Jesse's attention wandered. The woman looked disapproving. He wondered what he had said. Finally, when the man stopped giving his theories about Negro-owned factories and Negro-owned steamships and Negro-owned skyscrapers and why Negroes in the South didn't get together and buy up a heap of land and why those in the North didn't get together and make their own automobiles and distil their own whiskey and can their own vegetables and why those in South Africa didn't mine their own diamonds, Jesse said, "It was just an idea."

He felt quite sober as he looked about at the many-hued faces of the diners, here and there an interracial couple, and three tables in the rear seating large groups of whites, probably families. Although it was located on 125th Street just off St. Nicholas Avenue, in the heart of Harlem, when Jesse first came to New York eight years before, blacks had only been served at the tables along one side. Now they ate all over. "You see, boy," he said to himself. "Someday we'll all wake up and find all this race business gone and everything changed, people living in complete harmony without any thought of color." Then, blowing laughter through his nose, added, "But old Gabriel is going to have one hell of a job blowing."

The waiter brought him a check for a roast beef dinner with soup and salad extra. "I must have eaten it," he muttered, and then in reply to the waiter's perplexed look, added, "It's always good to know what one eats."

"You can always depend on Frank's," the waiter beamed.

The bill was for $3.05. "Damn right," Jesse thought. "Too bad I didn't get here first."

Outside was a soft warm night and the Harlem folk were crowded in the street. Jesse walked through the milling crowds, jostling and being jostled. The neon-lighted bars were jumping and the red buses bullied through the tight stream of traffic. Here and there a big braying voice pushed from the bubble of noise. The unforgettable scent of smoking marijuana pierced the gaseous mixture of motor fumes, cheap colognes, alcohol, foul breath, sweat stink, dust, and smoke that passed for air. "Going to float to heaven in a dream." Jesse thought.

He went down to Seventh Avenue and stood for a moment watching the fat black boys with their bright gold babes glide past in their shiny Cadillacs. "Can't beat that, son," he said. "Heaven already. No need of going any further." Then he turned and went back to the Apollo bar and began drinking gin and beer. A big sloppy black prostitute sidled up to the tall black man in a light green gabardine suit on the stool beside him and asked in a thick whiskey voice, "Wanna see a girl, baby?" The black man looked her up and down. "Where she at?" he asked. Jesse laughed to himself.

The next thing he knew he was in the balcony of the Apollo theatre watching a gangster picture on the screen. Weird faces in graduated rows appeared dimly in a thick blue haze of marijuana smoke like grim trophies of a ravenous cannibal. On the screen two thieves were quarreling over a pile of loot when suddenly one drew his gun and shot the other dead, and Jesse thought, "Solved now!"

Over to one side a high boy stated, "Easy come, easy go," and from another section someone added, "Get yours in heaven." Not to be outdone a third cried, "Open de door, Peter." Jesse said, "Your people, son."

He found himself getting a marijuana jag from inhaling the

smoke and the black and white film began taking on patches of brilliant technicolor. "If I sit here long enough the problem will solve itself," he thought. "Everybody will turn green."

Then he was walking north on Seventh Avenue beneath a bright purple sky and the dingy, smoke-blackened tenements were new brick red with yellow windows and green sills and the lights of the bars and greasy spoons slanting across the dirty walk burned like phosphorescent fires. "No wonder the cats smoke gage," he thought, then said aloud, "Every man his own Nero."

"What?" a feminine voice asked.

He looked about and found a woman on his arm. "Hello," he said.

"Hello," she said, thinking he was teasing. He had been buying her drinks at Small's bar for the past hour and now she was taking him home. "In here, baby," she said, steering him toward the entrance to a violet-colored apartment house. He gave her a good look then and saw a pretty brown-skinned woman in a soft blue suit. Her full-lipped mouth was deep purple like a lamb kidney and her black eyes shiny as twin cockroaches. "Is it good?" he asked. She smiled with teeth as yellow as canary birds.

At one-thirty he found himself having trouble with the locks of the front door at the apartment where he lived. He didn't know whether he'd gone to bed with the woman or not, for by then he had forgotten her. Nor did he know how long he'd been fumbling with the locks to the door. Finally he got it open and found it almost as difficult to get it locked again. Slowly he groped his way though the dark hall. Napoleon growled from the dark but did not attack, being uncertain whether it was a bona fide burglar or just the roomer. Jesse noticed immediately that the bedding was gone. Then his gaze went next to the rejected manuscript.

Up until then nothing had seemed strange. Now he was plunged into a state of mind where nothing seemed natural. Becky was gone and the book was returned. You couldn't marry a book. "No matter how much you sleep with it, you don't get any babies," he thought. "Else, son, you would have sired more manuscripts than the whole Victorian age." He looked at his reflection in the mirror. His greasy face was haggard, his eyes glazed and sunken, deep weary lines framing a catfish mouth. "Jesse Robinson," he said. "Can't eat bitter, son. No more than natural, anyway. Christian nation. Don't forget that. Pagans nutted all black slaves. Christians let them keep their God-given nuts. Profit in it too. Don't forget the profit. More nuts more pickaninnies grow. Just don't get bitter, son. Remember it was business; strictly business. Funny, really. Funny as hell if you just get the handle to the joke. Like the Englishman said to the cannibal, You may eat me, you savage, but you'll play hell digesting me. Or would an Englishman say 'play hell'? Doesn't matter. Nobody's ever digested an Englishman yet. Black men not that hard to digest but our Christians have weak stomachs. Can't even digest their own Christianity. Too bad, son. Too bad, so sad, you're mad. No point in being mad, son. Better get your black ass glad." He stared at his ugly reflection. "Don't blame them, either," he said. "Hard a time as they had getting this world, make no sense to give it away, share it up with some whining idiot like you. Sensible people. Look what they did with Christianity. Here a poor martyr died to bring his people freedom. And these people used his philosophy to enslave the world. If that ain't smart it will have to do. Get smart too, son. Be happy. Smile. A nigger's big white teeth are worth more than a college education. Show your teeth, son. Show your worth. Pry those gums open with a smile." He looked for his bottle of whiskey, found it nearly finished. He had no recollection of drinking the greater part of it. "No wonder," he said, emptying the bottle into his glass. He raised the glass to his reflection. "Smile." He grimaced as the sharp liquor burnt down his throat.

Before he'd finished undressing, the dirge had started faintly in the back of his mind:

> *dee-dee-dee-dee-dee dee dee dee*
> O   O   O   °dooooooooooooooooooooooo

For a short time after he'd gone to bed he tried to decide what course to take with the manuscript, whether to buckle down and try to do the necessary revisions himself before his money ran out, or whether to try to find another publisher and get a contract first. "A writer writes, a fighter fights," he muttered finally. "You jumped the gun, son. This is the age of the great black fighters. Next century for great black writers. They played you a dirty trick. You might have been a great fighter. But some practical joker put a pen in your hand. You should have stuck it in the bastard's ass."

dee-dee-dee-dee dee-dee dee dee dee dee
O O O O O O O
dooooooooooooooooooo

When he lay flat the room swam. His heart beat with great slow strokes, like an artesian pump, shaking his entire body. He felt physically exhausted but his mind kept churning at fever pitch, twitching convulsively as if in the throes of death. He decided to read and took down his volume of Gorki's *Bystander*. The book fell open at a page and he found himself reading over and over again in a strange feverish daze the two lines he'd already read a hundred times: "Clim heard someone in the crowd question gravely, doubtfully: *'But was there really a boy? Perhaps there was no boy at all!'* " He was convinced that those words contained a message, that through them some force was endeavouring to communicate some profound knowledge to him, perhaps the whole solution to the mystery, which he couldn't interpret . . . *Perhaps there was no boy at all . . . Perhaps there was no boy at all . . .* "Upon the churning water there floated only a black caracul cap. Small, leaden pieces of ice swam about it. The water heaved up in little waves, reddish in the rays of the sunset . . ." *Perhaps there was no boy all . . .* Beating the boy! That's the way black intellectuals referred to discussions of the black problem. Beating the boy! . . . *Perhaps there was no boy at all . . .* That's the sheet you got to bleach . . . What's your plan, Charlie Chan? . . . He felt the solution was contained in one sentence. In two words, perhaps . . . He tried combinations of words . . . Black-love . . . black-thin . . . white-right . . . white-light . . . repeat-defeat . . . change-same . . . change-stay . . . change-ever . . . Adam-atom . . . beige-age . . . blood-black . . . blood-mix . . . time-fall . . . time-level . . . But his thoughts returned again and again to the combination, white-woman . . . He suffered a frenzy of frustration . . . problem-woman . . . problem-black . . . problem-white . . . white-woman . . . The mental effort made him dizzy. Nausea grew in his stomach like a bomb about to burst . . . The room began to spin . . . He closed his eyes to steady it . . .

He dreamed he was in a house with a thousand rooms of different sizes made entirely of distorted mirrors. There were others beside himself but he could not tell how many because their reflections went on into infinity in the distorted mirrors. Nor could he see their true shape because in one mirror they all appeared to be obese dwarfs and in another tall, thin, cadaverous skeletons. He ran panic-stricken from room to room trying to find a familiar human shape, but he saw only the grotesque reflections, the brutal faces that leered from some distortions, the sweet smiles from others, the sad eyes, the gentle mouths, the sinister stares, the treacherous grins, the threatening scowls, hating and bestial, suffering and saintly, gracious and kind, and he knew that none of them was the true face and he continued to run in frantic terror until he found a door and escaped. The house sat on a hill higher than the Empire State Building and from the front steps he could see all of Manhattan Island from the Battery to the Cloisters, the East side and the West side, and he could see all the people in their streets and in the buildings at work and in the houses at home as if the walls were glass, the white people and the black people, the Gentiles and the Jews, the people of all the nationalities who dwelt and worked therein, side by side, day after day, all normal in physical form, their faces bearing normal everyday expressions, and he could see into their minds and read their thoughts and they were normal thoughts which had been associated with human mentality since the beginning of recorded history, but from his point of view this normal struggle for existence appeared so greatly distorted by emotional idiocy, senseless loves and hatreds, lunatic ambitions, bestial passions, grotesque reasoning, fantastic behavior, that he turned in horror and fled back into the house of distorted mirrors where by comparison everything seemed normal.

He threshed about in his sleep, grinding his teeth and groaning, and once he struck out with a stabbing motion, crying aloud through clenched teeth in a voice of insensate rage, "I'll kill you!"

At nine o'clock he awakened, got up and looked at his nude body in the mirror. His face was swollen and had the smooth greasy sheen of overdrinking; his eyes were glassy, almost senseless. He skinned back his lips and examined his dull yellow teeth. As yet he had no hangover, but his senses were deadened. For five full minutes he stood and stared at the paper-wrapped manuscript without any conscious thought. The room seemed to undulate almost imperceptibly. Outside the windows the day was gray. He turned his attention to the clock and watched the minute hand move from 9:07 to 9:10. Without being conscious of his reason for doing so, he picked up his big clasp knife, opened it, then stood with the naked blade and stared at his manuscript for another two minutes. Abruptly, with a cry of stricken rage, an animal sound, half howl, half scream, he stabbed the manuscript with all his force. The strong forged blade went deep into the pages without breaking. Then all of a sudden thought surged back into his mind.

He grunted a laugh and said aloud, "Really protest now!" The combination of this thought and the sight of the knife sticking from the heart of his manuscript amused him vastly. "You're some boy, son," he said. "Pope should see this now." Then, smiling grimly, "But it's a Freudian knot, not a Gordian knot, son." The thought steadied him somewhat. "Deserves a drink," he said. For the first time he noticed the empty whiskey bottle. "Dead, too." And then, half-laughing, "Kill 'em all."

Slipping into his robe and house shoes, he went to the bathroom. Leroy's door was open but he and his boy were out. Napoleon came to the kitchen door and growled as he passed. Through the half-open window he looked down on the convent wall.

On his way out he glanced into the kitchen and noticed two partly filled whiskey bottles amidst the orgiastic debris. On sudden impulse he knocked upon Mr. Ward's door and receiving no answer stepped into the kitchen and poured a gobletful of whiskey, half from each of the bottles. Napoleon stood at a distance and growled threateningly. Nero blinked sleepily from his deathbed beneath the stove. The sink was stacked with dirty dishes. Behind the door, crab shells overflowed the garbage pail. He drank half the whiskey at a gulp, gasped and grimaced. Then said laughingly, "They beat me to it; they got the still." On second thought, "Maybe they just drank it straight."

The pop-eyed cur answered with a nasty growl. Carefully Jesse put down his glass. "Son," he said to the dog. "This is going to be your Waterloo." He got an old leather belt from the broom closet. Sensing his intention Napoleon retreated to the protection of his sire beneath the stove. "Your pappy can't help you now, son," he said, advancing. "And your play-pappy's not here." He flicked the bundle of cowardly fur with the end of the strap. The dog yelped and ran from the kitchen. He flicked its rump as it went through the door. The dog slipped on the polished floor of the hall. Following quickly he slapped it again, just before he also slipped and crashed into the chest of drawers. The dog yelped and the man cursed. The dog ran into Leroy's room. He followed. The dog cowered beneath the bed. He got down on his knees and hit at it from one side. The dog ran back into the hall. He pursued, and got in another good lick before he slipped again and knocked over the white marble statue of a nude, that blocked the passage. He made a desperate lunge and caught the statue before it hit the floor, breaking its fall, then fell on top of it. He got up bruised and shaken and restored it to the table. "Good thing you're not in Georgia, son," he told himself. "Open and shut case of rape."

Returning to the kitchen he noticed the dog shaking like a dust mop in the corner beneath the stove. "And let that be a lesson to you," he said to it, returning the belt to the broom closet. Laughing, he added, "Yes sir, just like the white folks beating us niggers. Gave that black son of a bitch a good lesson; I beat that bugger's head until I fell over dead."

He drank the remainder of the whiskey and went back to his room. The walls had steadied and he felt almost normal. "Call Kriss at noon," he reminded himself.

After bathing, shaving, brushing his teeth, he donned his sport ensemble, went to the bank and drew out fifty dollars, ate a breakfast of fried sausage, scrambled eggs, hominy grits, toast and coffee. On his way home he stopped in a bar and had two gin-and-beers, then bought a bottle of cheap bourbon whiskey from the liquor store to take with him.

134

He found Napoleon hovering in the front hall, peering cautiously from beneath the zoo-parade table to see whether it was friend or enemy. "Enemy!" he snarled and the cur fled to the kitchen. The "birds" were still flown, so he uncorked his bottle and refilled their bottles from which he had drunk, then got some ice cubes and a bottle of ginger ale from the refrigerator. Sight of the stabbed manuscript on the dresser accused him. "Since no one's come to bury you, Caesar, I'll bury you myself," he said and stored it into the cabinet beside his bed. Then, sitting on the sofa by the windows, he sipped the mellow highballs and stared at the gray city in the gray day. For a moment he felt brilliant and creative.

"Seven million people. If each person has one half-pound of brains, that's three million, five hundred thousand pounds of brains. Seems like that amount of brains ought to produce the solution," he thought. "Doesn't though. Come out the wrong barrel. Solving kind still in heaven. Barrel's never been tapped. Got an angel in charge of the brain room who can't read. Still passing out those brains God condemned for lack of reasoning ingredients. If God doesn't replace him soon going to lose the world. Too bad, too. Excellent brains but for that one flaw . . ."

At twelve o'clock he put on his hat, hung his trench coat on his arm, went down to the basement and telephoned Kriss. Her line sounded the busy signal. He left the building and sauntered toward 145th Street, staggering slightly, but he didn't feel drunk. Wraithlike people floated past and the buildings rocked gently in the gray day. He felt a remote, sardonic, self-deprecating amusement. "Looking for the fountain of miracles, eh, Son?" he thought.

It occurred to him as he staggered along that since his return to the city he'd not once met anyone on the street whom he knew. "You're a pipe dream, son," he said. "Just something you dreamed up. Other folks smoking a different gage."

At 145th Street he turned downhill to the bar of the Chinese restaurant. After drinking two gin-and-beers he telephoned Kriss again. Still the busy signal. "Break it off," he muttered irritably, and two more gin-and-beers, wondering the while to whom she was talking and feeling vaguely jealous. After telephoning again he began to feel frustrated. "All right, babe," he said. "This is Sugar Hill—if one won't, another will."

The scent of frying peppers from the basement kitchen made him hungry and he sat in a booth and ate an order of peppers and pork, then an order of egg foo young. The food relieved him of his irritation but when he stood up to telephone again he found himself quite tight. "Fine," he said, deciding to go down to her apartment instead of telephoning again. When he stepped outside, a brown heart-shaped face caught in the angle of his vision and he thought it was Becky. Before he'd seen his error his heart turned over in agonizing shock. He realized he was gasping. The familiar scene went strange in a blurred distortion. "Not that street, son," he said, and reentered the bar, lingering over his gin-and-beer to study his reflection in the mirror.

A handsome, well-dressed, tan-skinned woman two seats down from him observed, "Looks familiar doesn't he?" In his slightly blurred vision she seemed about Kriss's age, lonely but cautious; then his attention returned to himself. "You see that son of a bitch—" he began, pointing toward his reflection. "That's what the white folks call a primitive." She smiled at his naivete. "Don't let that worry you, baby. They like primitives." He went on as if he hadn't heard her. "He's dangerous, a menace to society. He'd just as soon be white, rich and respected as black, poor and neglected. Proves right there he's crazy—" and the next thing he knew it was five o'clock and he was reentering his own apartment house, on his way up to see Susie, consoling himself with the home-made adage, "One cockroach in today's soup is more nourishing than all of next year's honey."

He had no memory of his bitter tirade against himself: "That s.o.b. thinks he's a writer. That s.o.b. once wrote for publication, *I consider it my duty to write the truth as I see it.* And he made more people unhappy, stirred up more anger and animosity—let me tell you—he made more enemies by his version of the truth than Jesus Christ himself."

"Why do you do it then, baby?" she asked calmly.

The question startled him. After a moment's reflection he said,

136

"See what I mean. Crazy beyond all doubt. Wants to tell the truth. Crucify that s.o.b. quick before he finds a fool who'll believe him."

He had no memory of telephoning Kriss three times during the discussion; of finally calling the operator and having her tap the line; of deciding that Kriss had taken off the receiver to keep from talking to him because she had someone else there; of storming back to the bar and paying his bill with the intention of going down to Kriss's and breaking in; of the woman stopping him, sensing his intention: "Why bother a white woman, baby, if she doesn't want to see you?"

"How do you know she's white?"

"I heard you give the operator a Gramercy number."

No memory of his buying her lunch and having another lunch himself—this time sweet and sour pork; of their going up St. Nicholas to Jimmy's Bar-and-Grill and listening to a natural-born comedian give a marvelous piano rendition of "What Makes Corn Grow," reciting the lyrics in a husky singsong voice:

> Oh, it's dark and cosy in the shucks . . .
> Two little grains been bellyrubbing . . .
> Now they begins to—rhymes, baby rhymes . . .
> Where there were only two grains before . . .
> Now there is three, four or even more . . .

No memory of going across the street to a blackjack game with this woman and another they'd picked up, of losing fifteen dollars and getting into an argument; of starting home for his knife, then changing his mind and taking the subway down to Kriss's and pressing her bell continuously for five minutes; no memory of his blind rage at her refusal to answer; of going around to the airwell beneath her window and shouting curses at her until the super came out and threatened to call the police; of sitting in the White Rose Bar at 23rd Street and Fourth Avenue, drinking gin-and-beers and telephoning her at fifteen minute intervals; of finally giving up at four-thirty and taking the subway uptown . . .

So now he wondered vaguely why he should console himself, because when he came to, he didn't know he had intended visiting

Susie and thought only that he was going to telephone again. He went down to the basement and telephoned Kriss in the same frame of mind in which he had first telephoned her, without any memory of his hours of rage and frustration.

In the back of his mind he was humming *da-da-dee* in a light, gay motif as he listened to the phone ringing clearly and finally to Kriss's forthright office voice: "Mrs. Cummings speaking."

CHAPTER 9

THE FAINT SOUND of the telephone clicking awakened Kriss at four-thirty. She had slept through the din of Jesse's doorbell ringing an hour earlier and the faint clicking sound which echoed at the other end as the busy signal had been going on for some time. She came awake abruptly and unnaturally alert. She saw at once the receiver was off the hook and had fallen behind the night table, but by the time she'd retrieved it the clicking had ceased. She divined instantly the caller had been Jesse and chuckled gleefully. She suffered none of her usual panic at awakening alone because of his call. Instead, she derived a delicious delight from his thinking she was talking to someone else. Then she noticed that it was four-thirty and she'd asked him to call at noon. Perhaps he'd been calling ever since noon and had got the busy signal each time. She felt a slight sense of guilt for standing him up for so long, and a slight trepidation of fear he'd not call again. But these tiny qualms were quickly dispelled by an abnormal sense of well-being. She felt more rested and refreshed than at any time in years, and for a moment she didn't care whether Jesse called again or not. For a time she luxuriated in the resolve not to answer when he called again, and he'd think she'd gone out with someone else. It would serve him right, she thought. Niggers! Niggers! Niggers! All they wanted was to drink your whiskey and sleep with you—he'd be furious if she broke their date . . . She smiled with malicious sensuality . . . Let him find some bitch in Harlem. Sleep with Maud. She'd always wanted to have him . . . But the thought of Maud started a train of memory she couldn't bear, as she had not yet taken her pill for "mental and emotional distress." They threw me to the niggers themselves, she thought accusingly; although whom she accused by the pronoun *they,* if not her entire race, she wasn't sure. She only knew that she wanted to be married to some decent cultured successful white man and bear his children as much as did any other white woman. It wasn't her fault, she reasoned, that she was sterile, diseased and rapidly becoming an alcoholic. She wasn't certain that she was diseased. Five years after she'd first contracted gonorrhea it had recurred, and she had been hospitalized four months. But she wasn't certain that she was completely cured. At that time she'd been with the Institute just a little over a year. In addition to the strain and worry that someone on the job might discover the nature of her illness, and the humiliation and mortification of having the nurses know, were the pain and the terrible headaches that had come from the countless injections.

She loved Nat Gold, her doctor, because he'd kept her sane during that awful time. She'd told him everything, about Ronny and the Negroes too—and all he'd ever said was: "Kriss, people are always asking, Would you have your daughter marry a Negro? To me my two daughters are the most precious girls in the world. But if one of them wanted to marry a Negro, I would just ask her, Do you honor him as much as you honor me?" She felt a maudlin gratitude toward him because even he treated her with respect, more as a friend than a patient.

Then her mind flared in venomous hatred as she recalled the circumstances of her husband giving her gonorrhea. He'd been sleeping around with all manner of tramps, on a binge half the time, but she hadn't minded because she'd begun sleeping with Harold by then. And then one night he'd come home weeping with guilt and remorse—had probably been sleeping with some Clark Street bouncer—and had begged her to give him a son. "Give me an heir, Kriss. Please, darling. I'm the last of my line. I can't let my family die out with me." She'd been certain at the time she couldn't have children, nevertheless she'd slept with him. And that was when it had happened because the night before Harold had gone to Tuskegee and was away for two weeks and she hadn't slept with anyone else since his second wife had left him and he'd tried three times to kill himself. There'd been some of her friends in for a drink that afternoon, ten days later. By then Ronny was on another binge, only God knew where, and she'd put on the red silk housecoat she'd owned then to entertain her friends. But she'd felt so sick after her second drink she'd turned pale and had had to lie on the sofa to keep from fainting. The sofa had just been done over in pale green and her friends accused her of posing for some newly patented aphrodisiac. But the next day she and her bleary-eyed unshaven hungover husband had been admitted to the hospital. She'd been furious because he hadn't suffered half as much as she. It was after their release Ronny first learned she'd been sleeping with Harold, although Harold had been positive he'd known it all the time. Harold had picked them up at the hospital in his car and had taken them to supper, trying to cheer them up by saying he'd had the clap seven times and, like the boys on State Street said, it was no more than a runny nose. But afterwards, sitting in the car before their apartment house, he'd said, "I told you to be careful, Kriss, but you wouldn't listen to me."

"After all, goddamit, I got it from Ronny!" she'd flared.

"Well, it's a bitch, it's a bitch all right," he'd said. "He's your husband. But count me out from now on. I'm getting too old to take any chances."

"He said he wanted an heir," she'd said without thinking, and had suddenly giggled.

They had turned simultaneously to stare at Ronny who'd been sitting silently in the outside seat, and he could no longer pretend he didn't understand.

"You bastard," he'd said to Harold. "All this time you've been pretending to be my friend you've been sleeping with my wife."

"Don't tell me you didn't know it." Harold had replied. "I've seen you leave the house so we could go to bed."

140

"You son of a bitch! If I was in Mississippi you wouldn't say that to me," Ronny had protested crying.

"You dirty pansy bastard!" Kriss thought as the vivid memory stung her. "You and your State Street whores! You ruined me, you son of a bitch . . ." And then: "I wish I'd told your mother, when she was telling me of all the beautiful Southern belles you could have married, you couldn't screw a decent white woman. And God knows I wish you'd married one of them instead of me—or married some Southern man. Maybe you'd have been happy lynching Negroes to get your courage up to screw your wife every two or three years so she could bear children for you. Maybe Southern women are used to homosexuals for husbands; maybe that's the reason they get so excited when they come North and meet a Negro man face to face. Maybe they've been dreaming of getting one good screwing before they die and can't resist the first temptation . . ."

She smiled maliciously as she recalled Ronny's married cousin, Sissybelle, who'd visited her in Chicago the second summer of the war. Ronny had been in England and his mother had written to caution Kriss against introducing her to any Negroes who might be connected with that "charity you work for." She'd underscored the lines: *"Sissybelle is very sensitive and highstrung and the sight of a negra in the same room with herself might give her screaming hysterics."* She had screamed all right, because Kriss had heard her, and Kriss had no doubt but what she had been hysterical too. Because she had not only been in the same room with Negroes, but she'd spent most of her visit in the same bed with them. She was a beautiful blonde woman of the extreme nervous temperament that comes from sexual frustration, and the letter had so annoyed Kriss that on the night of her arrival she had arranged a party and had invited all the best-equipped Negroes of her acquaintance. Although, for the most part, her own knowledge of their equipment had been hearsay. But during her two weeks' stay Sissybelle had become an authority on the subject; and had returned to Mississippi five pounds fatter and fresh as a daisy. Ronny's mother had written: "I don't know what you did to Sissybelle but she's a changed woman; she looks so rested and she isn't a bit nervous anymore and Toliver says she's even prettier. Although I bet he just says that because he says she's a better wife to him than she used to be; and he says if he knew your treatment he'd recommend it for all his friends' wives. *Thank Glory you didn't let her get close to any negras or she'd have been an hysterical wreck.*"

Kriss giggled, recalling the great glee that had reigned in the sophisticated circles of the Black Belt when this letter had made the rounds.

When the telephone rang again, she felt certain it was Jesse, but she picked up the receiver and said in her office voice: "Mrs. Cummings speaking."

"Hello, Kriss baby, did you have a good time?"

"I don't understand you, dear."

"It's understandable enough. You had your receiver off the hook. Has he gone?"

She smiled to herself but made her voice sound sharp and angry, "It's five o'clock, Jesse, and I'm hungry—"

"Five o'clock!" he echoed in amazement.

"Where have you been, dear?"

"I've been calling you since noon; the time slipped up on me," he said defensively.

"I must have jarred the receiver when I went to bed," she said, smiling maliciously at the knowledge he didn't believe it. "You should have come down and rung my bell."

"I intended to."

"It doesn't matter. I had a good sleep."

"I'll bet," she heard him mutter, and prodded his jealousy further by saying, "I am very hungry, dear," deriving a delicious sexual sensation from it.

"No wonder," she heard him mutter, and continued to prod sadistically, "A good sleep always makes me *so* hungry."

"I've had enough of that shit," he thought angrily, but said aloud, "You're stealing my lines, baby."

She giggled but made her voice sound matter-of-fact. "Bring a steak with you, dear. My butcher is closed by now."

"Right. Anything else?"

"Whatever you'd like for tomorrow."

"Fine. I'll see you soon."

142

"Hurry, baby, I'm lonely."

When she went to the bathroom she saw the sleeping pills scattered about the floor, and memory of Dave's visit the night before brought futile despair. "Oh shit!" she exclaimed, half in chagrin and half in regret. But she had no memory of either her call to Jesse's house, her telephone conversation with Harold, or her subsequent attempt to kill herself. She thought she had spilled the sleeping pills accidentally when taking her accustomed dose. Her chagrin came from memory of Dave's angry and abrupt departure, and her regret was for letting him see her such a drunken bitch. She had often raved at him but had never before made such a disgusting spectacle of herself. And after once having been so near to marrying him, she profoundly regretted giving him such a real cause for relief in having escaped. She felt her first need for a drink, but on her way to the kitchen saw his check on the sitting-room storage cabinet and his keys on the hall table, and even two drinks didn't help.

After she'd picked up the pills, brushed her teeth, rinsed her mouth, showered, shaved her armpits, emptied and washed the highball glasses and ashtrays, placed the check beneath the keys on a vase on the hall table so Jesse could see it, having decided with sardonic malice to keep it; thereby ridding both her person and environment of all signs of last night's debacle, her sense of defeat was dispelled and her self-confidence restored. She dressed in lemon-yellow terry-cloth rompers and gilt mules, combed her hair, painted her lips and nails, applied blue shadow to her upper lids, and surveyed herself in the full-length mirror on the hall closet door. Her yellow-and-white reflection with its blue-eyed, china-white, mongoloid face, seen against the backdrop of the deep maroon drapes in the sitting room, affected her like a painting of a sex dream by a twentieth-century Rubens with the colors of Van Gogh. She loved her legs with such ecstasy that for several minutes she stood voluptuously caressing them, then, with brisk efficiency, more like a business woman than housewife, she telephoned her liquor store for two bottles of Scotch and one each of gin, vermouth, and sherry; then telephoned her favorite delicatessen on Third Avenue for frozen peas, broccoli, whipped potatoes, a pound of butter, a jar of Hollandaise sauce, a carton of uncooked Pepperidge Farm club rolls, one pound of ripe tomatoes, green salad, and six bottles of Canada Dry sparkling water, proving the adage that whiskey drinkers never eat dessert. After which she mixed a sturdy highball with the last of her Scotch and took it to the sitting room. While leafing through the pages of the current *New Yorker,* she savored its flavor. Her first drink was always the best. She thought smilingly of that classic bit of dialogue by Hemingway:

> "What are you thinking, darling?"
> "About whiskey."
> "What about whiskey?"
> "About how nice it is."

The first time the bell tolled it was the boy with the liquor. She wrote a check for twenty-five dollars and he gave her three dollars and thirty-five cents in change. She tipped him the thirty-five cents and he gave her a nice smile.

The next bell was Jesse. In his damp trench coat, dark snap-brim hat, dark green goggles, greasy tan face, arms filled with parcels, he looked like a gangster on the lam from Florida. Kriss grinned with genuine amusement. "No one recognized you, I hope?"

"I couldn't get the damn things off with my hands so full."

He unloaded on the kitchen table, hung up his coat and hat, pocketed his goggles, and came back and kissed her. She was opening the bags with a pleased expression; she liked to be given things, for men to spend on her. She found a porterhouse steak, a ham steak, a pound of veal kidneys, two pounds of Pennsylvania pork sausage, two bottles of Scotch, one each of Bourbon, gin, and vermouth.

"At least you don't intend to waste away," she said, giggling.

"You said you were hungry, baby," he said, looking at her mouth, breasts, and legs. "You know the Harlem Trinity." She felt her smile going sensuous beneath his lustful stare. "Eat, drink, and fuck," he said, and they kissed.

"That's what I ought to write about," he mumbled against her mouth as his fingertips caressed her legs.

"What?" she asked inside his mouth, feeling him.

144

"Fucking. There are sixty-nine ways to fuck. I could write a chapter on each way."

"Do you know all of them, dear?"

"No, but those I don't know you can tell me."

She smiled sensuously.

The doorbell broke it up. A man came with the groceries and while Kriss was paying him Jesse busied himself emptying the ice cubes into the glass tray and refilling the ice pans. Suddenly she recalled telephoning him the night before, and when the grocery man left she turned on him and said viciously, "Jesse! If you slept with another woman last night I want you to go home right now."

He didn't feel at all surprised by this sudden outburst. "I haven't slept with anyone, baby," he said as he opened a bottle of her Scotch and made himself a drink.

"Make me one too," she said as she went to the bathroom to repair her lip paint. "My glass is in here."

He returned hers to the coaster on the storage cabinet and placed his on a coaster on the glass-top cocktail table, seating himself on the sofa. Coming from the bathroom she paused for a moment before the mirror to worship her legs, then stood in the arch so he could admire them also.

"I called you at two o'clock this morning," she lied, "and you weren't at home."

He had no idea when he'd returned to his room and couldn't dispute her. "I got a rejection on my book and went on a binge."

She grinned delightedly although she didn't know why she felt so pleased by his ill-fortune. "I like your slack suit," she said, tucking up her rompers to reveal more of her thighs so he would return the compliment.

He did. "I like your legs," he said. "You've got gorgeous legs, baby."

She melted with sensual ecstasy and her blue eyes swam glassily with passion. "Ronny used to say I missed my calling; that I should have been a chorus girl."

"I thought you were going to say call girl," he said, then impulsively knelt before her on the carpet and kissed each of her legs. Tenderly she massaged his kinky hair. Then savagely she pushed him off and threatened furiously, "If you ever sleep with your wife again, Jesse, I'll kill you."

She took her seat, shaking with repressed fury, and they began drinking as if it were their night's work and they were being paid by the drink.

"I've had enough of Negro women accusing me of stealing their husbands," she continued to rave.

"After all, baby, you can't blame them. You slept with their husbands enough."

"I didn't care a damn for a single one."

"You got your kicks."

She grinned malevolently. "If I told them what I thought of them in bed it would kill them."

"Why did you do it then?"

She emptied her glass and held it out to him. "Fix us a drink, baby."

He emptied his and made two more.

"I just wanted to know them," she said, smiling secretly. "I wanted to know what they were like inside."

"Ditto," he said. "After all, what better place to study origins than in the egg."

"When I was studying anthropology at the university, the kids used to say it was the study of man embracing woman."

"Race relations is the science of black man embracing white woman," he paraphrased.

She giggled. "I learned more about Negroes in one night than Uncle Whitney knew from twenty years of association." Uncle Whitney had been the President of the Foundation.

He blew laughter through his nose and finished his highball as if it were a drink of water. "Damn right! What was that French novel about the woman masquerading as a man, the one where she wears a squirrel's tail?"

"A squirrel's tail? Ambitious, wasn't she?"

"May as well be shot for a lion than eaten as a lamb? *Mademoiselle de Maupin!* He stood up to get another drink and she finished hers and gave him her glass.

"She could have taken half of Lacy's and there'd been plenty left for both." Her voice had the indistinct blur of one who's suffered a brain hemorrhage. She hadn't eaten since lunch the day before and the whiskey affected her brain.

Jesse felt a flicker of disgust, then was suddenly amused. "That reminds me of a joke one of my landladies used to tell—" he began but she interrupted rudely, "Are you going to make the drinks, Jesse?" He gave her a quick look, seeing her double, and thought, "I'll take the one who can't talk." On the way to the kitchen he staggered slightly and the abstract painting danced on the walls like an orgy of skinned cats. Mad genius, he thought, vastly amused by his blurred perspective. While mixing the drinks he called, "Shall I start dinner, baby?" and heard her reply something about "whipped potatoes." He found the package in the carton of groceries and placed it on the stove atop the pilot jet to thaw.

When serving her drink he said, "You came too late, Kriss baby. If you'd lived in the eighteenth century you'd have been a famous courtesan and would have made history, instead of sociology like now."

For reward she pulled him down and kissed him. "Why didn't you marry me in Chicago, Jesse? I would have married you in Chicago."

He resumed his seat and gulped half his drink, suddenly feeling old. "To tell you the truth, baby—" he began, intending to tell her he didn't remember a damn thing about their weekend in Chicago, that he'd been blotto all the time and it hadn't meant a damn thing to him, but she didn't hear him, so moved was she by her own maudlin memory.

"I loved you that weekend, Jesse. Why did you do it?"

"Fern is crazy," he said. "I'd never so much as touched her. The time we had our weekend I hardly knew her. All I—"

"She told it all over town that she was going to divorce Mose and you were going to divorce your wife—"

"I don't see how in the hell—"

"I heard her telling Alice and that group at a party. I was so hurt. Why did you tell her that? And she's so ugly too. Even Mose couldn't sleep with her, he just kept her—"

"And you told me you were going to divorce your wife and

marry me." She turned on him in a flurry of rage. "Jesse, if you ever sleep with your wife while you're sleeping with me—"

"That I'd like to see," he thought, but when she persisted, "I'm not going to have some black bitch after me with a knife," he also flew into such a violent rage the room turned white hot in his vision. "This bitch wants me to kill her," he thought, gripping the sofa for control. "Even Maud thought I was after Joe. They crucified me. Nigger bitches!" He started up to slap her when the telephone rang, and he lowered himself to his seat, the room dancing crazily in his eyes.

She staggered heavily as she went to answer it, and he finished his drink and sucked the ice to cool his head. He heard her saying in what no sober person on earth would take for a sober voice, "Miss-sess Cummings speaking," and he thought, half-amused, "What price we pay for respectability." Then her natural voice in drunken enthusiasm, "Oh, baby, come on over, Jesse's here and we're . . . Why do you drink that awful stuff, baby? You earn enough to buy decent . . . You make more than I do, you son of a bitch . . . (giggling) You've got to ration it . . . And bring your own whiskey, the last time you were here you drank up . . . I'll let you in, baby . . . Of course we're sober, we just got started . . . Take a taxi . . ."

"Harold's coming over," she announced from the hall. "I hope he's sober and doesn't fall out on my floor."

"I haven't seen Harold in years," he said as she took the glasses to make drinks. "Not since he came to New York. I saw Bebe once and she said he was living with you."

"That lying bitch." She put the glasses down, sloshing them over and flopped into her chair. "She used to call up here all the time and ask to speak to Harold and I hadn't seen—"

"When I was in Chicago in '48 he gave a party for me and Bebe—"

"—in five years and he came in here one day with the dt's and fell out in the middle of my floor and asked me to telephone his psychiatrist in Chicago—"

"—he was sick then and she wanted me to have her. He was taking morphine—"

148

"—It was the Saturday and she wasn't in her office—"

"—The same one? Nancy what's her—"

"—Rothchild . . . And he didn't know her home number, it's not listed. She was Ronny's analyst too and I called the restaurant where she always—"

"—All these people getting cured of something—"

"—and when I told him I couldn't get her he just turned over on his face and gave up. I had to call Nat—my own doctor—and—"

"—Why didn't you just let him sleep it off. He'd have—"

"—That son of a bitch wet my carpet and trembled so I thought he was dying. I called Nat and had him sent to my own hospital. I had to sign him in and it cost me twenty-four dollars a day. Nat wanted to have him sent to Bellevue—"

"—Why didn't you let him? Hell—"

"—Oh, I couldn't bear it. Bellevue sounded like the end of the world—all those skid row drunks—and Harold was a great man once. Nat said I was a fool. He wanted me to call the police and tell them he had no means of support—"

"—Where was Bebe? She had a little money from—"

"—Divorced the year before—"

"—I'd have let him go to Bellevue. They're used to handling dt patients—"

"—Went himself . . . two days checked out my hospital and went back to his flat—had a cold water flat on Houston—called the police and told them he was sick and destitute—"

"—time is it, baby?"

She glanced at her watch and leaped from her chair, staggered across the floor to her television set as if gone berserk. "Sid Caesar and Imogene Coca. Mix drinks dear while I dial—" The screen lit up and showed the flashing of jagged lines. "Oh shit!" he heard her cry as he staggered toward the kitchen bearing the empty glasses like a man dying of thirst staggering his last mile across a burning hot desert in a blinding snow storm, and when he got back to the sitting room with the refills he thought of Donavan staggering into his apartment where they were having the last WPA party—the time they were let off for two days shortly before the end—his dirty white shirt flapping open, suspenders hanging down and his pants about to fall from his long lean frame, blue eyes glazed, red hair flagging across his bloodless forehead, ugly bony face set in grim determination, a bottle of Paul Jones whiskey in each hand, looking about triumphantly at all his goggle-eyed coworkers, and saying, "I made it," before falling on his face.

She took her drink from his hand and gave him a quick friendly kiss, then sat on the sofa beside him. "I just love Imogene Coca, don't you?"

He peered at the blurred pygmies on the screen, trying to focus his vision, and the next thing he knew Harold was stepping down into the room, hand extended, saying in his jubilant tenor voice, "Jesse, what you say, old man?"

Jesse jumped to his feet and they shook hands warmly. "Damn, Harold, I'm glad to see you!" he exclaimed with drunken emotion. "Really glad to see you. Goddamn folks are getting me down again."

"It's a bitch, man, it's a bitch. I've been thinking of wearing a turban and posing as an Indian like that Sam preacher who went all through the South. Stayed in all the best hotels and—"

Kriss had served him a drink on the storage cabinet beside her three-legged chair and on resuming her seat on the sofa cut him off irritably, "Harold, will you please sit down so I can see the screen."

He was a big heavyset man with strong bold features of a ruddy tan complexion, appearing rugged and forceful in brown tweed jacket and gabardine slacks, and when he gave Kriss a half-hurt, half-indulgent smile, and obeyed like a scolded child, Jesse felt another tremor of violent rage. "Thinks she's God!" he thought, and then half-amused, remembering the current crop of jokes, "Not God, MacArthur!"

Harold was sitting, leaning forward, talking around Kriss: ". . . pecks bowing and scraping—" when she cut him off again, "If you and Jesse want to talk, go outside. This is my only pleasure, only—" she laughed childishly at some antic on the television screen, and now Jesse was half-amused, thinking of those magazine cartoons of a man cast away on a tropical island with a beautiful woman and complaining that his radio wouldn't work. "Bitch cast away with two men . . . Island not tropical . . . no palm trees—but shade of skyscrapers—just as good . . . only pleasure television . . ."

150

He stood shakily and said, "I'ma maka drink."

Kriss held up her glass and Harold hastened to empty his.

"I smell somp'n on fire," Jesse said, hugging the empty glasses to his stomach.

Kriss giggled. "It's Harold's paraldehyde."

Jesse sniffed. "Paldahyde? Smells like formaldehyde."

"They give it to alcoholics at Bellevue," Kriss said, forgetting the program in her enjoyment of Harold's discomfiture.

"Don't laugh, my dear, you might be taking it yourself some-day," Harold said acidly.

Jesse staggered kitchenward, laughing to himself. "Poor sona-bitch embalming himself 'fore he's dead." When he stopped to place the glasses on the hall table to get a better grip he noticed for the first time the three keys atop a check. He poked the keys aside and studied the check, trying to concentrate. But all that made sense was the amount and he thought, as he continued on, "Son, if meat's so high you gonna have to drink soup."

When he saw the potatoes on the stove he decided to start dinner. Taking a short drink straight, he pulled out the grill, placed it on the table, lit the oven, put the steak on the grill, and the next thing he knew he was sitting on the sofa beside Kriss, asking Harold, ". . . happened about that Chicago letter you were going to write for the *New Democrat*? I bought it for a time but I never saw your pieces."

He felt reasonably sober and quite lucid.

"Never heard from them . . . after that lunch at Cheerio's . . . was going to review your book . . ."

". . . killed everybody ever liked it . . . rank poison those things—"

". . . 'sa book, Jesse ol' man, 'sa book . . . these white folks 'rnot gointa letcha—"

Kriss turned on Jesse in a rage and cried, "If this book is like the last one I'll never speak to you again!"

". . .'ll never forgive you, ol' man, 'll never forgive you. They'll—" Harold was saying while Jesse glared at Kriss, "Did you read it? All you people—"

"I hated it—'n what's more—"

"—count all the white people—"

"—all of 'em, Hal, all of 'em. No goddam except—"

"—son of a bitch, if you ever write another book like—"

He looked at her glazed eyes filled with senseless hatred and felt the sickness coming over him. "—wrote it for you . . . wrote it to please you—" he was saying without realizing what he said, and she was saying, "—ever mention it again in my house!—'n Harold, I'm sick o' your whining! Negroes!—'d think—only people matter . . ."

Harold was staggering toward the kitchen to get another drink and Jesse was muttering half to himself, ". . . took a beating . . . took a headwhipping . . ." and Kriss was laughing maliciously, and it was unbearably hot in the small apartment, and Jesse was talking to himself. ". . . only time you ever tried to be fair . . . fair to everybody . . . made all of 'em much good as bad . . . hated nobody . . . thought they'd say, at last a nigger's who's fair . . . and they stoned you . . . they gutbutted you, son . . . knocked you down and kicked you in the nuts . . . it's funny . . . take the hate but hate the compassion . . . hate the objectivity . . . hate the analysis . . . hate it! . . . makes sense though . . . only reasonable . . . guilt invites hate but hates reason . . . hates pity . . . hates forgiveness most . . . never forgive forgiveness . . . hate that sonabitch forever . . . great race though . . . right too . . . conquered the world . . . proves they're right . . . never hate hate—first commandment . . . love hate . . . hates what makes conquest . . . love that sonabitch like mother . . . never loved mother either though . . . never loved anything but hate . . . love that sonabitch though . . ." And from this disjointed mental soliloquy he went into a stage of kaleidoscopic remembering: they'd cancelled all his radio appearances, all public contacts, removed his books from the stores, returned them to the publisher, because the blacks had hated it as much as had the whites . . . in the communist press it was likened to the biased ravings from the "rotted mouth of Bilboa!" and himself was compared to those depraved slaves who betrayed the slave revolts; while writers for the capitalist press labeled it sordid, bitter, the most poorly written book ever published, said hate ran through it like a yellow bile, likened it to the graffiti on walls and termed him psychotic . . . he was showing his

152

father Rockefeller Center on his father's visit to New York for the publication and his father looked up at the tall buildings of the city that had hurt his son so cruelly and said, "Had they built the Terminal Tower in Cleveland before you left, Jesse?" trying to tell his son there were just as big dwarfs elsewhere as in New York City . . . he was hurrying from a downtown bookstore where his autographing hour had been canceled and just missed the telephone call Becky took canceling him off his first scheduled radio appearance, so he said nonchalantly, "Fine, I'll take you and Dad to Luchow's for lunch" . . . he was crossing the grounds of Skiddoo four o'clock of an April morning, thinking, "I'd just like to find some goddamned short one-storied street of simple folk whom I could understand" . . . And then the disjointed thoughts again: ". . . what makes these people—big important people—hate a simple sonabitch like you . . . tell you so many lies . . . simple sonabitch like you . . . can't hurt anybody . . . yourself . . . can hurt yourself but nobody else . . . what are they afraid of . . ." And finally: "What you never knew, son, what you never knew—" His head seemed to burst with the effort of trying to catch that one simple thing he never knew which in extreme moments of extreme drunkenness was always so close . . . "What you never knew . . . Jesse Robinson . . . what you never knew . . ." and all the while the dirge going on in the back of his mind:

deeee-do-deeee-do-deeee-do
                                    d
                                    e
        eeeee-do-daaaaaaaaaaaaaaaaaaaaaaaaaaaaa

". . . 'sabitch, Jesse, 'sabitch . . . hated white folks so much had to be a whore for 'em . . ."

And Kriss saying: ". . . whore when you married her . . ."

". . . no more than you, my dear . . . you nigger men . . . she white men . . . all part of problem . . ."

And Jesse saying: ". . . surrenderin' myself . . . made private peace . . . screw 'em now in peace . . ."

And Harold saying: ". . . she couldn't be my wife . . . not wife of a nigger . . . had to be white men's whore . . ."

And Kriss, remembering when she'd first tried to make him, thinking him so great and exciting and dangerous, and so superior to herself, forgiving him for his condescension and indifference, his caustic comments such as at the interracial dinner party when she was relating some joke about "Uncle Mose" who'd been her step-mother's handyman in Mississippi, he'd turned to her and said, "Your mother's brother, no doubt?" and even after she'd been sleeping with him and loved him dearly and went to sleep one night drunk with a cigarette and set her bed on fire and telephoned him to come and put it out to have him say crossly, "Just throw a bucket of water on it, my dear," and how he'd married a Negro bitch, a one-time streetwalker who'd married a homosexual racketeer and got up in the world, and then married Harold and got up farther, and had let her break him because he came and slept with her sometimes when she needed him, his wife going around sleeping with all his white friends, sometimes two and three at a time, and saying she wondered why Harold could never make her happy when Kriss liked it so well . . .

The memories fired her with such blind rage, remembering in addition that she, herself, had never been able to break him, that she lurched to her feet and screamed at him hysterically: "Niggers! niggers! niggers! That's all you niggers talk about . . . Niggers! niggers! niggers! You're just as bad as she is! All *niggers*! I'm sick to death of *niggers*! Ever since I've known you you've talked of nothing but *niggers*!" her rage causing her to talk distinctly. "I'm tired of you niggers always whining around me. I am sick of all you niggers . . ."

Jesse staggered to his feet and with a violent action threw her on the sofa. "One more *nigger* out of you—" he began, peering through a blinding blur of rage to find her face to hit it. But instead he saw Harold kneeling before her, embracing her hips, tears streaming down his sweaty tan cheeks, his big strong face piteously distorted, pleading hoarsely, "Don't say that to me, Kriss. Don't try to hurt me. We've been through too much together, my dear . . . just alike . . . you and me . . . no difference . . . white woman black man . . .

154

broke us both . . . white woman black man always broken together
. . . don't try to hurt old Harold . . . don't my dear . . . in the same
river together . . . you married homosexual . . . I married whore
. . . you can't do without black men . . . no more'n I can do without
white women . . ." And she stroked his hair and consoled him.
"Don't cry, baby . . . Kriss didn' intend hurt you . . ." And feeling
such perverted pleasure at having made him cry it turned to sexual
desire for him more intense than she had ever felt in all the years
of his critical arrogance. "Kriss 'll take care you baby . . . put you
to bed . . . make you happy. . . ." Feeling his hot wet tears on her
dry palms with orgastic ecstasy.

Jesse vaguely realized through his senseless rage and stupefying
drunkenness that he was witnessing a sex ritual of laceration, the
two of them slashing each other in sensual excitement, and he
thought some deep frustrated love between them was frothing out
in cruelty. And when she too began to cry, her tears streaming down
a face gone ugly to fall on his head where he felt them through his
hair, Harold also felt a sexual urge for her and buried his wet face
in her lap.

This was too much for Jesse; he'd come to screw the bitch
himself. Savagely, he clutched Harold by the collar and jerked him
to his feet. "Godammit make love t'her w'en I'm not 'ere!"

Harold spread his hands in a gesture of innocence as if to show
he had no aces palmed, ". . . don' be jealous of me, ol' man . . .
flame's out . . . truth it was never lit . . ." Then with a deprecating
laugh, "Kriss tried t'make great romance . . ."

Kriss gave them both a venomous look through red-laced eyes
. . . "Sonssabitches!" she muttered and got up dizzily and staggered
into her bedroom and slammed the door.

"Bitch is sick," Jesse said from a sudden subconscious realization. "Really sick . . . Negroes hurt her . . . really hurt her . . ."

"'sabitch, Jess, 'sabitch, ol' man. Once a white person works
for the Sam cause never get over it."

"'ow bout a drink?"

"God bless whiskey. Man couldn't live without it."

The next thing Jesse knew he and Harold were sitting at the
table eating hot burnt rolls, warm raw steak, hot soapy potatoes

swimming in butter, and cold sliced tomatoes with Hollandaise sauce. Harold was saying in a fairly sober voice: ". . . the popcorn got mixed up with the head juices and the bloodstream rushed it to the brain, you see, and the popcorn on the brain caused a burning fever, you see, and the heat popped the corn with such force it came out through the skull into the hair, and that's how you get dandruff, old man."

Jesse laughed boisterously, feeling quite sober. "Economical, too. Saves buying a popper. But I don't like popcorn."

Harold chuckled. "That reminds me of a joke—"

"Where's Kriss?" Jesse asked.

Harold looked at him questioningly. "She's in her room unless she's eviled on away as the boys used to say on—"

"I ought to wake her up; she hasn't eaten anything." He looked about at the closed bedroom door. "Was she sick?"

Harold chuckled maliciously. "You should know, old man. You went in and asked her if she wanted to eat."

Jesse felt embarrassed because he didn't remember his doing so. "What did she say?"

"You could hear better than I, ol' man. You were right there beside her, but if I remember right I think she told you to go to hell and take your food with you."

Jesse laughed. "You know, that bitch is crazy." Then seriously, "But she's been hurt. I wonder what happened between her and Ted."

"He caught her sleeping with Joe and broke her jaw."

"No wonder! I thought it was Maud who—"

"Maud quit her after that." Harold licked his lips, relishing the vicious gossip.

"I always wondered what the setup was."

"These dikers are a bitch, old man. Maud got Kriss to divorce Ronny and get engaged to Ted, and when she'd married Ted Maud intended to sleep with both of them. But Kriss took so long Maud couldn't wait and began sleeping with Ted during the day and with Kriss after she came from work at night and Kriss got irritated, you see, and slept with Joe."

"I didn't think Maud gave a damn who slept with Joe," Jesse

said. But he didn't fully realize what he was saying for his mind had gone into a daze wherein his conscious mind was torn between incomprehension and subjectivism.

"She didn't," Harold said. "She got mad because Kriss let Ted know. And when Ted quit her, Maud didn't want just bare cunt, so she—" He broke off as the bedroom door opened.

Kriss came into the hall, red-eyed from crying. Her face was tear-stained and the flesh indented by the wrinkles on the coverlet, but she felt a cold contained rage of such violence it had sobered her. "I heard what both of you said," she announced. "Both of you get up from my table and leave my house." But the ludicrousness of herself ordering two drunken Negroes to stop eating and leave her house in the early hours of morning tickled her so that she giggled.

However, Harold chose to be offended. Clambering to his feet with a great show of dignity, chuckling with insouciance at her bad manners as if that was the correct thing to do when one was ordered from a house, said, "Certainly, my dear. Your company doesn't interest me. I only came because you invited me to come—"

"—inviting you to leave—"

"—to see Jesse, with whom—"

"—may take him home and sleep with him too, you—"

"—wants to sleep with you, my dear, although whom you want to—"

"—for you to leave at once, this—"

"—on my way, my dear—"

"—want you to go too, Jesse!"

Scraping back his stool, Jesse heaved to his feet and began, "I'm not going any goddam where and if Harold wants to stay and drink my own liquor—"

"—not me, old man, not me. As Bert Williams used to say:

> *When the fellows*
> *get to fighting*
> *and the law is at the door . . .*
> *somebody stay*
> *and the law delay*

157

and make himself a great hero
—but somebody else
not me . . .

—not me, old man. But I'll have a drink for the road."

Jesse staggered with him into the kitchen and poured two half glasses of straight whiskey which they gulped down without strangling, barely tasting it, then they staggered to the door and shook hands and Harold said in parting, "She likes to be whipped, old man. Uncle Whitney brought a bullwhip from Mexico to whip her with. Used to tell me how she liked it." Jesse closed the door on him, momentarily sobered by the last drink and tired of Harold's malice. He found Kriss mixing a drink and said, "You ought to eat something, baby," but she turned on him furiously, "I'm never going to sleep with you again, Jesse!"

"Don't give a goddam!"

"Go back to your wife, you son of—"

"Why not to some other white bitch? Why always back to my wife?"

"You hate me, you son of a bitch!" she blazed.

"Don't hate you. Just want some peace. A piece," he corrected. "A piece in peace. You goddam white women always want to be raped. I don't feel like raping you. Too old, too tired. Can leer at you though, if you like that. Best I can do. If that doesn't satisfy—"

"You hate white people!"

"Don't be too sure about that," he said, thinking of some half-remembered joke about the white man who said to the black, "You don't hate white people, do you, Mose?"

She took her drink to the table and poked at the cold partly eaten steak. "It's raw," she said, giggling.

"What you expect from two cannibals? Cook it for you though, baby. White ladies like well-browned meat. Fact can't get it too black . . ."

"You son of a bitch! I'm never—"

He felt a sudden violent impulse to beat her into silence. The next thing he knew he was down on his knees before the oven trying to place the steak on the grill that was located at the bottom of the firebox. The acrid scent of raw gas had brought him to his senses. "Damn oven's on!" he exclaimed and leaping to his feet struck a match and threw it into the grill. The flame blasted out with a whooshing sound.

"Hydrogen bomb!" he thought. "That's the way to do it, son. Blow 'em all up!" And after a moment, "Just be patient. They'll do it they own damn selves."

And the next thing he knew he was sitting at the hall table with a cleared space before him scrawling the words at the bottom of a page of typewriter paper:"—and just don't be so goddam challenging because I will kill you . . ." He had already written on the page: "Dear Kriss, you like feeling being hated because it offers you absolution for your sense of guilt. Also helps you bear defeat. You've always felt the need to pay for adulation—fact for everything—good will, good morning, good time—every Goddam thing—pay for it with your body. Pay pay pay. Somebody tell you you're pretty. Pay. Tell you you're smart. Pay. Take you to dinner. Pay. Way you used to be. Pay for it in ass. Pay with ass—get discount. Liked you then. Sell you this nigger. Pay for him in ass. Fair exchange. Everybody happy. Lot of fun. No frustration. No fighting. Just fucking and fun. Way it should be. They take the credit but you take the fool. American way. No more though You've gone un-American. No more pay for nigger with ass. Now whip nigger with ass. Use it as cheap dirty weapon for fighting. Don't blame you. Happens to most women. Just don't like the women it happens to. Don't try whipping me with it. Too much like the south. Been whipping nigger with white ass three hundred years. This nigger's been whipped with enough other things to leave ass out. Don't try whipping me with ass because you know baby I can hurt you more than anybody. Because I can kill you. Only person you ever knew who could kill you. So don't press me. Be a good girl and pay ass—"

Suddenly the smell of something burning alerted his senses. On sight of smoke pouring from the kitchen doorway he jumped to his feet and rushed into the smoke-filled room. For a moment he was in complete command of his senses. He realized instantly that the steak had caught fire. Calmly he turned off the gas, threw open the window, speared the burning steak with a long-handled fork, tossed it into the sink and turned the cold water on it. "Black enough for Kriss now," he thought.

And the next thing he knew it was Sunday afternoon.

CHAPTER 10

*K*RIS NEVER DREAMED. But physical discomfort ofttimes penetrated her unconsciousness in a manner similar to a dream. In her sleep she became conscious of being chilly and awakened immediately. Before opening her eyes she flung a bare arm searchingly across the faded blue sheet. It encountered only emptiness. Every event of the previous night returned in one flash of memory. She became rigid, scarcely breathing, her emotions shattered by the blind panic she always experienced on awakening and finding herself alone. "Oh shit!" she exclaimed in acute chagrin. Not that she regretted having ordered Jesse home, but that he had gone. She felt as if her fair white body had betrayed her. It had been bad enough when Dave walked out, but for Jesse—for any Negro . . .

She opened her eyes and saw she had slept uncovered. Critically she examined her neglected body. From her prone position she saw the hill of a soft white belly between two flat-top mounds of breasts, one arm outflung and the other curved around breasts and belly with the fingertips sunk in the straight sparse leaf-brown hairs surrounding her cloaca, and beyond, the square-toed feet in vague silhouette against the dark gray slit of open window. She thought of the time she used to have a lovely flat stomach and resolved to stop drinking for a month. Remembering how much she had drunk the night before she became enraged. "Damn Jesse to hell!" she muttered, as if he'd forced her to drink against her will. And then, tickled by the indignant thought: "At least he should have had the decency to screw me before leaving—even if I were unconscious," she began to giggle. It was dim in the room; the door was open to a gray hall and outside it looked like a gray night. She turned on the night light and looked at the gold-plated Swiss clock. The hands stood at 6:11. She picked it up and found that it had stopped. She dialed "Time" and while waiting looked at her nude body with distaste. A woman's controlled contralto voice purred affectedly, "When you hear the chime . . . the time will be . . . one thirty-two and one-quarter . . ." It struck Kriss as being a sexy voice, whereas a man would have been irritated, and she listened for it to speak again, wondering what the woman looked like, blonde or brunette, buxom or petite, young or elderly, if she had been screwed last night, if she had liked it, if she screwed quietly or intensely or with a lot of pitching and gasping and crying or with the dull indifferent application of a woman trying to get it done; and when she heard her voice again she decided she did it in the first way and thought, "Come up to my house, baby," and the next instant was shocked by such a thought. She got up and set the clock and started across the hall to the bathroom but heard a voice muttering, "Going to fuck you goddamit—open your goddam legs," and stepped to the arch of the sitting room. In the semidarkness she saw clothes strewn haphazardly over the floor and a nude brown body curled grotesquely on the sofa, a wrinkled sheet beneath it and one of her extra blankets wrapped about the head and shoulders. It faced outward, the buttocks pressed tightly against the sofa's back, and erected penis pointing roomward with which the right hand struggled spasmodically as if to tear it off. By his presence she was instantly relieved of her panic and chagrin and when she heard him scream in muffled frustration, "Don't play around, goddamit!" she giggled with delight and felt warm and good all over. She felt an impulse to tickle his penis with a broom straw to see what he would do but was afraid she might awaken him, so instead she stood silently and listened. For a long time he didn't speak again, then he cried in a voice of rage, "kill you!" and kicked out so violently his toe hit the cocktail table and sent a glass spinning across the floor. "Uhn!" he grunted in pain but didn't awaken. Then quickly he turned on his stomach, pressing his erection against the sofa and

161

she heard a jumble of words which sounded like, "Now that's better, baby—but your skin feels rough." His tan body minus its head was like a bronze statue in the dim light and she felt a strong desire to kneel beside it and kiss the firm smooth buttocks and hard slender thighs. But her curiosity proved stronger and she let him sleep.

She performed her morning's toilet as quickly as possible, brushed her teeth and showered briefly, slipped on a pair of rayon panties and then, as she was standing before the mirror surveying her legs, one ear cocked to listen, abruptly her stomach fell. She had felt no hangover on awakening but was now so suddenly hungry she felt nausea. In the doorway of the kitchen immediately after turning on the light, she stood stock still in consternation. The window was open wide on the rusty wet fire escape and a face peered from the window of the apartment across the murky air well. It was raining grayly with that desolation of a miserable big city Sunday and she went quickly to shut the window and draw the blinds to close out the gloomy day and the leering face of the fat baldheaded salesman across the way who'd been vainly trying for the past two months to meet her accidentally in the corridor. The grill at the bottom of the oven was pulled out and charred black, and a soggy cinder of meat lay in the greasy sink. Atop the stove was a pan lined with burnt whipped potatoes, a charred paper container and some green stuff in a pot that resembled scum on a stagnant pool. On the table the cardboard carton in which the groceries had been delivered had been hacked to pieces, and then she saw the knife sticking from the centre of the door. Four of the white doughy uncooked club rolls were skewered on the blade like corpses of newborn quadruplets and the blade stabbed into the center crossbar of the door with such force it remained in position as if awaiting the fire to barbecue. Kriss stared at it for some time, more out of curiosity than fear, wondering what had been in Jesse's mind, and from what she knew of how he thought, the skewered rolls took the form of the four outsize testicles of the great-grandfathers of the whole white race pinned as a grim love token by a bitter Negro on a lush white woman's door. She was so sexually excited by the sadistic thought that when she endeavored to draw out the knife she found her fingertips caressing the dead white mutilated testicles and her mind picturing the black erection of the tan body on the sofa. Suddenly she was weak from hunger to the point of fainting. She ate a plain slice of white bread, then put on water to make coffee and boil eggs, and stepped back into the hall to clear a space on the table. Not until then did she notice the scrawled note, and as she stood reading it, ciphering the scrawled words, her sexual excitement was again heightened by the veiled frustration behind the drunken threats. This, combined with the telltale erection and the mutilated mammoth white testicles, conjured up a picture of frenzy that made her frantic, her mouth turning strange with opening glands, and she would have gone and turned him over if she hadn't heard the water boil.

She made coffee, two pieces of dry toast, softboiled one egg, got the Sunday *Herald-Tribune* from the mat outside her door, cleared a space on the table, and while sipping her black coffee and munching her egg-dipped toast, began methodically reading the paper from cover to cover. She read rapidly, making mental notes of all items concerning foundations and the India Institute, her brilliant mentality with its wide research experience rapidly condensing the facts and discarding the journalistic repetitions, functioning at the high degree of efficiency attributed to Harvard-trained scientists who live normal lives, eat balanced diets, are happily married and sexually complete, and have never tasted an intoxicating beverage. With one corner of her mind she listened to Jesse grinding his teeth and muttering angrily in his sleep and once, giggling with the therapeutic amusement which humans derive from the antics of monkeys in the zoo, paused for a moment to watch him thresh about like an eel in a net. "Kill you!" he shouted in a fit of rage and struck out with his fist, striking the wall with such force she crossed the room to see if the paint was scarred. After that he turned onto his side, and tucked his bruised hand between his legs. He blew a snort of laughter and said in a distinct voice, "I got mine, now you get yours." Kriss laughed girlishly with incurious delight and resumed her perusal of an address delivered for U.S. President Truman by U.S. Secretary of State Acheson to the effect that unless suffering was wiped out in underdeveloped countries it might be used by a new dictatorship "more terrible" than the Soviet Union.

Since the first instant of sleep Jesse had dreamed countless horrible scenes of violent rape and murder and savage fights and apoplectic arguments, all of which had been blasted from memory at the moment of awakening by the last macabre dream of millions of black men, women, and children being driven off a cliff into a bottomless gorge by a genial mob of white horsemen, himself watching them disappear, wave after wave, like mute zombies without anger or protest or entreaty, but when it came his turn he cried out in a voice of terror, "But I signed the paper!" and the laughing horsemen spurred their beasts toward him, one of them saying, "Who said you could write?" and trampled him over the edge, and as he fell turning over and over, he caught glimpses of columns of horsemen galloping through the sky and thought, half-amused, of a story his father used to tell about two slaves raiding the ham-house one dark and rainy night; old master was waiting inside and when the first slave reached underneath a loose board to swipe a ham, old master whacked his hand with a hammer, and hearing his buddy jerk back his hand, the second slave asked, "You get it?" to which the first slave replied, "Ah got mine, now you get yours."

He awakened instantly in the middle of his fall and feeling the blanket wound about his head thought someone was trying to strangle him, and took a desperate leap backward, clawing at the murderous hands. He landed with a loud thud on his side in the middle of the floor. When finally he'd torn off the offending blanket from his face he saw Kriss sitting at the table, grinning at him.

"You've been having a bad time, baby," she said. "Was some woman's husband trying to trap you?"

"I thought I was being strangled," he confessed sheepishly.

She giggled. "You shouldn't fight so much, baby. You wouldn't be so afraid."

He stood up, threw the blanket on the sofa and rubbed his bruised hip bone. "Those bastards jump me while I'm sleeping," he said self-mockingly. "Won't come out and fight when I'm awake and sober."

"When is that, dear?"

164

He noticed his clothes on the floor, the knocked-over glass, slept-on sofa, heaped ashtrays, dirty dishes and blew laughter through his nose. "Kilroy was here. On a bender, too." Then to himself, "Not *Kil* roy, *Le* roy!" Suddenly realizing he'd slept on a sheet, he asked wonderingly, "Did you make the sofa?"

"No, dear, when I went to bed you were cooking." She grinned. "You were having a cooking good time."

He remembered the burning steak and laughed. "Damn right!" Then he noticed her staring analytically at his nude body. "What am I bid?"

"You have a beautiful body, Jesse," she said with honest lascivi-ousness.

"It ought to be," he thought. "All those workouts I got pushing that mop in White Plains."

"If we still owned slaves I'd pay a year's wages for you—"

"Don't be so goddam cheap!"

"I'd keep you in my bedroom for a pet and give you a gold collar and nameplate—"

"Be the envy of all the bitches with the Pekineses because I can talk."

"You can do more than talk, baby. You're much better equipped than a Pekinese!"

"Don't have their finesse, evidently."

She grinned. "You are having a hard time getting started, aren't you, baby?"

"If this keeps up—" But in the middle of it he had a sudden attack of diarrhea and had to dash. "Actions speak louder than words," he thought, then, "Phew! Bastards not only beat me in my sleep but made me eat with the buzzards." Afterward he examined his drink-swollen face in the mirror. It had the smooth greasy sheen of a syphilitic pimp's, and his glazed stunned eyes, now a jaundiced yellow, looked inhuman. "Black Dracula," he said. He felt pleas-antly dazed and slightly tickled as if a bubble of laughter floated about in his delightful derangement, yet perfectly normal, other than that his body felt sore and bruised. "Kiss, baby," he called, sticking his head out of the doorway, "you haven't by any chance been beating me with a poker in my sleep?"

"No, dear, I regret to confess. You were beating it yourself."

Turning back, he shook his head at his reflection. "Jesse Robinson, what's the matter, son? You've been with this bitch for two whole nights and still haven't scored." Then, while showering, "If you don't get started soon, son, they're gonna farm you out to the Bush League." He put a new blade in her safety razor and shaved, applied her comb and brush to his wet kinks and used the first toothbrush he touched, thinking, "Don't let those hygienists catch you, boy."

Returning to the sitting room he dressed in shorts, socks, and shoes, hung the remainder of his clothes in her clothes closet, after which he went behind her and bent down and kissed her on the nape of her neck, noticing with a slight revulsion a faint rash on her back.

"Get me my glasses, dear," she commanded. "They're on the night stand in the bedroom."

He fetched them obediently, thinking, "That bitch would love to switch me." Aloud he asked, "How about breakfast, baby?"

"I've had my breakfast, dear. I was eating while you were fighting your enemies in your sleep."

He started to say, "You call that a breakfast for a big girl like you," but instantly realized she was *too* big a girl for that remark.

Then on entering the kitchen he exclaimed, "Great damn, Kilroy brought his whole fuckin' family," adding amusedly when he saw the knife sticking in the door, "Blazed a trail for Mr. Ward too!" Then, to himself, "Damn, son, you'll never be a Hamlet at this rate." But for an instant he was shocked out of his nice sensation of deranged normality and felt a tremor of fear. "I ought to get the hell out of here!" he thought, but quickly drowned it with a drink. They'd drunk two bottles of Scotch and a half bottle of bourbon, he noticed, as he started on the remainder of the bourbon.

"Jesse!" Kriss spoke so sharply at his back he gave a violent start and dropped the empty glass in the sink where it shattered into pieces. "Goddamit, Kriss—" he gasped protestingly.

She was vastly tickled by his frightened start but repressed it long enough to say viciously, "I want you to have that door fixed.

I'm not going to have you niggers break up this apartment. Maud hacked my dining room table to pieces with a kitchen knife—"

"Maud? I thought—"

"That was in Chicago. She tried to make Harold pay me some money he owed me and he slapped her—"

"Good for him!"

But she wouldn't let him off that easily. "It cost me three hundred dollars to have this place painted and I'm not going to let you hungry niggers—"

"—Three hundred dollars? Before I'd have paid that I'd have fucked and got myself another one."

Grinning, she moved into him and squeezed him painfully. "You would?"

"Ouch, goddamit, that hurts!"

Their bodies locked together and they kissed with mechanical skill, but the sight of her clad only in shell-rimmed spectacles and rayon shorts kept reminding him of the cartoons of Africans clad only in top hats and interfered with his passion, and he took them off and began all over again. For the moment following her vicious abuse of him she felt passionate, but it soon waned and she broke away, "Jesse, I want you to clean up this mess you and Harold made—" Such animal rage spewed from his yellow eyes she broke off to giggle. His hands trembled as he poured a drink to steady himself. Gulping it, he gasped, "One of these times, baby—"

"Oh, Jesse, why didn't you drink the bourbon," she complained with genuine emotion. "You and that son of a bitch drank up my good Scotch—"

"He's your friend, baby."

"I hate him!" she said, venomously, and returned to her paper.

"Well, as long as there's food, there's hope," he said to himself, and after making a tall iced bourbon highball, prepared for himself a breakfast of four sausages, four slices of kidney, three fried eggs, and two browned rolls.

"You going on a journey, baby?" she asked at the sight of his plate.

"You called me a *hungry nigger*."

"Hungry, anyway."

"No, I like the *hungry nigger* better. I like to think of myself as a nigger when I'm fucking you."

She smiled her secret sensual smile and turned his face toward her and kissed his greasy mouth and after that he had a hard time swallowing it, but he made it.

When he had finished eating, he washed the dishes, cleaned the stove, scoured the grill, and wiped up the floor while she made her bed, straightened the sitting room, ran the carpet sweeper, and emptied the garbage into the incinerator in the hall. Then he put on his trousers and shirt and she dressed in her red silk Chinese Mandarin robe and Turkish-toed slippers and they sat in their respective seats, he on the sofa and she in her three-legged chair, tall iced civilized highballs in silver coasters within reach, to watch a television program called *Zoo Parade*. At that moment they formed a picture of Manhattan domestic tranquillity on a Sunday afternoon, painted by some idiot who has never been east of the Hudson River. The charming director of Chicago's Lincoln Zoo, who conducted the performances of the animals on the show, had just reached a climactic scene, handling a couple of poisonous snakes, when the telephone rang. "Oh shit!" Kriss exclaimed. Snakes fascinated her, the more poisonous the greater the fascination, in addition to which the director had twice been snakebitten on the show before, and she wouldn't want to miss seeing him bitten again for the world. Her first impulse was to ignore the telephone, but after letting it ring to within one split-second of the end of any male caller's patience, she dashed in to answer it. Over the sound of the television Jesse heard her gushing incoherently with a warmth she never showed toward man or woman and thought dreamily, "Take a card, any card." With his fourth drink he had entered a blurred, half-heard world of complete indifference to which he could give vague attention or even choose another. He only pretended interest in the television programs to please Kriss, now he closed his eyes and began to play with words:

I bit a tit
to twit a chit
but the chit had the grit

to sit on her split and would not submit
though I smit and she fit and I hit and she spit and I grit
I must admit I could not outwit the sprit and had to quit ...

"That was Don," Kriss said, and he opened his eyes. "He's coming over. You like Don, don't you, baby?"

"Oh, sure," he said, thinking, "I like de big gut, do you like de big gut ..."

"He's on the wagon, drinking nothing but cola." She was all excited as if her closest girlfriend were calling, and when she added, "I love Don, he's so sweet when he's sober," her face took on a look of melting sympathy.

"Can't be a successful fag without being sweet sometime," he said, and she became suddenly cross. "Jesse, if you're going to be nasty—"

"—baby, baby, I love—"

"Don's been an angel to me and—"

"Let's not argue any more, baby."

She relented. "Make us drinks, dear, while I order Coca-Cola. Mine Scotch this time." Calling to him in the kitchen, "Make some ice, dear."

"Make some ice, dear ... make some drinks, dear ... wash the dishes, dear ... scrub the floor, dear ... climb a tree, dear ... fuck yourself, dear ..." he muttered to himself as he melted the ice from the trays, but the back of his mind was still playing with the rhyme:

but if you will permit
I most humbly remit
I desire only to transmit
what would most befit
nay, benefit
any slit
oh, definite!
to whit:
I would emit
so exquisite a pit
as to acquit—

"Jesse!" He gave such a start the ice tray flew birdlike from his hand and clattered in the sink. Kriss stood in the doorway, grinning, "What are you thinking about, dear?"

He'd been absently running water over the ice cubes in the sink, melting them. "Abwout Twitty, bwaby," he said lispingly on recovering.

"Well, think about the ice now, dear. Don will be here in a minute."

He began putting the cubes into the glass tray. "Yes, baby. I'll think about the ice cubes, baby. Anything else you want me to think about, baby?"

A scholarly-looking, dark-haired Harvard-type young man who turned out to be the delivery boy from the delicatessen brought twelve bottles of Coca-Cola, four bottles of sparkling water, tins of cheesebits and assorted nuts, and to show how broadminded he was, he gave Jesse a confidential wink. "Ain't what you think, bub," Jesse thought. "I've been sleeping on the sofa."

Then Don came with six bottles of Pepsi-Cola for himself and a bottle of Scotch for Kriss and she flung her arms about him like a proud mother-bear and kissed him. They came into the kitchen, talking incoherently:

"—look much better, baby—"

"—not had a drop in ten days, and—"

"—so worried about your health, baby, when—"

"—eating like a horse—"

Hearing the word *horse* Jesse was reminded of a joke going about in psychiatric circles:

Psychiatrist (interviewing young man charged with murdering his mother): Do you care for girls?

Young Man: That's the trouble, I don't.

Psychiatrist: Do you care for boys?

Young Man: No.

Psychiatrist: What do you care for?

Young Man: Horses are the only thing that make me feel passionate.

Psychiatrist: Mares or stallions?

Young Man (horrified): Do you take me to be a fairy, doctor?

Kriss was grinning idiotically. "—so happy, baby—"

And Don was drooling spitty words between gasps of embarrassed laughter as if he'd been running for the past hour and was now chewing on a stone. "Jesse ha ha . . . son of a bitch ha ha . . . puking on my sofa . . ."

"—are you, Don. Sorry about—"

"—didn't mind about the sofa myself ha ha but Ralph had to clean it up ha ha. Been knocked on the head since I saw you last ha ha. Did I tell you, Kriss?"

"I was still living there, baby."

She gave him a tall glass of iced cola and he gulped greedily, laughing even while drinking, and looking at Jesse with a bright-eyed inclusiveness as if to say, "All us turds here together." He was a tall well-built Anglo-Saxon, with the unhealthy flush of alcoholism, and his strong-boned handsome face was corroded by constant dissipation and incredibly distorted by deliberate subjection to sexual perversion. In addition to which he hadn't shaved. On this dismal rainy day he'd gone bareheaded and his wet brown crewcut hair was plastered to his head. He wore a pea-green cashmere sport jacket over a pink shirt open at the throat, old soiled bagged Oxford-gray flannel trousers, and rope-soled canvas-top sneakers that had once been white, over bare feet that had also once been white. Had it not been for the spitty incontrollable laughter that indicated a definite deterioration of the brain, he might have been considered human. Anatomically he was male. He had attended Harvard for three years until, at the beginning of his senior year, he was secretly jailed for a year on a homosexual charge—the secrecy costing his family twenty thousand dollars.

Considering these facts Jesse thought, "Adds up. Harvard man all right. No two ways about it."

Being the descendant of a very old and very wealthy Bostonian family of the highest social prominence, obviously he couldn't stay in Boston. Don's family, rather than run the risk of his prison record becoming duck-soup gossip for the columnists by applying for a passport, had exiled him to New York City in lieu of some hot Mediterranean island where he might drink himself to death on the cheap potent brandies along with other Bostonian exiles, hoping he might find the native bourbons just as lethal. However the boy had a better constitution than they had any reason to suspect.

On arriving in New York with Ralph, his black companion, he had established himself in a penthouse on Riverside Drive and had become a patron of the blacks. This had come about by Maud's discovering him. Naturally she had discovered him immediately. She could smell white homosexuals with money within a radius of one hundred miles. With her assistance he had endowed various black benefits and had established scholarship funds in several black colleges for promising black art students. He felt he'd found his life's mission in the black cause. His interracial black-benefit parties had become so celebrated and successful he'd bought a big old house in the Gramercy Park district to accommodate more black benefitters and do more benefit. The first time Jesse had attended one of Don's penthouse parties, he'd arrived uninvited at eleven o'clock to find everyone roaring drunk, and a handsome young man in a white silk shirt laughing boyishly had put a huge heavy dark-green expensively cut crystal tumbler, containing a pint of Myer's rum chilled with cracked ice, into his hand. He had drunk it politely and had begun dancing closely with a convenient woman, and the next thing he remembered he was sitting in the kitchen opening one tin after another of anchovies, eating them with his fingers and throwing the cans into the corner, watching the dull gray Hudson River flow sluggishly through a rainy day. Now, looking at this pink-shirted derelict, two hops from idiocy, he thought, half-amused, "Ain't nobody here that ain't been here before, boss."

They took their drinks to the sitting room, Don stopping on the way to "wee-wee"—"most *awful* stuff imaginable; weakens your bladder something awfully ha ha," afterwards remarking, "—feel like a baby ha ha—" To prove which he brought a wooden stool from the hall table to sit on like a baby. Then he began telling breathlessly of how in his favorite Harlem bar—"I've been going to Bucky's for *years;* everybody knows me—" sitting in his customary seat; he *merely* asked the man next to him to have a drink—"I didn't know him from *Adam,* dear—" and a woman he had not even seen—"assumed I was trying to make her man ha ha—but I assure you dear ha ha *nothing* was farther—"

"—your trouble, baby, you were always buying those hungry niggers drinks and—"

"—Bucky will tell you, dear, I *never*—"

"—just liked you for your money. All that money on those niggers' drinks—"

"Must have bought a lot of drinks to get rid of a quarter million dollars in six years," Jesse thought.

"—but never attempted to take any bitches man ha ha. All I *ever* had to do was whistle—"

"—hope you've learned your lesson, baby—"

Jesse thinking: "I'd have bought me three grown niggers and three pickaninnies to raise and saved the rest of my money."

This woman he hadn't even seen hit him over the head with a whiskey bottle and knocked him unconscious—"Jesse ha ha I bled like a stuck pig ha ha. I don't know *how* I got home ha ha. Bucky must have—"

"—sent in a taxi, baby. You had a towel about your head and some black guy—"

"—took care of me like a baby ha ha. I had *oodles* of friends everybody—"

"—and Ralph was so mad he went back with his pistol—"

"—just so afraid they might beat up the bitch ha ha and I couldn't have *borne*—"

This incoherent account being interrupted every two minutes by: first, his going to the kitchen for a fresh drink of cola; and secondly, his going to the john.

"The pause that refreshes," Jesse thought.

"—through your kidneys like needles ha ha. I drink six dozen bottles a day ha ha and it has the most *terrible*—"

"No wonder the son of a bitch makes like old Faithbue," Jesse thought.

"—but you *must* drink something ha ha—"

"—but you look so well, baby—"

Kriss just loved that man—*one*, rather, *one of those*, like the joke about the men counting off in the army: one-two-three-four . . . one . . . "Oh, I'm *one* too"—just *loved* that *one* because he was just like a sister and they could tell each other all about their affairs and discuss, Oh so candidly, the anatomy of last night's lover. Besides which he was a Harvard Bostonian socialite, which made everything right, and once he'd taken her on a visit to his ancestral mansion—when all of the family were away of course—and they'd had a glorious time hopping about the Boston nightclubs in search of men; so different from that son of a bitch Ronny, who sneaked off with the lowest kind of bums. But that was the difference between Boston and Mississippi; Bostonians were cultured.

When he next came from the john, Kriss said, "Why don't you eat some nuts, baby, maybe they'd help stop—"

"Don't look at me!" Jesse thought, pointing toward the bowl on the cocktail table. Then suddenly his mind went off, shutting out the sounds of voices, and he began again to play with words:

> *be there a knight*
> *without affright*
> *to blight the white*
> *and smite the spite*
> *that men call right—*
> *or even once a night*
> *will be quite*
> *alright*
> *especially if one is tight—*

And when his mind came back he heard Kriss saying, "How is it with you and Garner, baby?" and Don began telling the sad tale of the slow death of his glorious romance with a handsome dark-skinned curly-haired black army officer, which romance had reached its peak three years before when they sailed on a cruise to Martha's Vineyard and were so delighted with the blind tolerance and idyllic isolation of that New England Eden they decided to stay there in ecstatic inebriation for the remainder of their lives. Don bought and furnished a huge old-fashioned house and bought a station wagon to drive back and forth to town, but that first winter they did not get to town very often and did not have a single unpleasant moment of sobriety. But the following summer Garner's brother Jack, a Philadelphia lawyer, and his wife Geraldine, a very brainy newspaper columnist, along with their young son and heir, a lad of twelve, came to visit the honeymooners and liked it so well they stayed. And Don was so delighted he deeded the house to them jointly, thinking they would all live there pleasantly as two married couples for life. But Geraldine was a prominent socialite and her house guests, who were all quite distinguished blacks, found the arrangement puzzling and the presence of a drunken unshaven young white man clad only in an old bathrobe wandering about the premises at all hours somewhat disconcerting, even though he was a Harvard-Bostonian socialite, so Geraldine soon stopped introducing him to her distinguished guests and began devising ways and means to get him out of her house.

"—and she even went so far ha ha well, she was driving the station wagon to town to pick up some of her guests at the ferry station and I asked to go along to do some shopping because ha ha I'd never learned to drive the thing myself and daddy was sleeping and I heard her whisper to her guests ha ha that I was the gardener ha ha. I cared nothing about that but she took my television set down to the living room for her own guests—"

"—you didn't let her do that, baby? Your own—"

"—she's such an awful bitch ha ha and I positively could not *hear* in the condition I was in ha ha to make a scene involving—"

It finally reached the place where they lived in the house as strangers, each with their own set of guests, eating at different hours, sitting on opposite sides of the living room to carry on separate conversations, passing each other in the house without speaking, each set acting as if the other were invisible.

"—so I told daddy if he would not take my part I would positively leave him. Now he is—"

"*Jesse!*" Kriss shouted suddenly. He gave such a violent start the cheesebits he was eating flew into the air like buckshot. She giggled. "Make some drinks, dear. And you might join us if you have no—"

"I'm listening to every word. Fascinating. Beats Rimbaud's *Season in Hell*. Beats *Macbeth*—"

"You know Garner, Jesse?"

"Oh, sure, met him at your house—"

"Get the drinks first, dear."

"Yes, dear."

When Jesse went to the kitchen to make the drinks, Don went to the john and when Jesse returned Kriss was reading a letter Garner had written to Don.

"He wants you back, baby."

"He will drink himself to death ha ha but I positively do not care ha ha."

"But your *house,* baby! You're not going—"

"They can have it ha ha. I positively can *not* be bothered—"

Gulping down great swallows of nausea, Jesse struggled to his feet. He tried to fix his vision on what appeared to be a great number of dismembered square fish-eyes bobbing on the surface of a sea of dark congealing blood, but the nauseous putrefactive taste-smell of whiskey-rotted guts came up from his stomach faster than he could swallow it back, and cramps of lightning-fast diarrhea struck down through his bowels with the gut-stretched, panic-stricken, anus-ache of enema. He felt on the verge of suddenly erupting filth from both ends into the dead-eyed sea of blood. Laboring under great difficulty, he said politely, pronouncing each word separately in a slow thick voice, "If—you—dears—will—excuse—me—I will—go—vomit—and—shit—" and staggered toward the bathroom, striking heavily against the corner of the arch. Don leaped up and took him by the arm. He remembered getting down his pants in the nick of time and sitting on the stool, and the presence of a vague shape-sound hovering above, and the knowledge of another shape-sound hovering in the hall, and of feeling half-amused by the really staggering stink of foul putrescence he was giving them to smell, and of trying to put into words what he was thinking, "Just tit for tat ha ha."

CHAPTER 11

IT WAS SEVEN-FIFTEEN when he came to, and he was in bed naked and half-uncovered. Through the partly opened window he could see it was a dismal night outside. He felt cold, sober, and dangerously depressed. Thoughts pounded in rational sequence: Book . . . rejection . . . Becky . . . blankets . . . Kriss . . . white woman . . . white man's world, son . . .

> naught is a naught
> and five is a figure
> five for the white man
> and naught for the nigger

"You hired out for the job, son, nobody made you," he thought, and then, "What I really ought to have told the son of a bitch—" His mind hit a wall. "What son?" he asked aloud.

He got from the bed, thinking with bitter amusement, "And, dear ha ha I was knocked speechless!"

He crossed to the bathroom in his bare feet and Kriss, sitting in her favorite chair with an iced highball by her side, watching her favorite television program, Mr. Peepers, and thinking herself unseen, was giggling like an imbecile and did not hear him. Between them, she and Don had cleaned up the mess, and now she had grilled the ham-steak Jesse had brought and made her dinner, and now, being entertained by modern science, delightfully intoxicated by aged whiskey, with a healthy anxious and qualified male Negro awaiting her in her bed in her own apartment in the greatest city in the world, with the whole night ahead, she felt wonderful.

Instinctively Jesse first closed the bathroom window to keep the neighbors from seeing a black man in a white woman's apartment, then studied his reflection in the mirror. "What do you keep looking for, son? A miracle?" he asked himself. "You're going to keep on looking at yourself until you see something you don't want to see." He then brushed his teeth, gargled, showered hot then cold until his teeth began to chatter. He was drying himself when Kriss looked in the door and asked, grinning cheerfully, "How do you feel now, baby?"

He toweled about his groin and between his legs, looking at her with detached camera-eye coldness. And what he saw was a definitely mature bloated-stomach fat-jowled blonde white woman with glassy blue eyes of a strange oriental shape and skin as white as a fish's belly.

A woman who had probably slept with a hundred or more blacks, mostly men, grinning at him in what he interpreted as that strange idiotic manner of white Americans laughing at every black they see, no matter how unfunny that black might be, as if laughing at blacks was as obligatory as standing for the national anthem.

"I feel fine," he said flatly.

But she was in a playful mood and reached out and clutched him hurtingly, as if shaking hands. "If you don't make good tonight, Peter, you're fired."

"Goddamit, cut it out!" he said angrily. "That isn't a subway strap."

"All aboard!" she said, giggling, and gave two jerks. "Toot-toot!"

His brain exploded with the quick blind rage of killing, and he would have hit her in the face involuntarily had she not pinioned his arms in a tight embrace and, still grinning, forced her tongue between his teeth. His obvious resentment enhanced her enjoyment all the more and she let go his arms and pinched his buttocks, drawing back her face to say, "You have a beautiful derriere, baby; if I was a man I'd like you."

He disengaged himself without comment, coldly and soberly hating himself for ever wanting to sleep with this white woman or any white woman, and yet thinking on the other side of his mind, half-amused by the sober picture of himself: "Logical enough, though. Unavoidable really. Nigger's got to want to screw white women. Got no choice the way they got it set up. Wouldn't be human if he didn't. Absolutely right too. Should want to screw 'em. Good for his ego; great therapeutic qualities in screwing white woman. White man kick his ass until he gets sick; get some white woman ass and get well. Good for her too. White man kick her ass till she gets sick; screw some black niggers and get even. Don't let him catch her though; but be sure and let him know about it, otherwise lose half its curative value. Not just logical and unavoidable and right, but essential in our culture. Necessary balance. Besides which, what the hell else is there to expect—the country's full of white women who want to be screwed and everything from *Saucy Dames* to Henry James says they're the firstest with the mostest . . ."

"Are you hungry, baby?" she asked solicitously.

Applying her best hairbrush to his wet kinks in a deliberate effort to annoy her, he replied shortly, "No."

But this only added to her enjoyment of his vexation. They say the best way to keep a woman is barefooted and knocked up, but she liked her men bare-bodied and knocked down. Grinning, she offered, "I'll make you a drink while you dress, baby."

"I'll make it myself," he muttered, pushing past her and going naked to the kitchen.

She brought her glass and made a civilized Scotch highball while watching him uncork a bottle of gin, pour a half glass, and gulp it down. He gasped and she giggled, her eyes brightly amused. For her, this was the best part of it, all her past hurts were dissolved, watching the symptomatic self-destructiveness of a frustrated Negro male in a white woman's room. She was sexually thrilled by the look of raw hatred he turned on her and was only deterred from clutching him again by the risk of getting smashed in the face.

"You gave Don a messy job, baby," she said giggling.

He poured another drink of gin to quickly blur his sharp-angled perspective, in which everything seemed so strange and incredibly depraved.

"It seems as if every time you see him you get sick and vomit, baby."

"Small wonder."

"He said it would be nice to see what you were like when you were sober."

"Fuck what he said."

Daringly, she gave him a quick painful jerk and ducked into the hall before he could react. "Hurry baby," she called cheerfully.

"What for?" he muttered, then to himself. "Son, you ought to go home." But the thought of leaving that small bright cell of debauchery and invading the outside darkness invoked an incomprehensible fear. It was as if, during his twenty-six hours in her apartment, the *outside* had become the *unknown,* and was infested with dangers and evils and, what was more to be feared, imponderables of what was termed normality too terrifying to be ventured. Inside he felt secure, when sufficiently drunk to pleasantly subside into a dementia praecox befitting the circumstances and complimenting the bitch. Besides which he hadn't yet screwed her. After taking another drink of gin he went naked into the sitting room and closed in on Kriss as she bent over the dials of the television set, taking her about the waist and drawing her to him. "Get off this goddam rag," he said hoarsely, "I'm gonna screw you on the floor."

She giggled, playfully shaking her derriere against him, but when he jerked savagely about, fumbling with the zipper of her rompers, she flushed with rage. "Jesse! If you knock over my television set—"

His mind went into a great white blinding flash and the next thing he knew she was struggling beneath him on the floor with a great rent down the front of her rompers, giggling with such intense sexual fury she felt an orgasm being forced unwillingly from her subdued body. The telephone rang and her glands closed in an absolute dispersion of passion, like a turtle drawing in its head. "Goddammit let me answer the telephone!" she cried. Her sudden animus had changed the very nature of her flesh into so much spongy and undesirable meat. His passion went out too, leaving him with a detached, almost clinical desire to hold her by the throat with one hand and slap her face with the other. But she began struggling, with the crazed panic of one being forcibly drowned—"That might

180

be my boss, you son of a bitch!"—and was out from beneath him and away before he could begin to slap her.

He lay on his side watching the zigzag streaks of white and black chase one another furiously across the television screen, as if it were the intention of the studio to depict continual distortion, and when he heard a faint voice from the television say, ". . . and that, ladies and gentlemen of the television audience, is the news of the world," he thought, half-amused, "Might be news to you, son, but I knowed it all along."

"Walter Martin and Lucille are coming over shortly," Kriss announced from the hall.

"That ass!" he muttered irritably.

"He's better than you think," she said, smiling her secret sensual smile.

"Who haven't you slept with?" he asked in disgust.

She grinned. "Not many."

"When you run out of these, there're plenty more in the jungle."

"Hurry and get dressed, dear, they'll be here soon."

"In addition to which there are the apes. Now an ape I'm told—"

"Jesse!" she said viciously. "If you're going to be disagreeable I want you to go home now."

"Kriss, baby," he said cheerfly, clambering to his feet, "the next time you tell me to go home I'm going to knock your teeth out."

They dressed in silent antagonism, she in the black square-neck party dress and heavy silver jewelry she'd worn to Nick's, even to the affectation of middle-class respectability; and he in his full regalia of a weekend lay for a sexually frustrated white business lady.

Walter came galloping in astride his aggressive personality like the mighty Richard Coeur de Lion astride his mighty horse and Jesse thought, as he was clapped mightily on the shoulder by the mighty man's mighty hand, "Knight me, big boy, knight me!" Walter was one of the editors of a successful black picture magazine and consequently knew everything knowable within the realm of human knowledge and much that was without it—a great deal without it. He was a handsome man with a handsome moustache and a complexion the color of dried cow dung. Every two weeks he went to a barber shop up on Seventh Avenue and for four dollars a treatment had a white lye paste applied to his thick kinky hair which made it as soft and as straight as white folks' hair. The hair was killed by this treatment. However, Walter preferred dead white-folks'-hair to live nigger-kinks.

Placing his drink on the seldom used desk, he turned the desk chair about to face the room. Then, seating himself in executive fashion, took command of the conversation: "I was in San Francisco last week interviewing Mayor Robinson—no relation to Jesse—on the problem of the new Negro slums that have grown up there since the war. What Mayor Robinson doesn't know—"

"You told him of course," Jesse thought and quit listening to examine Lucille who sat beside him on the sofa wearing a long-suffering look. She was a petite brown-skinned woman with a tiny waist, a rather pretty narrow face, a shyly sexy mouth and big legs. She smelled of woman-and-perfume and Jesse lit a cigarette to keep from being disturbed by it. Catching a moment when both her mighty man and his white woman audience were taking a drink at once, she said to Jesse, "I heard you've written a new book," but Walter was too quick for them, having a big gullet no doubt, and grabbed back the conversation before he could reply.

"The trouble with Jess is he writes for a limited audience—"

"—hates white people so much—" Kriss was trying to say, but Walter's big executive voice shouted her down:

"Got to write so people will read you, Jess boy—"

"—My writing teacher played a dirty joke—" Jesse was trying to get in edgewise but Walter had no liking for anyone's voice but his own:

"You write plain enough but what do they see? In my profession we say one picture is worth ten pages—"

"He'll never write a successful book until he stops hating—" Kriss piped up but Walter mowed her down:

"Take Dickens—clear picture on every page, great composition, hard black on stark white—"

Jesse slipped in with: "Your libido is showing."

Kriss had started to say: "White people are tired of being hated by you—" when suddenly she realized the meaning of Jesse's quip and broke off to giggle, stealing a furtive, sidelong look at Lucille.

"What I am trying to tell Jess is—" Walter recovered ponderously, and Jesse leaned his head back on the sofa and watched the bright, mottled color-sounds bob on the bloody blurred sea. He felt sealed within a vague amusement by the idiocy of it all.

"Why don't you and Kriss give Jesse a chance to defend himself?" Lucille interrupted the great man daringly, and Jesse said thickly, speaking in his careful drunken voice, "My next book is going to be an outstanding bestseller. It is going to be selected by all seven book clubs—all eleven that is—" and for once he had their undivided attention. Blowing laughter through his nose he said slowly, "At first I was undecided. I was going to write my autobiography and entitle it: *Massa's Old Black Mammy Takes Her Last Crap*, but my editors objected to the use of the pronoun *her*—they thought it should be *it*—" he was vaguely aware of Kriss giggling, Walter looking disgusted, and Lucille staring at him in amazement "—so I gave that one up. And now I'm going to write the biography of the great white ape who rules all the black apes in the jungle. Mister A., as he is known to the black apes. Of course the title will be, *Gone With The Apes*." He became so tickled he couldn't continue.

"You're joking—" Walter began.

"Don't tell me you knew all along?" he gasped.

"—but I'm trying to tell you something for your own good. You Negro writers—"

"Don't look at me, boss, I ain't done nothing!"

"—want you to listen, nigger! I'm telling you something—" Walter was getting angry.

"—catching every word, boss—"

"Jesse!" Kriss said sharply, furious at being ignored. But her good humor was restored by the sudden start he gave, knocking over his glass. "Make the drinks for us, dear," she said, grinning cheerfully.

He stood up, smiling, and said thickly, "For one sweet look from your big blue beautiful braised eyes, will cross deepest ocean, be it filled with gin . . ." and staggered about the room, clutching the glasses to his belly, then lurched teetering toward the kitchen, banging into the table and ricocheting against the opposite wall. Spontaneously, Lucille started from her seat to help him, but Walter, taking his cue from the malicious grin of Kriss, motioned her to stay seated.

Jesse poured a quarter of a glass of gin for himself and drank it quickly to steady the bottles that had begun acquiring reptilian life.

And the next thing he knew he was sitting in Kriss's favorite three-legged chair speaking in his normal voice with great animation "—without prejudice or favor and he'll hate you forever. But call him either a saint or a bastard and he'll either love you or forgive you—" to Harold who was sitting on a stool across the room with his back to the wall between the sofa and desk, listening with the appreciative relish of one hearing his enemies maligned. Kriss was sitting on the sofa talking shop with Lucille, who worked for a foundation in Brooklyn, smelling her femininity in much the same fashion Jesse had smelled it previously, staring with unconscious lust at the whip and coil of Lucille's lips which she wetted with her tongue-tip between every sentence or two. While Walter was leaning back in his desk chair, looking at the whole assembly with the expression of cynical disdain which he had assiduously rehearsed for such occasions as this, but seen from without in lieu of from within appeared a great deal more like the lowering expression of a half-treed coon. "—because if you're a nigger," Jesse went on talking to Harold, unmindful of the others, "he won't believe you can see him as he is. If you're a bad nigger he expects you to hate him and if you're a good nigger he knows damn well that you love him. But he doesn't know what to do with a nigger who neither loves nor hates him—"

"But to kill him!" Harold said, chuckling deprecatingly as if he'd warned that nigger to watch out. "Jesse, you know, old man, I've found out there's one thing drives a white man to murder—"

"Screwing white women."

"Jesse, ol' man, let me tell you something I've found out; the American white man *wants* you to screw his women—"

"—all you niggers can think about is screwing white women," Walter said disgustedly, and Kriss, attracted by the unconscious envy in his voice, deserted Lucille in the middle of a sentence and staggered across the room with her white body to console him. She sat on the arm of his chair facing him with her back to the room as if she were going to offer him a fat white breast to chew on, but instead she kissed him, grinning all the time, and mumbled incoherently, "—an' Jesse hates white people so. You don't hate white people, do you, baby?"

"—but if he ever suspects that you know how he thinks—" Harold was saying, with Jesse interposing: "—kill you sure as—" and Kriss mumbling sensually, "—tell me you don't hate white people too, baby—" and Walter stroking her breast as if to get milk but still trying to talk around her shoulder to Harold and Jesse: "It's time you niggers count your blessings—"

"—know how insecure he is, you give him a problem he can't solve and he's panic-stricken, can't think—"

"—ever tell you the story of—"

"—white race has never solved a single problem in all its history except by extermination. Dead Indians good Indians—"

"—I went up to Connecticut to work as a caretaker for this guy—New York City attorney, senior member in a firm that handled a lot of movie business—"

"—sa bitch, ol' man, itsa bitch—"

"—had a beautiful farm—used for breeding thoroughbred horses before he got it—beautiful stalls; wooden floors, electric lights in each stall—"

"—tell you, ol' man—"

"—were there, Becky and I, before the son of a bitch came up for the summer an' wanted us to do housework—we quit—but that's beside the story . . ."

There was a big fine yellow rooster in the pig pen, a little bantam hen that lived in one of the wagon sheds, and seventeen fat white ducks in the wire enclosed chicken yard. This attorney had decided to put in some laying hens, so he came out one weekend and killed the ducks by standing outside the wire fence and shooting them with a shotgun. After which he drove off to order two dozen pullets and pick up a Negro in the city to pluck the ducks, which Jesse had refused to do. The following week Jesse cleaned and whitewashed the henhouse, forked the chicken yard, bought two hundred-pound sacks of chicken mash and scratch, drove over in the Jeep and picked up the pullets and installed them in their new home. But he'd been feeding them from a sack of old mash, which happened to be pig mash, and the eggs were ill-formed and had soft shells. When this attorney came back the following weekend he examined the soft-shelled eggs and stated authoritatively their deformity was due to the rooster fertilizing them. The ignorant Negro who had plucked the ducks stopped by for his pay after dinner, and this attorney called Jesse to the kitchen and the three of them sat around for two hours, drinking Canadian Club whiskey highballs, trying to decide what to do with the rooster. This ignorant Negro suggested that the rooster be denutted but Jesse said he'd never seen any nuts on a rooster carcass, so this attorney went into his library and brought back a book on poultry-raising, but all he discovered about roosters' nuts was a section of the rooster referred to as *primaries*. Being an attorney who was familiar with all manner of terms, he was able to state authoritatively that the primaries were the nuts, but there was no way of separating them from the rooster. Jesse couldn't understand how this rooster who lived in the pig pen a half mile distant from the chicken coop could have fertilized the eggs, even with such portentous sounding nuts as primaries, or for that matter even had he been as well-equipped as a Man O' War. But of course he didn't say so, being as he was drinking this attorney's good whiskey. Finally the solution burst on this attorney like a brainstorm. He banged dramatically on the table with his open palm and said in the voice of a general giving the order to charge: "*Jesse!* KILL THE ROOSTER!"

"—and let that be a lesson, old man. He'll do it every time."

"Damn right. But what gets me—" In the edge of his vision he saw suddenly the face of Lucille as she watched her husband stroke Kriss's breast, and there was something in her expression of contained despair that reminded him of Becky—and the outside world came tumbling in. Breaking off in the middle of a sentence he lurched to his feet and staggered toward the kitchen, but his mind had become cold sober and flint hard. "That bitch is never happy unless she's making someone else unhappy," he thought, and then, "The way of a gringo—good movie title."

Stepping into the hall he called, "Kriss! Kriss! Come here a minute, will you baby." She heard the urgency in his voice and thought the liquor was giving out. He watched her come across the room with the high-shouldered almost masculine swagger she assumed when having made a conquest, and preceded her into the kitchen.

"Why don't you grow up," he said.

She knew instantly what he referred to and her sense of guilt gave her the face of innocence. "What's the matter, baby?"

"You know damn well what's the matter. You're making Lucille miserable pawing over Walter like that."

"She doesn't care, baby. It's just—"

"The hell she doesn't. Any woman would care. Besides you got all the advantage; you haven't got any husband to—"

"She knows I'm not trying to make Walter, baby."

"Then what the hell are you trying to do?"

"You're the only one who is worried, baby," she said, and smiling her secret sensual smile added in a thick anticipatory voice, "I'm just curious to see what makes him tick. You know how I am, baby."

"I know how you are all right. You think a man only ticks between sheets."

"I'm just curious about what's in a Negro's mind, baby."

"Just quit fucking with him, goddammit, that's all!" he said in a sudden scalding rage; and when, smiling at his resentment, she said, "Can hardly call it that, baby; both of us have got on so many clothes," he turned away from her to keep from knocking her down. Walter's loud voice came from the sitting-room: "—trouble with you niggers is—" With uncontrollable violence he picked up the kitchen knife and chopped off the head of an empty whiskey bottle. "What's happening to Jesse?" he heard Harold asking, and Kriss replying bitchily, "He's just being doggy in the manger."

"Bitch wants to die," he said.

Harold came into the kitchen and saw the knife in his hand and the headless bottle on the table. Chuckling, he said, "Dead now."

Jesse picked it up and shook it. "Dead before."

Harold tried the other bottles and found them all empty. "All dead."

Jesse began opening the last bottle of gin. "Let's not leave this sonabitch alive."

Harold gave his self-deprecating laugh. "As Bert Williams used to say: When the liquor's flowing freely, and your pocket's full of dough—I'm with you, man."

Jesse took a drink then staggered quickly to the bathroom. He leaned against the wall, but his knees kept buckling and he swayed from side to side, wetting the floor about the john like a lawn sprinkler. "More rain more ass grow," he thought, half-amused, then as he tried to steady himself and aim straight, he looked down blurrily at the enameled bowl and muttered, half-laughingly, "Grown since hell since I saw it last."

On returning to the sitting room he found that Kriss and Lucille had gone to the kitchen. Walter had a leg over the arm of his chair and was saying: "—It's time you niggers count your blessings." Jesse wondered if he was hearing double. "Bastard's brain got stuck,' he thought.

"You got to join the human race," Walter held forth.

"Come apart now," Jesse thought. "Knew it was going to happen. Overloaded." Aloud he said in his slow thick voice: "—been an ape too long to change now—feeling mighty uncomfortable as a human being."

Harold chuckled. "How'd you manage it, Walt? The man turned me and Jesse down."

"—said weren't no vacancies . . ." Jesse mumbled. "Knew the sonabitch was lyin'."

"You niggers want to clown," Walter said disgustedly and Harold put in, chuckling, "Fish swim," and Jesse mumbled: "—what you expect clowns to do—play *Macbeth*?"

"What those girls doing in there?" Walter muttered irritably, flicking up his sleeve with mighty elegance to glance at his watch. If he couldn't have an attentive and admiring female audience he was ready to leave.

Harold chuckled. "Don't get worried, Walt, you got the nuts."

"That sort of thing don't worry me; I *know* I *can*—" Walter muttered defensively, but Jesse cut him off, mumbling: "That's what you get for joining the human race."

Harold laughed. "Nothing's too strange for human beings, Walt. Now us apes, we got just one way—"

Laughing, Jesse lurched to his feet and staggered to the kitchen. Lucille greeted him with an accusing look. "You shouldn't have told Kriss that, Jesse, I didn't—" she began, and Kriss cut in: "—she knows I didn't mean anything—" but Lucille continued: "—think anything about it at all. Kriss always—" Kriss gave Jesse a sweetly malicious vindictive smile: "—she knows it's just my way . . ." Jesse trembled with a sudden squall of rage that left him momentarily sober. "Don't be so motherfucking cute, bitch!" he said to Kriss and seeing the first glint of outrage in her blue-glazed red-rimmed eyes he slapped her with such savage violence it spun her into the stove. He was going to hit her with his fist when Lucille intervened, saying indignantly, "You shouldn't have done that, Jesse! You're crazy! I'm not unhappy!" He looked at the anguish in her face and the rage drained out of him. "Now this hurt bitch had got to defend this other bitch who hurt her to prove to the bitch she wasn't hurt when the bitch knows damn well she was hurt and she knows damn well the bitch knows it," he thought disgustedly, and then, "Perfectly natural, though," and after an instant, "Maud's got the right idea; only defence a nigger bitch got against a white bitch is to screw her."

Kriss wheeled towards him with her face aflame. "You son of a bitch! I'm going to—"

He turned away as if unaware of her existence and went back to the living-room and sat defiantly in her favorite three-legged chair.

She came out and, standing behind him in the hall said, in an icy voice, "Jesse! I want you to go home," and he replied just as icily, "Kriss. Fuck yourself!"

Harold chuckled innocently and began reciting: "When the fellows get to fighting, and the law is at de door—"

Walter cut him off. "When niggers learn how to behave themselves—"

"Got it all figured out, haven't you, boy?" Jesse felt a cold sober malevolence toward everyone. "Got your big fat brain stuffed with solutions, eh, boy?"

Behind him Kriss was repeating: "Jesse! I want you to—" but Jesse's last remark had pricked Walter in a tender spot and he shouted angrily: "You goddamned smart-alecky niggers always mess up everything—"

"Why don't you turn that record over, boy? You been talking about the same thing—"

"I'll talk about whatever I please. I was invited here—"

"Well, go home then!"

"Go home your goddamned self! Kriss has asked you three times!"

"You take care of Lucy and let me take care of Kriss, son," and Kriss's blood-flushed jowls swelled like a puffing adder's at this last outrage to white womanhood: "You son of a bitch—"

But Walter suffered a blind fit of nigger-rage at being relegated to the sole defense of Negro womanhood—a great man like himself. "Don't call me son, nigger!" he shouted.

"Listen, son—" Jesse began in a patronizing tone, and before he'd finished Walter leaped to his feet and snapped open a switchblade knife. "I'll cut your motherfuckin' throat!" he threatened, advancing dangerously.

Kriss shuddered with a sadistic thrill, at once excited and repulsed by the prospect of seeing Jesse writhing on the floor with blood spurting from his cut throat because her skin was white.

Lucille sprang forward and threw her arms about Walter, restraining him, while Harold scrambled hastily to his feet to get out of the way. "Motherfucker, I'll show you—" Walter was mouthing, trying to free himself from his wife's arms.

Jesse sat silent and unmoving, watching the performance with a complete but detached curiosity; with no reaction to the danger whatsoever, scarcely realizing his own participation. It was as if he were watching with impersonal interest some vaguely valid but not very novel exhibition of idiocy, like a Hollywood treatment of a Negro theme. "Now the bitch has got us niggers killing off each other," he thought with vague chagrin but no surprise, and then, half-amused, "Now I really do believe the sonofabitch has joined the human race," and directly following, "Nigger's right too . . . right attitude . . . good nigger . . . footsteps of tradition . . . no wonder they let the nigger join . . ." Then his conscious awareness went off and came on at intervals, like billboard lights, leaving a series of jumbled and unrelated impressions: Walter was seated as before, grinning at him derisively: "I know what's eatin' you . . ." and himself still sitting in the same position, thinking, "The nigger's earned his, anyway . . ." Then everyone was standing, milling about, and he was patting Walter on the shoulder, saying with great benevolence, "I like you, man, hell, I'm only too glad you found the combination . . ." Then the Martins were gone and Kriss was standing in front of the television set, putting on a coat, and stating to Harold who stood to one side, with an attitude of deprecation: "I'm going home with you—" Harold shaking his head and replying: "—*make himself a great hero . . .*" and both talking at once. "You gotta take me home with you, baby . . ." "*But somebody else . . .*" "I'm not going to stay here with this son of a bitch . . ." "*Not me . . .*"

"You're not going any goddam where!" Jesse said in a clear dangerous voice.

"You son of a bitch!" Kriss flared, flashing him a look of supreme indignation, then taking Harold by the arm: "Come on, baby, take me home with you." She giggled. "Let Jesse screw himself." Then cursed viciously: "Son of a bitch!"

"Fix this bitch right now," Jesse thought and staggered to the kitchen to get the big kitchen knife.

"Don't cut her, man, don't cut her!" Harold said in alarm when Jesse returned, brandishing the knife. "Hit her with your fist but don't cut her."

"Don't tell that son of a bitch to hit me, you son of a bitch!" Kriss screamed in a rage now directed toward her erstwhile protector.

"Man's right," Jesse thought. "Bitch just needs a little blacking for the coming cakewalk." Aloud he said, "Right-O!" and, placing the knife carefully atop the storage cabinet so as not to scar the finish, hit her on the jaw as hard as he could. In amazement he watched her bang against the television set and crumple to the floor.

"White bitches fall on their ass just like all other bitches when they're smacked on the jaw," he thought.

"Don't kick her, man," Harold said quickly.

"Got you, coach," Jesse said. "Don't bruise the stuff."

Harold chuckled. "Consider the depreciation."

"Trouble with us niggers now—"

Neither of them moved to help Kriss as she struggled to her feet. With clinical curiosity Jesse watched her first straighten the television set on its stand, then pull down her skirt which had flown up about her waist, thinking, "Property first, virtue second—" and when at last she gave him the full malevolence of her look, added, "—hatred third. Good thing to know." She kept silent for fear he might hit her again, but said to herself, "Jesse! You son of a bitch! I'll never let you sleep with me again as long as I live!" dictating his ultimate punishment in much the same attitude as Puritans sentencing a witch to burning, or white southerners a Negro to lynching. Then, silently, she took off all of her clothes and threw them on the floor, staggered to the kitchen and mixed a gin drink, came back into the hall and posed naked long enough for him to see what he was missing; then she giggled and went into the bedroom and slammed the door with a bang that sounded like a shot.

"Ought to be hot now," Harold said, chuckling.

"Just exploded," Jesse said.

By accord they went to the kitchen to get a drink and finding the gin gone opened the bottle of sherry. "I'm getting good and goddamned tired of these hurt white bitches taking it out on me," Jesse muttered, finding himself slowly burning with what was the beginning of accumulated rage.

"You hear me!" His voice thickening with growing passion. "TIREDDDDDDDD!" And with that he took a huge swallow of sherry to cool his blazing brain. But whatever comment Harold made on this revealing outburst, he never knew, for with the warm pungent fiery wine exploding in his stomach, his conscious awareness blanked out again and did not return until he began to dream shortly before awakening.

CHAPTER 12

*H*E DREAMED he was writing a soft sweet lyrical and gently humorous account of his experiences as a cook on a big country estate somewhere, and as he completed each chapter it was being printed on pale green pages of stiff Irish linen, each page with an individual hand-painted border of various ancient Egyptian designs; the book itself with both the printed pages and those yet to be filled bound in dark green morocco leather with gold leaf corners and with the title *Hog Will Eat Hog*, branded on the leather, and his name in heavy silver letters beneath:

I discovered I didn't have to kill the hogs because they'd give six or seven inches of sausage each day, neatly stuffed in their intestines, and I'd simply have to go down to the pig sty and cut it off. There'd always be plenty for everyone and some left over, and by the next morning they would have grown an equal amount. The lady I worked for—I won't mention her name because she is very famous and might be embarrassed—didn't want to eat the sausage at first because she thought it was being cruel to the hogs to cut it off like that. But when I showed her that the hogs did not feel any pain whatsoever, and how happy they were to be giving a little sausage each day instead of being slaughtered all at once and butchered for hams, she consented to eat the sausage and liked it very much. The way I discovered she liked the sausage came about like this: She was sitting on the terrace with Proust's *Remembrance of Things Past* open in her lap, but instead of reading she was looking across her sunny acres with a dreamy expression.

"If I may be so bold as to ask, what are you thinking, madame?" I asked.

"About sausage."

"What about sausage, madame?"

"About how good it is."

It made me happy to see her happy, and the hogs were happy to see us both happy.

But one day one of the hogs refused to give his bit of sausage. I knew he was not going dry because he was eating as much swill as any of the other hogs and he was also just as fat. So after breakfast that morning I took him down to the slaughterhouse to have a good talk with him.

"Why do you refuse to give your bit of sausage, like the other hogs do?" I asked.

"I have run out of sausage," he said.

But I knew by his hang-hog expression and the guilty manner in which he avoided my eyes that the sausage manufacturers had bribed him.

"Why do you lie to me?" I asked. "I can tell by looking at you that you have gone over to the other side."

"But it is true," he contended. "Besides which I have no more guts."

"Would you rather be slaughtered and butchered by the sausage manufacturers, or give us, your friends, a little bit of sausage each day?" I asked bluntly.

"I don't know why I hate you so when you've been so good to me," he squealed pathetically, lard drops streaming from his little hog eyes.

On hearing this, the other hogs who had followed down to the slaughterhouse expecting to see him slaughtered, thought that I might forgive him and began shouting, "Slaughter the traitor! Slaughter the traitor!"

But when I saw their cruel sadistic expressions, I recalled the words of our Savior, and I said to them, "He that is without pork chops among you, let him first cut his brother's throat." Then I turned to the recalcitrant hog and said, "Let this be a lesson to you: hog will eat hog the same as dog will eat dog . . ."

At the moment of awakening he remembered the dream entirely and thought, half-amused, "Damn right!" Then, as he became oriented, he realized he was sleeping on the sofa in the living room. "Good thing you're not a hog, son," he thought as he reached

194

behind him and switched on the table light. "You'd have to eat your own sausage."

The room looked a worse wreck than it had the morning before. "I had Kilroy wrong," he thought, eyeing the signs of havoc. "McCarthy's been investigating here." Kriss's clothes were piled as she had left them on stripping, but there was no evidence of his own. He got up and found them hanging neatly in the hall closet. "Now I know I was tight," he said aloud.

Next he examined his face in the bathroom mirror. It looked the same. "Stuff embalms you good enough," he thought.

His head felt funny and he suffered streaks of sharp brain ache when he moved it too quickly, and his mouth felt cottony and tasted brown. His body was slightly numb as if his sense of feel was impaired, and did things contrary to the commands of his brain.

He had no idea what time it was. When he went into the bedroom to look at the clock, he noticed through the partly open window that it was dull gray and raining outside. Without turning on the light for fear of awakening Kriss, he stooped and peered at the clock. But the clock had stopped at 3:16 and he had to switch on the light to find her watch. In the meantime he took a good look at her. She lay flat on her back with her arms straight down as if laid out for burial and slept so peacefully she seemed scarcely to breathe. "Bitch is so quiet she must be dead," he thought. The covers were pulled up about her throat and only her face was exposed, and it was serene and very white and astonishingly beautiful. "All bitches look best flat on their backs," he thought as he studied the marble countenance, "Too bad they can't function in their sleep. When you wake up their brains the trouble begins." He saw by the watch on her dressing table that it was 8:23 and started to wake her so she'd be in time for work, but changed his mind. "Leave her to Gabriel, son, too late to score now," and then, "we got no twat but too late to plot another shot, eh wot?—bestseller . . ." and went to the kitchen for a drink. Finding only the two bottles of vermouth left, he opened one, drank a tumblerful and muttered sourly, "Ladypiss," quickly adding. "Some other lady's, not hers." Taking a bottle and glass back to the sitting-room he decided suddenly to dress and leave before Kriss awakened.

While showering he entertained himself by imagining an invention whereby one could bite into a set of electric brushes attached to the wall and have his teeth cleaned while taking a shower. "Wonder someone hasn't thought of it before," he said. "Typical American innovation. Fits smackdab into the American way. If so many million gainfully employed U.S. citizens spent thirty seconds every morning brushing their teeth, look how much time would be saved to earn more money to pay for this machine on the installment plan." Then, "It'd be the easiest thing in the world to sell; a natural for an advertising slogan: Why be whiny when Packer's electric shower-brush will make your teeth so nice and shiny?—Too long, though—Don't Beef! Shine your teeth! . . . That's better . . ." He could envision a fine, fat, somewhat paunchy but still bustling bald-headed businessman, B. Smart, taking his morning's ice-cold shower with his teeth clamped about the electric brushes when all of a sudden he has a spell of lockjaw brought on by staying beneath the icecold shower too long and trying to sing the chorus of "Old Shagging Riley" while his teeth were being shined. And before he can get loose his teeth have been worn down to the roots and the busy little brushes are busily polishing away his jawbone. "Nothing serious," he can hear the firm's executives saying. "People expect such things. Perfectly normal accident of our mechanical age. Good publicity, too. Couldn't sell the damn things without an element of risk. Great gamblers, the Americans. Got plates myself, thank God . . ." He laughed until he cried, thinking of old B. Smart chomping up fillets in "21" with his razor-sharp jawbones. "I got a beautiful sense of humor," he thought laughingly. "As typically American as the tooth-shining machine. Laugh my ass off at misfortune. But somebody else's, not mine. Must remember to tell them that next time I apply for membership in the human race."

The combination of warm shower and dry herb wine had a sobering effect on him and again he felt a dread of going outside into the unknown day. So instead of dressing as he had intended he went into the living room and sat naked on the sofa and finished the bottle of wine. "Courage, son," he said, feeling slightly better, "it's cheaper by the bottle—bestseller." But lacking the high proof courage of bottled-in-bond bourbon he still did not feel up to facing

196

the unknown outside. "Reason why Italians never won a war," he thought. "Drink this ladypiss." Then corrected himself, "Raped Abyssinia, though. So must be good for raping." Taking the empty bottle back to the kitchen for the full one, he thought, "Maybe if you drink enough of this, son, you'll get in some raping too. Do the bitch a world of good." Then, "But then Abyssinia was a nigger; don't know how it'll work on a white bitch." While drawing the cork he looked about the kitchen at the night's devastation. "Tell we won the war," he thought. "Don't know who we whipped but this is sure hell a liberated nation." Pouring a tumblerful of the aromatic wine, he drank it down without pause, then cautioned himself, "Just don't fuck up like Mussolini, son. That bastard got so het up over raping a nigger he set the whole world on fire." For some reason he didn't know, he was assailed by a feeling of remorse. Taking the bottle and glass to the sitting room, he stood for a moment as if bemused. With one part of his mind he thought, "They're all watching Russia. Better watch Mississippi too—more firebugs there than in the Kremlin," and with the other part, for no evident reason, "*Thus conscience does make cowards of us all . . .*" Then with the first part, half-amused, "No tonic manufactured good as whipping a nigger's ass. Makes you feel more powerful than cocaine," and with the second part, strangely depressed, "All his conscience in his dick, though, never yet no higher." Then with the first part, "Poor Kriss, too bad she's not strong enough to whip your ass, son; she'd give you all of hers to heal it," and again with the second part, "Can't change nature, son, nuts and brains taste just the same; fact, nuts taste better, got more soul."

Involuntarily he went over and tuned in the television set, then sat wide-legged on the sofa, staring absently at his penis and thinking the while, "Doctors know. Can't prescribe it enough. Whip nigger's ass—unlawful even in Latin. But know just the same. Aphrodisiacal, too, just like whipping a bitch's ass. Works the same way. In the glands. Tightens them. Glands back? Whip a black!—spot add . . ."

The voice from the television drew his attention: "—peace treaty reestablishing Japan as an independent and sovereign nation, will go into effect. On May 6, a federal law requiring gamblers . . ." On sight of the two faces grinning at him from the television screen, he realized that Gloucester was conducting his weekday morning interview with the prophetic chimpanzee, and involuntarily rushed in to call Kriss, thinking, "She'll want to hear this." But his call didn't awaken her and he could hear the chimp saying: "East Germany will announce plans to form an army to protect itself against aggression . . ." So he let her sleep on, thinking, "We must have been drinking different stuff," and went back to his seat.

"—twenty-seven year old Negro porter, Irving Greene, will confess to setting twenty fires in Brooklyn during the past two years, including the June 18th fire in which seven persons died. When asked why he did it, he will reply that he liked the excitement."

"—black Nero—" Jesse thought.

"—U.S. will allocate a fifteen million dollar working fund to aid business in West Berlin—"

"—thicker than conscience—"

"—new series of reports of flying saucers over Washington and other parts of the nation resulted in an Air Force announcement that the objects were not a menace to the U.S.—"

"—McCarthy nightmares—"

"—August 7, Florida Supreme Court will dismiss pleas of five Negroes who seek entrance to the University of Florida, and rule they are not entitled to admittance while equal facilities are available at the Florida Agricultural and Mechanical College for Negroes—"

"—Southern mathematics—"

"—General Eisenhower will urge Southerners to protect the rights of Negroes—"

"—shell-shocked—"

"—beautiful world—"

"—will be tried for the first-degree murder of Mrs. Kristina Cummings, white, a divorcee employed as assistant director of the India Institute. State-appointed defense attorneys for Robinson will enter a plea of temporary insanity, based on the allegation that Robinson, after a weekend of excessive drinking in the Gramercy Park apartment of Mrs. Cummings, had become intoxicated to the extent that, during the commission of the crime, he was not conscious of his actions—"

"—battle fatigue," Jesse thought. "Same thing as shell-shocked, just sounds worse—"

"—prosecution will establish that, following a previous quarrel, during which he knocked her down with his fist, he entered her bedroom armed with a kitchen knife, stabbed her through the heart while she lay in bed, after which he washed the body clean of blood, changed the bedding, and arranged the body in the fresh bed in the position of sleeping with the eyes closed and the arms extended at its sides, then took a shower, dressed, packed the murder knife, bloodstained towels, and bedding into two paper shopping bags, pocketed an extra set of keys to her apartment which he had formerly noticed in a bowl on the table, walked down 23rd Street to the East River and threw the shopping bags containing the bloodstained evidence into the river, returned to the apartment on 21st Street, let himself in with the extra set of keys, undressed, hanging his clothes in Mrs. Cummings's hall clothes closet, made a bed on the sofa in the sitting room, and went to sleep immediately—"

"—what you get for reading too much Faulkner, son," Jesse said, half-laughing.

"—defense will allege that he was completely blotto all during this time; that if, as the prosecution will maintain, he stabbed her in a rage because she refused to succumb to his advances, he was entirely unconscious of making advances and of feeling outraged, and could only have been acting out of a subconscious resentment toward the woman who invited him to spend the weekend in her apartment for immoral purposes, and then, after two days of continuous drinking and sexual enticement, reneged on her part of the bargain—"

"—you tell 'em, bub! Give a little sausage or get slaughtered for ham."

"—will dismiss the insanity plea—"

"—must be sure to get a copy of the transcription to show all those critics who've been calling you psychotic—"

"—and Robinson will be sentenced to be electrocuted in Sing Sing prison, December 9th—"

"—elementary progression—"

"As a rule, on this program, we don't consider murder a news-

199

worthy event," Gloucester rebuked the chimp, somewhat superciliously. "What do you find so unusual about this case?"

Chimpanzee (leering): "There will be no evidence of rape."

Jesse: "Son of a bitch was too drunk. Only reason."

Gloucester (embarrassed): "Oh! You don't say!"

Chimpanzee (grinning maliciously): "But I do say. And furthermore, on May 17, 1954 the U.S. Supreme Court will render a decision against racial segregation in all U.S. public schools—"

Jesse (with drunken clairvoyance): "Then the agony begins—"

Gloucester (sardonically): "I say, my little friend, aren't you letting your imagination run away with you. As much as I abhor any form of discrimination toward our darker brother, I doubt if the South would stand for it—for the end of segregation, I mean—"

Jesse: "Boy's shooting with history. Doesn't know it—"

Gloucester: "—by the Federal Government, I mean—"

Jesse: "—thinks he's playing with sentiment; harmless stuff, he thinks; killed more people than—"

Gloucester: "—feel very strongly about State Rights. They consider the problem—"

Jesse: "—time integrates; man liquidates—"

Gloucester: "—will fight valiantly for what they deem right. But I have no doubt—"

Jesse: "—kill the rooster, son! Do it every time. Only answer to enlightment man's ever figured out—"

Gloucester: "—if you understand the problem, my little friend, and the issue of the rights involved—"

Jesse: "—more rights, more grave grow, all I said, massa—"

Chimpanzee (with bored indifference): "My dear sir, I report the news as I foresee it." After all, chimpanzees have never been segregated in U.S. public schools.

Gloucester: "Why the South might even go to war again."

Jesse: "They laughed at Hitler too, when he sat down to play, 'Deutschland, Deutschland über Alles!'"

Chimpanzee (brightening): "That reminds me of a joke they tell about Generalissimo Franco—"

Gloucester (startled): "Generalissimo Franco?"

Chimpanzee: "There was great poverty in Spain and the Franco government couldn't get a penny from the U.S. And they had a grave beggar-problem similar to your Negro-problem which had to be solved, besides which Franco's uniforms were getting somewhat frayed. So the Generalissimo met with his ministers to see what could be done about these problems, especially about the problem of his uniforms. After a week's deliberation, the ministers suddenly struck upon a foolproof solution. In a body, they rushed to the palace and demanded an immediate audience with the Generalissimo.

" '—What's the answer, boys?' he asked.

" '—Declare war on the U.S.!' they chorused exultantly.

" 'Generalissimo Franco considered the suggestion. He thought of the prosperity in post-war Japan and Germany. It seemed to be a flawless solution. But he was assailed by one grave doubt.

" 'But what if I win?' he asked."

Jesse: "Damn right! Suppose the South had won the Civil War . . ."

The interview had overrun its time and abruptly the commercial came on. A disembodied hand held forth what appeared on first sight to be an ordinary cigarette lighter.

"PRESTO!" the mealy-mouthed voice of the adman shouted, and the disembodied thumb pressed a button on top and a flame shot upward. "Light your cigarette." Disembodied lip holding a cigarette leaned into view and the cigarette was lit.

"PRESTO!" A disembodied little finger pressed a button on the bottom of the lighter and a flame shot downward. "Light your pipe." Disembodied teeth clamping a pipe leaned into view and the pipe was lit.

"PRESTO!" the disembodied hand pressed both buttons at once and what had been a simple two-way cigarette-pipe lighter became a modern kitchen fully equipped with all the most modern appliances in shining chrome and gleaming white enamel. "Why burn your candle at both ends?" the mealy-mouthed voice asked solemnly, "When PRESTO, the greatest gadget of them all will not only do the trick slick, but cook you a meal just as quick!" And sure enough, there was a precooked self-roasting turkey basting itself in a self-heating oven, while on top of the stove was a self-frozen vegetable garden complete with gardener, self-thawing itself; self-washing breakfast dishes were slopping about happily in a sink full of self-foaming suds; self-washing shirts were hard at work in the self-operating (invisible: takes up absolutely no space at all) laundry, washing and drying and ironing themselves and turning the collars where needed; and over by the four-way kitchen door (just turn handle and it opens from either side or top or bottom) the PRESTO Atom-atic Refrigerator, equipped with the famous PRESTO NO DOOR (just press a button and the door disappears completely) was busily engaged in freezing and defrosting, cheese-and-butter keeping, juice-and-dairy barring, and many other necessary functions, such as crisping various items and mixing rye high-balls, and all the while operating itself entirely on stale air at absolutely no cost whatsoever to the owner (perfect for city apartment dwellers); while across the room in the self-opening-and-closing window a self-containing air conditioner was washing and rinsing the air until pretty soon the PRESTO Atom-atic Refrigerator called over, "Look, bub, I eat stale air, you're taking the food out of my mouth!"—to which the self-containing air conditioner retorted, "Food for the mouth yet, he says, in this self-eating nation!"

"Won't be long now before they have the main problem solved," Jesse said, laughing, scratching his testicles and peering curiously at his penis. "How man and woman can screw with both on top. No more beefs about who's being screwed. Both being screwed. Be a good thing, too. Solve the woman problem, too . . ."

"Mawnin," a flat Negroid voice greeted from behind.

He turned with such a violent start he almost denutted himself, and on sight of an amazonian black woman clad in professional rags grinning at him slyly from the hallway, leaped to his feet and started to run.

But she said, "Ah'm Mattie," and he caught himself. "That's a relief!" he said. "I wondered what had happened to Kriss."

Her sly little eyes appraised his manly physique, took in the spread sofa and the consolatory bottle, then she went about her work collecting the dirty glasses and ashtrays as if finding a naked black man laughing and scratching his nuts and talking to himself in a white lady's fashionable apartment of a Monday morning were as commonplace a Manhattan incident as finding cockroaches in the kitchen. But he could tell by her sly silent laughter she didn't give much for his chances. "She doesn't think much of the Robinson label, son," he thought, half-amused, as he picked up his bottle and glass and went into the bedroom. "Can't depend on those self-starting genitals. Choke up every time. Nothing to beat the old fashioned crack. Give it a turn and it never fails to start. These modern jobs got to be babies and petted every minute. Then if you happen to put a couple of quarts of booze in the tank, the automatic nuts will go dead sure as hell."

Placing the bottle and glass beside the telephone on the nightstand, he made certain the door was shut, then sat on the side of the bed and poured a half glass of wine and drank it. Everything was delightfully blurred again and he felt relaxed and indifferent. "Your maid's here," he said to Kriss. Then, recalling the maid's sly scrutiny of his equipment, he thought, "She probably wonders how they missed throwing me back into the Harlem river." Listening to her moving about the apartment, cleaning up the night's debris, he realized he'd been given a short reprieve from having to face the unknown outside. There was a vaguely drunken delicious atmosphere of safety in the small dark room with the gray chill dangerous day locked out. He began feeling a warm half-amused friendliness for Kriss. "Kriss, baby," he said tentatively, and started to awaken her, then changed his mind and decided to take a nap himself. He slipped beneath the covers without disturbing her and went to sleep instantly.

He dreamed horribly of running naked across endless glaciers and awakened seven minutes later, deathly chilled, without being aware he had dreamed. "Damn, Kriss, aren't you cold, baby?" he asked. She didn't reply. He got up and slammed the window shut with a bang, then sat on the edge of the bed and poured a glass of wine. His teeth chattered against the rim of the glass. "Bitch must have self-heating blood," he thought. He felt certain that now she was awake and was keeping silent to annoy him. "You know, Kriss baby, you can be a very unpleasant bitch," he said angrily, and as

203

his rage began to ride, added, "You're going to get yourself good and fucked up someday." Then, prodded by her continued silence, he turned on her furiously, saying, "And whether you like it or not I'm—" His voice stopped short when he clutched her naked white shoulders. Her ice-cold flesh burned his hands.

His next action of which he was aware occurred two and a half minutes later. He was kneeling on the bed, astride her naked body, trying to make her breathe by means of artificial respiration; and seeing his tears dripping on the purple-lipped knife wound over her heart, thought she was beginning to bleed again. He felt such a fury of frustration he began beating her senselessly about the face and shoulders, cursing in a sobbing voice, "Breathe, Goddamit, breathe!"

The next thing he knew he was kneeling beside the bed, sobbing into the sheet, praying between gasps: "—have mercy on her, God . . . forgive her, God . . . she was a good girl, God . . . we were the bastards . . . You've got to forgive her, God—" Suddenly it struck him, "Here you are asking God to forgive her for what you've done to God," and he broke off and stood up and finished the bottle of wine. It soothed his panic sufficiently for him to look at the body again, and he thought, "You don't really know you did it," but in the next flash, "Who're you lying to, son? You knew before anybody. You knew it two days before it happened. Perhaps two years. Perhaps from the time they first hurt you for being born black." Unaware of what he was doing, he leaned over and covered the body completely with both sheet and blanket as if to bury the deed itself and for the first time noticed the yellow spread piled in the corner on the floor. In a daze he picked it up and examined it in the dim light and when he saw the one dark spot of congealed blood, shaped something like a hand, he knew he could not bury the deed—only the dead. Letting it fall back to the floor he felt for his pocket to get a cigarette. He realized then that he was naked, and instinctively closed the venetian blinds before turning on the light. There were no cigarettes in sight but he found one in the gold case in Kriss's purse that lay open on the dresser, and lit it with her gold-plated lighter. From that part of his mind which persistently analyzed his own behavior came the realization that he was not frightened. "Too late to run, anyway," he said. "Too late to make it straight," his thoughts continued, then, "Your fate," adding, "P.S.—tragedy."

On a sudden impulse he leaned over and uncovered Kriss's face, tucking the covers about her throat as they'd been before. Sighing heavily, he said to the marble-like face, "Sorry, baby," then with bitter self-condemnation, "Son of a bitch kills you and says excuse me," after which he had to exert tremendous restraint to keep from praying again.

He sat on the side of the bed with his back to the dead body, staring unseeingly at the framed picture of Kriss's mother on the dressing table. "You finally did it, son," he said, and when the full realization of what he had done penetrated his intelligence, his mind turned inward and became sealed within a sardonic self-lacerating humor, so that now he realized the body of his victim as the final result of his own life. "End product of the impact of Americanization on one Jesse Robinson—black man. Your answer, son. You've been searching for it. BLACK MAN KILLS WHITE WOMAN. All the proof you need now. Absolutely incontrovertible behaviorism of a male human being. Most human of all behavior. Human beings only species of animal life where males are known to kill their females. Proof beyond all doubt. Jesse Robinson joins the human race. Good article for the *Post*: He Joined The Human Race. All good solid American *Post* readers will know exactly what you meant were a nigger but killed a white woman and became a human being. Knew they'd keep fucking around with us until they made us human. They don't know yet what they're doing. Fucking up a good thing. Best thing they ever had for all their social ills . . . Be Happy—Go Nappy . . . Feel Low? Lynch Negro! . . . Can't Fuck? Shoot A Buck! . . . Suffer From Rigor? Chase A Nigger! . . . If Hubby's a Prune, Get Yourself a Coon! . . . Banned From The Hierarchy? Take Up With A Darky! . . . Why Whine? Screw A Shine And Feel Fine! . . . When All Your Money Affords You No Ease—Then Sambo Will Please!" Placing the dead cigarette butt in the ashtray on the nightstand, he stood up and lit another from Kriss's case and sat back in the same position. "Your trouble, son," his thoughts continued without interruption. "You tried too hard to please. Showed right there you were a primitive. A human being never tries to please. Not restricted by conscience like a primitive. Reason why he's human. All other animals restricted by conscience. Call it instinct but conscience just the same. Reason why your own life was so bitter, son. Had conscience." He realized then that in the back of his mind he was thinking also of Becky. But he couldn't visualize her anymore; she seemed only a wraith. "No such person, really," he told himself. "Just your conscience. Give one to all primitives. But gone now. No more worrying about what is right and what is wrong. You're human now. Went in the back door of the Alchemy Company of America a primitive filled with all that crap called principles, integrity, honor, conscience, faith, love, hope, charity, and such, and came out the front door a human being, completely purged. End of a primitive; beginning of a human. Good title for a book but won't sell with the word *human* in it. Americans sensitive about that word. Don't want it known they're human. Don't blame them, though. Poses the only problem they've never been able to solve with all their gadgets—the human problem. But they'll know damn well you're human. Be in all the newspapers: BLACK MAN KILLS WHITE WOMAN. Not only natural, plausible, logical, inevitable, psychiatrically compulsive and sociologically conclusive behavior of a human being—and all the rest of the shit the social scientists think up—but mathematically accurate and politically correct as well. Black son of a bitch has got to have some means of joining the human race. Old Shakespeare knew. Suppose he'd had Othello kiss the bitch and make up. Would have dehumanized the bastard. Didn't take much to know, however. All right there in little figures. Two plus two equal four. Some happy-headed bastards are beginning to claim they equal five. And of course we've always had those mite-hearted sons of bitches who claim they make only three. But equal four regardless. Way the system works. Got to change the whole damn system to get either five or three. Wonder by this time the sons of bitches haven't made up their minds to accept this. Their own fucking system, too. Yours too now, son. Too bad Kriss not here to see that you made it." His face relaxed in a slow sympathetic smile. "She'd be the only one who'd understand."

A knock sounded on the door but the sound did not penetrate his closed and sealed perceptions.

"Miz Cummons, anything mo y'all need?"

"—too bad, Kriss-baby," he was thinking. "Spent ten best years of your life trying to get us niggers into the human race and not here to see your first recruit."

He did not hear the diminishing sound of footsteps down the hall, not the faint sound of the front door opening and closing. In the act of lifting the telephone to call the police he stopped abruptly, thinking, "She would never forgive you for being undressed, son." He went across to the bathroom, shaved, brushed his teeth again, and dressed completely, retying his tie several times before he'd fashioned a perfect V-shaped Duke of Kent knot. "Now you can tell them you just dropped by for the killing. Nothing disrespectable about that," he said as he examined his face in the mirror. Tears flowed uncontrollably down his pale tan cheeks. "Don't cry, son," he said. "It's funny really. You just got to get the handle to the joke."

Returning to the bedroom he said to Kriss's body, "Now we're all even, baby," and smiling slightly beneath the steady seep of tears, he picked up the telephone and asked for police headquarters. On receiving an answer he asked to speak to Homicide, thinking, "Damn good thing I read detective stories; wouldn't know what to do otherwise."

Finally a bored voice said, "Yeah . . . Homicide."

"My name is Robinson, Jesse."

"Yeah . . . Robinson." Whoever he was sounded as if his ass was filled with lead.

"I'm a nigger."

There was a slight pause before the voice said, "What's that?"

"Where you been all your life, boy, you don't know what a nigger is?"

"All right! Cut the comedy! What's the beef?"

"I'm a nigger, and I've just killed a white woman," Jesse said, giving the address on 21st Street, and hung up. "That'll get the lead out of his ass," he thought, half-amused.